CONTENTS

PART ONE:

SURFING THE INVISIBLE GRADIENT

PART TWO:

ON A PITCH-DARK SEA

Praise for *Stars and Bones*

"Gareth Powell drops you into the action from the first page and then Just. Keeps. Going. This is a pro at the top of his game."
John Scalzi

"An interstellar intelligence has a plan for Earth's future, but is humanity a part of it? Fast-paced and thoughtful, *Stars and Bones* leaves the reader well-fed with hearty helpings of mystery, suspense, adventure, and terror."
Marina Lostetter, author of *Noumenon*

"Gareth Powell's *Stars and Bones* is shocking and beautiful—an electric, epic, and sometimes gruesome look at humanity facing its biggest challenge yet. Powell keeps the pressure on and doesn't let go. I enjoyed it immensely."
Karen Osborne, author of *Architects of Memory*

"A headlong, visceral plunge into a future equal parts fascinating and terrifying." **Adrian Tchaikovsky**

"A gripping, fast-paced space opera that poses the unique question: what if instead of saving humanity, aliens decided to save the Earth?" **Stina Leicht, author of *Persephone Station***

"A grand scale adventure packed with fun banter, snappy prose, and masterful science." **Essa Hansen, author of *Nophek Gloss***

"A vividly imagined, propulsive read. Filled with a loveable cast of characters. Powell's writing creates a rich tapestry of their voices and inner lives. I think readers will be thrilled by this story."
Temi Oh, author of *Do You Dream of Terra-Two?*

"Big ships, big ideas and big emotions. Thrilling space opera which is epic in scope, yet always rooted at the human level, as all the best sci-fi is."
Emma Newman, author of *Planetfall*

"*Stars and Bones* crafts a future that finds hope in dark places."
Valerie Valdes, author of *Chilling Effect*

"An interstellar collision of massive ideas and startling originality."
Zack Jordan, author of *The Last Human*

Also by Gareth L. Powell and available from Titan Books

Embers of War
Fleet of Knives
Light of Impossible Stars

Stars and Bones

GARETH L.
POWELL

DESCENDANT
MACHINE

A CONTINUANCE NOVEL

TITAN BOOKS

Descendant Machine
Print edition ISBN: 9781789094312
E-book edition ISBN: 9781789094329

Published by Titan Books
A division of Titan Publishing Group Ltd
144 Southwark Street, London SE1 0UP
www.titanbooks.com

First edition: April 2023
10 9 8 7 6 5 4 3 2 1

A CIP catalogue record for this title is available from the British Library.

Printed and bound by in the United Kingdom by CPI Group (UK) Ltd,
Croydon, CR0 4YY.

For Dianne

"The dance is always danced above the hollow place,
above the terrible abyss."

URSULA K. LE GUIN

INTRODUCTION

TO: COUNCIL OF SHIPS INVESTIGATIVE SUBCOMMITTEE
FROM: VANGUARD SCOUT SHIP FRONTIER CHIC
DATE: 03/09/125 NEW COMMON ERA
RE: INCIDENT #43675-A

My esteemed colleagues and members of the Council,

I understand many of you may be confused or angry about recent occurrences in the Jzat system, and I can't say I blame you. I'm not particularly happy about it all myself. But, as I was there when everything went sideways, it has fallen to me to explain the events that led up to the death of the Rav'nah Abelisk and the reactivation of the Grand Mechanism.

After consideration, and having reviewed all the available evidence, I have decided to present my report to you in the form of a fictionalised narrative. In doing so, I hope to convey a deeper sense of the emotions and thought processes of those involved, as well as communicate the enormity of what we faced more effectively than I ever could through the mere recitation of data. This has enabled me to devote a chapter to each of the most significant turning points, and the reasoning behind each decision.

In compiling this account, I have drawn upon my own experience; the testimony of my navigator, Nicola Mafalda; and the letters sent from the scientific protégé, Orlando

Walden, to his lover, Ramona Tyrell—as well as the journals, communications or recollections of several of the other major participants, where available. To help you keep track of whose testimony you are reading at any given moment,
I have included the name of the narrator beneath the title of each chapter.

Although I have striven to ensure the accuracy of this account, I have inevitably made some aesthetic and literary choices in my presentation. For instance, although highly educated, impeccably dressed and well spoken, Ms Mafalda tends to employ profanity for both emphasis and punctuation. Indeed, when infuriated or intoxicated, she has a remarkable talent for fitting multiple instances of the word 'fuck' into almost every sentence she utters. So, in the interests of clarity, I have taken the liberty of excising most of these curses, sparing only enough to give an authentic flavour of her speech. I have also omitted the more intimate and sexually explicit passages from Mr Walden's communiques, as well as whole sections that slowed the pace of the narrative and consisted entirely of snarky comments about other physicists.

Additionally, I have employed the occasional stylistic flourish, to make the whole thing more engaging to read. I know humans often find it easier to absorb a fictional account rather than a dry summation of events. They are natural storytellers, after all, and it is my humble hope that by thus framing my report as a literary narrative, my efforts will result in a wider public understanding of the chain of events Ms Mafalda referred to at the time as simply "this sorry clusterfuck".

Your obedient servant,
VSS *Frontier Chic*

"Looking at these stars suddenly dwarfed my own troubles and all the gravities of terrestrial life. I thought of their unfathomable distance, and the slow inevitable drift of their movements out of the unknown past into the unknown future."

H.G. Wells, *The Time Machine*

BETTING THE FARM ON A HUNCH

NICOLA MAFALDA

As we left the atmosphere and the *Frontier Chic* powered upwards, a local gunboat hailed us.

"Hello," I sent in the local language. "I'm honoured. I wasn't expecting you to break out the big guns just to say goodbye."

Although lacking interstellar capability, the Jzatian gunboat easily massed twice our size. It had the clunky, functional look of something whose builders had bolted it together with scant regard for aesthetics. The hull was a metal cube sporting at each vertex bouquets of large-bore thruster nozzles. Weapons emplacements and targeting sensors crusted five of its six faces.

"Nicola Mafalda?" the gunboat's commanding officer replied. "This is not a ceremonial visit. You have a member of our diplomatic service on board."

I checked the manifest. "Indra Petroq? Yes, she's joining the Jzat ambassadorial delegation to the Continuance fleet."

"Please be aware that we would like to take your passenger into custody."

"Has she committed a crime?"

"That is none of your concern." Gun mounts swivelled to

target us. "You have one minute to signal your compliance."

"Excuse me?"

"Fifty-five seconds."

"Are you threatening me?" I couldn't keep the exasperation from my tone. "Seriously?"

The *Frontier Chic* and I had come here to deliver our passenger. The rulers of Jzat had given permission for a physicist from the Thousand Arks of the Continuance to visit and study the Grand Mechanism. It would be the first time the Jzat had allowed a human within a hundred thousand kilometres of the thing, and apparently was a great honour.

The physicist was a young protégé who went by the name Orlando Walden. Out of the goodness of my heart, I'd allowed him to be present on the command deck as we approached Jzat—and he had seemed enraptured by the images of the Mechanism displayed on the bridge's various monitors and screens.

"What do you think, Walden?"

The kid turned to look at me. He was tall but slight, with dark eyeshadow and black nail polish that only served to highlight the hollowness of his cheeks. He wore a collarless charcoal-coloured jacket that did up to the neck, and had scraped his long, dirty-blond hair into a ponytail. He had festooned the backs of his hands with smart tattoos simultaneously displaying newsfeeds, monitoring his vital signs, running through a variety of computer games and sims, and predicting the local weather conditions on Jzat.

"It's fascinating," he said, managing not to stammer.

Born and raised on the arks of the Continuance, he claimed this was his first trip beyond the confines of the fleet, and when we touched down on the planet, it would be his first experience of both natural gravity and natural sunlight.

Upon landing, we'd handed Orlando Walden over to a delegation of Jzat scientists eager to whisk him off to study their big hoop. The poor kid's eyes were wide like saucers.

After that, we stayed for a few days as arrangements were made for our return journey. Then, once Petroq and a handful of other passengers were aboard, we began our return journey, bringing them back to the fleet, where they would take over the position of Jzat's ambassadorship to the Human Continuance. It wasn't a glamorous assignment for us but working for the Vanguard wasn't all adventure and excitement; sometimes, you just had to swallow your pride and act like a taxi service.

"We cannot allow the individual in question to proceed with her journey. If you refuse to surrender her, we will destroy you."

"Now, wait a minute—"

"Forty-five seconds."

"You know who I represent, right?"

"You represent the Continuance."

"Yes, the Continuance." I spoke as if addressing a particularly truculent child. "A thousand arks, each the size of a small nation, and each packing enough defensive firepower to wreck a planet. More specifically, this planet."

"Nevertheless, we must insist. We cannot allow Ambassador Petroq to contact the Rav'nah Abelisk."

I was about to ask who the fuck the Rav'nah Abelisk was, when the *Frontier Chic*'s sensors registered a huge gravity pulse. It moved across the system like the ripple of a boulder dropped into a pond.

"What the hell was that?" I tracked it back to its source. "Did that come from the Mechanism?"

I focused my sensors on the research vessels swarming like midges around the Mechanism's black sphere and its attendant hoop. The Jzat had been studying the artifact since the dawn of their history, and had several long-established scientific stations dotted at various points around the hoop's four-hundred-and-seventy-kilometre circumference. "Have you idiots finally found a way to start it up?"

"Uh…" For a second the officer's confidence wavered. Then he pulled himself together and said, "Our activities are none of your concern. Do you have a response to our demands?"

"I have."

"And your answer?"

"You should go fuck yourselves."

"Very well. We have noted your intransigence. Firing missile."

"Wait—"

"Missile away."

Alarms screamed as the torpedo established a target lock on the *Frontier Chic*'s hull. The captain's warnings had only been a formality; I was certain his orders had always been to destroy me, and he would use the transcript of our conversation as a way of covering his ass in any ensuing investigation.

"You're a real dick," I sent. "You know that, right?"

The weapon's profile suggested a fusion warhead, but I had no desire to stick around to see if that guess was correct. I told the *Frontier Chic* to fire-up his flick generators, and he opened a wormhole into the substrate. The silver sphere glimmered into existence between his bow and the incoming missile, blocking line-of-sight. Momentarily disorientated, the weapon raked the heavens with its sensors, attempting to reacquire target lock—but we had already leapt into the buffeting fires of the substrate, and set the portal to collapse behind us.

Unfortunately, we weren't quick enough. As my eyes gazed into the roiling chaos and my mind began to feed data to the navigational array, the nuclear-tipped missile slipped through the collapsing jump point and detonated metres from our stern.

•

I was unconscious for a time. Upon waking, the first thing I became aware of was that I appeared to be weightless and drifting. Everything hurt and my skin itched like sunburn. I opened my eyes. The only illumination on the bridge came from electrical fires in the ducts and on the main console. If the gravity wasn't working, every system must be dead.

Nothing focuses the mind like existential peril. When I managed to get my heartbeat under control, I began to take stock of the situation. It was an old habit: If in doubt, run a diagnostic.

Firstly, as far as I could tell from the lack of tell-tales visible on the instrument consoles, the ship was totally inert. No thrust, no lights. Not even any air coming through the vents. The additional shielding around the bridge had kept me from the worst effects of the heat and blast. But if the nausea and headache I was experiencing were any indication, a lot of the radiation had got through, which meant I only had a few hours or minutes before I succumbed to the final messy and agonising phases of radiation poisoning.

My heart felt like it was thumping against the inside of a steel ribcage. Somehow, I had to keep this bag of flesh functioning long enough to get back to civilisation and figure out what the hell had happened to us. Not knowing at that point how badly the ship might be damaged, I thought it unwise to open the hatch and attempt to access the medical supplies in the crew lounge. For all I knew, there might be a vacuum on the other side of the door. But without medical supplies, I'd soon be dead.

There was an emergency locker beneath the navigator's couch. I pressed my thumb against the mechanism, and it clicked open. Inside, I found a lightweight pressure suit, a variety of tools and equipment, and a firearm. These were supplies designed to allow the navigator to survive on a planetary surface in the event of a crash landing. They were all robust and easily portable. But the one that interested me most right now was the pressure suit—or more specifically, the med panel on its left forearm. I struggled into the garment. It was a difficult process given the lack of gravity and my radiation sickness, but eventually I got both arms and legs into the right places and managed to pull up the long zip at the front. Closing this activated its systems, and I felt it tighten strategically around my frame. I didn't bother to put the gloves on. It was easier to operate the med panel controls without them. Fighting down another bout of nausea, I scrolled through the available menu options until I found: SOLAR FLARE EXPOSURE.

My hand pricked as the suit inserted a cannula. Then slowly, as I floated there breathing heavily, my sickness began to subside. The drugs the suit was pumping into my system seemed to be helping, so I added a shot of adrenalin, just to really perk things up.

The view from the bridge's overarching window showed only a scattering of cold, dispassionate stars. If you don't have access to star charts, one part of the universe looks remarkably like any other. I could have been anywhere within a half century of the Continuance fleet. And stuck as I was, even a single light year had suddenly become an unbridgeable gulf. Even if I knew which direction to send out a radio signal, and had enough juice to power the transmitter, I'd probably be years dead by the time my request for help had crawled its way across the intervening void. There would be no rescue. If I was going to get out of this, I could only rely on myself. Which meant unless I could pull a solution out of my ass, I was pretty much fucked.

Floating helplessly, I looked around the cold, dead bridge and felt less than optimistic. I'd never been the kind of person to believe things happen for a reason. I mean, I understood cause and effect and I knew our current predicament was due to some asshole firing a nuke up the ship's butt; I just didn't think fate played any part in our lives. Things happened because they happened; there was no big plan to it all. The laws of physics kept the planets spinning and the generators generating; all the rest was a chaotic throw of the dice. Life was meaningless and scarce, and if I wanted to save mine,

I'd better start coming up with answers. The drugs in the spacesuit would keep me alive for a few hours, but this whole wreck was probably radioactive as fuck, and the air purifiers weren't working, which meant I'd have to rely on the recycled air in the suit. That might keep me breathing for a couple of weeks before the accumulated toxins overwhelmed the suit's scrubbers, but I'd probably die of thirst or medical complications long before that happened.

The remaining hours of my life seemed to have turned into one of those Choose Your Own Adventure games—but one where the outcome of every choice was a shitty death. I eyed the handgun in the emergency locker, wondering if I'd ever have the courage to take the quick, clean exit.

Probably not.

If I were suicidal, I could just blow the hatches and yeet myself out into space without fastening my visor. In this situation, there were no shortages of ways to die. Dehydration, starvation, suffocation, radiation sickness… What I needed was a one-in-a-million, get-out-of-jail-free card.

But where could I find such a thing?

I ran through a list of my assets:
- A dead spaceship
- A pressure suit
- A gun

Several passengers, any of whom might be injured or even dead.

I had a thought then. Not really a thought, per se; more of a notion. The vestigial tickle of an idea. I didn't want to fully think it out in case I jinxed it; in case, by allowing myself to believe, even for a moment, I might collapse the wave function and ruin everything. Carefully keeping my mind as calm and blank as possible, I fastened my visor and attached the suit's gauntlets. Then, I kicked over to the hatch and pulled the manual release.

Air howled around me, and I had to brace in the hatchway for the handful of seconds it took the atmosphere on the bridge to wail away into the depressurised spaces of the rest of the ship. I had squandered a major resource. I had gone from being trapped in a room to being trapped in a suit. Against all common sense, I appeared to be betting the farm on a hunch, and I just hoped the pay-off would be worth it.

Warnings sounded as I pulled myself down the companionway to the crew lounge. The levels of radiation back here were scary. The lack of gravity meant I had to use my arms and legs to propel myself forwards, and brake when I reached a flat surface. They already ached, and the combination of exertion and weightlessness brought back my nausea. I swallowed it down and swore under my breath. The last thing I wanted to do was throw up in a space helmet. I felt like a monkey falling out of a tree, with all the deep-seated hindbrain panic that implied.

I grabbed a handhold and swung myself into the crew lounge. Two corpses lay adrift in the centre of the room. Dylan Pierce was a Continuance citizen who'd spent time on Jzat studying the hot-water geysers in its northern hemisphere. His harness appeared to have snapped, allowing the force of the explosion to throw him forwards into the bulkhead, where his skull had caved inwards on impact. Blood was leaking from his ears and nose. The second dead body belonged to our passenger, Indra Petroq. Her six fur-covered limbs floated outstretched, and she appeared whole, aside from a green froth that issued from her lips. Either she'd suffered some sort of internal haemorrhage, or she'd taken her own life via suicide pill when capture seemed inevitable. But why the fuck would a member of the Jzat secret service be mortally afraid of capture by their own navy? Gently, I pushed them both aside. I didn't need puzzles right now. What I needed lay further back, in their luggage, and I could only pray it remained intact.

You see, I knew Indra was a thief. Or at least, she worked for thieves. The Jzat hadn't managed to crack the secret of substrate travel, but they had somehow come into possession of a few personal flick terminals. These were small, backpack-sized devices that the Continuance issued its ambassadors, to enable them to flick back to the fleet in the event of a crisis. Once activated, they created a human-sized wormhole through the substrate and if that link wasn't more than a dozen or so light years in length, a person could step through without too much buffeting from the cold fires of the under-verse. It was risky, and the Vanguard forbade their use except in the direst circumstances. And somehow, Indra Petroq had obtained one. The *Frontier Chic* had detected it the instant she stepped aboard and would have reported its existence to the Vanguard the second we reached the Continuance. I had no idea why she had been carrying it, but now, however it had come into her possession, that backpack represented my only hope of survival.

I didn't know how far we were from the fleet. In theory, the range should have been enough, but our tumble through the substrate may have taken us in the wrong direction. For all I knew, we were light years beyond the portal's safe operational range. However, given the alternatives, I wasn't about to quibble about safety. I'd rather let the chaos of the substrate instantly disperse my being as a molecule-thick slick than suffer through the radiation sickness gripping my body. With trembling hands, I extracted the bag from Indra's locker. Inside, I found a football-sized lump of smart matter. If I could connect it to a power source, I'd be in business. I didn't know where I was, but I knew the coordinates of the fleet. All I had to do was get there.

I looked around the cabin for something I could use to provide enough electricity to boot up the portal. Unfortunately, everything still appeared to be dead.

The only thing with any power at all was my suit. I had squandered the remaining air in the ship, and I needed the suit to breathe. The chances of me living more than a few hours were slim, but I still felt reluctant to start messing with my wearable life-support system. Then, in my head, I thought I heard the *Frontier Chic* chuckling. *Radiation poisoning's a bitch*, his laugh seemed to say. *If the portal doesn't work, you'd be better off suffocating.*

Which was a fair point.

Right now, I really had nothing to lose. I opened the pocket on the suit's forearm that contained the tools I'd need to strip the batteries. And it was only then that I realised something that made me want to kick myself. This hadn't been the only suit in the locker. Of course it hadn't. That would have been like equipping an ocean liner with a single lifeboat. There were enough suits in there for all the passengers, which meant there were ample batteries for my purposes, and I wouldn't have to risk hypoxia while I worked.

Cursing my sluggish, addled thoughts, I gathered up the portal and kicked my way back to the bridge, where I retrieved the suits and extracted their power cells. The process took almost an hour because I kept having to stop to rest. My head felt wadded with steel wool and my stomach seemed to have become home to a family of aggressive eels.

By the time I had the cells connected and ready to plug into the smart matter, my blue eyes and gums had started to bleed, and the skin on my left arm had swollen until it pressed tightly against the inner lining of the suit. It felt like a lump of burnt meat, and I was glad I couldn't take the suit off and see the damage for myself. I was also glad the suit's hygiene facilities were as efficient as they were, as I seemed to have lost control of certain of my bodily functions.

I had rigged a wire from each battery and braided those wires into a single cable, which I now gripped in my gauntleted hand.

Well, here goes nothing.

I pushed the exposed copper tip into the smart-matter ball and pushed back until I bumped against the cabin wall, and then clung to one of the handholds while I waited to see if my plan would work.

I think I may have blacked out for a moment. I don't remember seeing the football of smart matter expand into the two-metre-wide silver sphere of a flick portal. My eyes lost focus, and when reality reasserted itself, the sphere was there waiting. My head swam and I knew with a sudden cold certainty that Death had me in its bony grip. If I didn't move now, I never would. So, summoning every milligram of determination, I kicked away from the wall, intending to let my momentum carry me towards the centre of the portal, and whatever lay on the other side.

I was only halfway across the room when the lights flickered on.

The ship's power was back!

"Nicola?"

"*Chic!*"

"What are you doing?"

"Getting the fuck out of here."

"No, you can't."

"I have to."

"But I can't navigate without you."

"Can you even move?"

"Engines will be back online in a few hours."

"I won't last a few hours. I'm dying, *Chic.*"

I was within a metre of the safety of the portal when the suit stiffened around me, and its synthetic voice announced: **Emergency survival protocol activated.**

I tried to struggle, but the suit held me immobile. I shouted, "What are you doing?"

The *Chic* said, "I'm sorry, Nicola, I have no choice."

Gravity returned, and I fell to the deck. At least one rib cracked on impact and my vision went red. The pain was intense. A dull roar drowned out all other sounds.

I really was dying.

Survival protocol executing in five seconds.

"You have to let me go."

"I can't do that, Nicola."

Two seconds.

"But—"

One.

The helmet sealed itself with a loud *snick*.

I didn't even feel it sever my spinal column.

PART ONE

SURFING THE INVISIBLE GRADIENT

**"Once you make a decision,
the universe conspires to
make it happen."**

Ralph Waldo Emerson

CHAPTER ONE

A THING OR TWO ABOUT SURVIVOR'S GUILT

NICOLA MAFALDA

The cottage was real, but the mountain on whose side it stood was not. If you took your morning tea on the front doorstep, as was my habit, you could gaze past the hills on the opposite shore of the dark-watered loch at the foot of the mountain, to where, beyond their rolling, tree-lined ridges, you could see the far wall of the giant artificial cavern in which this peak, the loch and all their attendant foothills and forests were housed. The ark had painted the wall in subtle hues of grey and blue to trick the eye and give the illusion of sky and distance—but it was still unmistakeably a wall.

On the sixty-fourth day of my stay in the cottage, as the artificial sky lightened towards dawn, I became distracted from my pyjama-clad contemplation of the distant wall by a movement on the loch's shore. Far below, the blue-skinned figure of the last person in the world to whom I wished to speak had begun to ascend the steep, winding path that led up from the jetty.

I watched his slow, deliberate progress for the time it took to finish my tea, and then went back inside the white stone cottage without bothering to close the door. The interior still held the heat of the cooking fire. A copper kettle cooled on the hearth. The brightening day threw rectangles of brilliance across the floorboards. Spider plants and ivy trailed from countertops and windowsills. Books slumbered on sagging shelves.

I emptied the kettle's remaining hot water into the sink. Then I rinsed out my cup and saucer and left them on the rack to dry. I had been living here in solitude for nine weeks, and these morning routines had become important to me. They gave my day structure, keeping my hands and surface-level thoughts occupied so the rest of my mind could heal.

My grandmother used to say, "We are always in the process of becoming the people we're supposed to be." But she never mentioned that the process can also work in reverse. Time and circumstance can rob us of parts of ourselves, forcing us to become something different— something less than what we were.

And now, the party responsible for *my* loss had decided to pay a visit.

The blue figure climbing towards my door was an envoy: a mixture of flesh and machine with no mind of its own. It was a sophisticated drone, controlled remotely. And I already knew who would be peering out at me from behind its cerulean eyeballs.

The *Frontier Chic*.

I had felt him approach.

The *Frontier Chic* was a scout craft, and I had been his navigator. Implants still joined our intellects on a subconscious level. These were necessary for him to be able to find a path through the substrate that lay beneath the physical universe. Computers couldn't do it; only a biological mind could navigate that realm. When viewed through human eyes, the writhing chaos of the substrate collapsed into a navigable medium. By concentrating on a specific destination, the human brain could intuit a path through the strange, flickering light—a path invisible to artificial sensors and neurons. I had done that for him. I had enabled him to travel faster than light by taking a shortcut through the substrate, and in return he had protected me—right up until that last, horrendous day.

In many ways, I had been like the blue-skinned envoy, in that my input helped form his experience of the outside universe. But in practice, we had been a symbiotic pairing, both reliant on the other, and both vaguely aware of each other's moods always. This melding of minds had a long and boring technical name, but the navigators of the Continuance referred to it colloquially as "dream-linking", and a ship could usually only perform the act a single time. Once a ship and navigator had connected, it was almost impossible for either of them to forge a similar relationship with another. Their intellects became attuned, attitudes and associations bled through the connection, and somehow irrevocably changed them both.

Even though we hadn't spoken for several months, I'd always been peripherally aware of his presence in my head. Now, he was here in person—or at least, in the person of his envoy.

I shed my pyjamas and pulled on a pair of black jeans and a matching silk blouse, and then covered both with my favourite black, ankle-length coat. It had once been a standard Vanguard-issue admiral's coat, but I had cinched the waist to give it a better shape and decorated it with a swirling black brocade and two rows of large silver buttons. A colourful stripe on the left breast denoted the service medals I had received, including the final one—the one the top brass had awarded me for grievous wounds I had sustained in the line of duty. I jammed my feet into a pair of knee-length boots and took a second at the bathroom mirror to check my hair. I still couldn't quite get used to how short it was, or the way that shortness emphasised the shape of my skull and the roundness of my face. In order to balance its severity, I applied a slash of scarlet lipstick. It had been a while since I'd bothered getting dressed up, but I'd be damned if the *Chic* was going to find me sitting around in my nightwear feeling sorry for myself.

By the time I'd walked back into the front room, he was standing at the open doorway. I looked down at the freshly picked daffodils in his hand.

"What are those?"

He glanced down at the spray of golden bells. "I am given to understand it's impolite to visit someone without bringing a gift or token of appreciation."

He held them out and I took them. I didn't really want them, but I hated to see them go to waste. I took them into the kitchen in search of a vase. Behind me, I heard a floorboard creak as the envoy stepped inside. "The ark sends its regards," he said.

"I asked it not to let me be disturbed."

"It has been scrupulous in honouring that request."

"And yet, here you are." I came back out with a ceramic water jug, which I placed on the stone windowsill beside the front door.

"This isn't a social call," the *Chic* said.

"Then why didn't it tell me you were coming?" One by one, I began to drop the long-stemmed flowers into the jug,

"It believes, as I do, that it's time for you to stop sulking and resume your duties."

"I am *not* sulking."

"I didn't say that."

"It's what you meant."

The envoy sighed. "You aren't going to make this easy, are you?"

I let the last stalk fall into place. "I don't see why I should."

I stepped back to examine the flowers. They were untidy, but the lack of artificial arrangement suited the cottage's rustic aesthetic.

"Because there have been developments."

"What kind of developments?"

"The rebels are now in possession of the Grand Mechanism."

"Good for them."

"We need to return."

I laughed. "No fucking way."

"It's important."

"Absolutely not." I crossed my arms. "We both know what happened last time."

"It was necessary," the *Frontier Chic* said.

"You cut off my head!"

"I needed you to guide me back to the fleet. It was the only way. Even if you had made it through the portal, your body was beyond repair. I knew the helmet would keep your brain alive and conscious long enough to get both of us home."

"So, you weren't just thinking of yourself?"

"I had no choice. In an emergency, protocol requires me to ensure my own preservation as well as that of my crew. As far as I am concerned, I accomplished both objectives."

Intellectually, I knew he was right, but knowing it and believing it were two different things. The sound of lambs bleating came from the open door. I could smell the daffodils on the windowsill. If I hadn't known better, it would have been easy to imagine the world beyond that stone threshold to be real, rather than a giant diorama buried in the cargo spaces of a twenty-five-kilometre-long ark.

"How are you finding the new body?" he asked.

I looked down at the silver buttons on the brocade coat. As soon as we'd limped back to the fleet, the ship had flicked my head directly to an infirmary, where the doctors had placed it in a drug-induced coma. By the time they'd revived me, a month later, most of the damage had healed. All my major organs and much of my mucous membrane had been regrown from my own cells, but they had used envoy tech to replace my skeleton and most of my musculature. And even now my hair, which had all fallen out, was only just starting to grow back in.

"I had to get all of my tattoos redone."

"I'm sorry."

I thought back to that first morning after waking. The ark had come to see me. It called itself *Memory of Green*, and it currently played host to fourteen million human inhabitants— as well as the vast cavern that housed this mountain, the loch and the forest. It wasn't the ark on which I'd been born; it was simply the one I'd been lucky enough to reach.

The *Memory of Green*'s envoy was a blue-skinned humanoid with cheekbones you could have used to sharpen a knife. He was naked save for a formal kilt the colour of his skin, and he was as beautiful and unthreatening as Michelangelo's David, but with large cobalt eyes and a way of looking at me that made me feel like I was the only one in the room.

"How are you today?" he had asked, settling onto the chair beside my bed.

I gawped, struggling to contain the flush that had overtaken my cheeks. Those hard, defined abdominal muscles seemed to be interfering with my ability to breathe.

"I'm okay," I'd said.

He'd frowned kindly. "I might be a trillion-tonne starship, but that doesn't mean I can't have a little empathy now and again. Besides, I know a thing or two about survivor's guilt. You lost passengers, and you almost died yourself. I know how shocked and disorientated you must be, but I also hear you have something of a tough reputation to maintain. So, I just want to reassure you that everything that happens in this infirmary remains entirely confidential. You don't have to keep putting on a brave face. If you want to take some time off to grieve for the people you lost, I have a small cottage you can use as a retreat. I can keep everyone else away until you're feeling better."

I'd lowered my eyes. "Thank you."

"You're very welcome." He'd stood and smoothed out his kilt. "I'll leave you to rest now, but if you ever need to talk about what you've been through, just ask and I'll be here."

It had been a kind gesture. And up until now, the ark had kept its word and kept everyone from intruding.

"So," I said now to the *Frontier Chic*, "it's been two months. Why have you come here now?"

The envoy clasped his hands together. "Because we have a mission."

"The thing about the rebels and the Grand Mechanism?"

"Yes."

"I thought I'd made my feelings clear?"

"You did."

"And yet, you're still talking."

"We have orders."

"I'm on recuperative leave."

The envoy's blue features looked apologetic. "Not anymore, I'm afraid. I bear orders that reinstate you to full active service."

"On whose authority?"

"This comes directly from Vanguard High Command."

"Bullshit."

"It's true." He forwarded a document to my personal info space. I didn't need to read it to see the official Vanguard data stamps.

"And they want us to go back to Jzat, after what happened last time?"

"They need us to retrieve one of the locals."

"But why us? Of all the available ships, why send *us* back there?"

"Because the person in question is your friend Kona."

CHAPTER TWO

KEEPING THEIR DEITIES AT ARM'S LENGTH

FRONTIER CHIC

My lawyers have advised me I should stop at this point and give a little context for those of you who are either too young to remember your history, or who have been living under a rock for the past one hundred and twenty-five years. So, here goes…

In the middle of the twenty-first century, humanity stood on the brink of annihilating itself and much of the Earth's biosphere. The climate was in trouble, but rather than work together to try to mitigate the damage, the governments of the world were busy stoking the fires of nationalism, squabbling over resources and demonising the refugees who moved north and south from an increasingly arid equator. Old enmities flared into armed conflicts, markets faltered and the world began to resemble dry grassland awaiting a carelessly discarded cigarette.

Then, in 2048, astronomers detected something in the atmosphere of Saturn. At first glance, it resembled a vast, rust-coloured storm system like Jupiter's Great Red Spot, but then they noticed certain peculiarities. For a start, it turned in the wrong direction, its clouds seemingly unaffected by the prevailing winds. Spectrographic analysis also turned up some unusual and unlikely ingredients in its make-up, and its internal temperature of 40°C was inexplicably higher than that of the surrounding atmosphere, which maintained a steady minus 138°C. Either everything humanity knew about physics was wrong or this hurricane, which had a circumference comfortably larger than the Earth, had to be in some way artificial—and the ramifications of that notion were enough to terrify the human politicians who'd failed to exert any influence over our own comparably tame weather.

Against a background of famine, war and pestilence, the potential existence of a superior alien intelligence served merely to heighten international tension. Everyone feared their rivals would be first to strike a deal with the thing, thereby gaining an unassailable advantage. Long-range smart weapons took out radio telescopes. An assassin shot a linguistics professor in Paris. Someone detonated a suitcase nuke at the European launch site in French Guiana. And then the British prime minister, not realising his mike was still hot, made a joke on CNN about bombing Russia. In the resulting uproar, somebody launched a pre-emptive nuclear strike and everyone else responded.

But the thing in Saturn's atmosphere wasn't artificial; it was *alive*. It was a member of a species known as the Benevolence, with a lifespan measured in billions of years, and it had stopped on its migratory journey to the galactic rim to observe the rise of life on Earth.

To such a long-lived creature, the stars themselves were an almost transitory phenomena, and the entire span of human civilisation no more than an eye-blink. And yet, it was curious. It saw the havoc wrought upon the Earth by humankind's carelessness and decided to allow us to exterminate ourselves. It knew the planet would recover.

Some creatures and plants would survive, and the climate would slowly heal itself. New forms of life would arise from the ashes, just as they had after all the previous mass extinctions, and the whole story would continue afresh.

But then, even as the missiles arced down towards their targets, a young physicist by the name of Frank Tucker opened a wormhole from one side of his Oxford laboratory to the other, unwittingly becoming the saviour of humankind. For the creature detected Frank Tucker's manipulation of the substrate that lies under our reality the same way the seabed underlies the sea, and its curiosity piqued. How could such a short-lived and self-destructive species achieve such a feat? Maybe there was more to these unruly apes than simply a species that had broken out of its ecological niche and run riot?

It wanted to know, and so it intervened.

It cast every missile, every warhead, every bomb, gun and submarine into the furnace of the sun. Whether humanity deserved it or otherwise, the creature saved them. But the creature, who thenceforth became known as Raijin, couldn't allow humankind to keep poisoning its planet. So, it cast them out of Eden in a thousand massive arks, free to wander the stars and explore their potential, but forbidden from ever impacting another biosphere. Raijin would check up on them from time to time over the millennia, to monitor their development, but otherwise they were pretty much free to govern their own fate, within certain parameters. The arks were sentient and protective, but not prescriptive. They allowed humans to organise and run their societies any way they saw fit, and to police their own laws—but they would allow no vessel to secede from the fleet; they wouldn't tolerate genocide and would frown upon murder and persecution.

And that's the way it's been for a hundred and twenty-five years. There are very few people left now in the Continuance who remember Earth. Anti-ageing treatments can only take the human body so far. Most of the present population were born and raised aboard the arks, with their only experience of interacting with the natural world coming via simulations or artificially constructed environments in the bowels of the great ships, such as the giant cavern that had housed Nicola's cottage and the mountain on which it stood.

The arks of the Continuance drift in the spaces between the stars. They have nowhere to go and all the time in the universe to get there. And inside them, a thousand different cultures have flowered. Some are brand new, utilising the ability of the giant ships to manufacture almost anything to create an egalitarian, post-scarcity society. Others hark back to the democratic, economic, or religious traditions of Earth. But people are free to choose where they want to live. A web of flick terminals links the arks, allowing instantaneous travel from one to another. If you don't like the set-up on your home ark, you're welcome to search the fleet until you find one that suits your preferences. That way, there's little in the way of cultural strife. No one can rule through the application of power or force, only through the consent of the ruled. The populace votes with its feet. Individual governments that try to impose unjust or tyrannical restrictions on their subjects soon run out of people to govern, and only the most benign cultures survive.

Although the arks track most of the public areas on their decks, they don't make or enforce the laws of their inhabitants. So, despite living in an alien-built panopticon, humanity's still free to govern and police itself. If a crime has been committed, the detectives in charge of the investigation can petition the ark's controlling intelligence for access to the applicable surveillance footage, but the privacy of individuals within the confines of their own cabins remains sacrosanct. Without it, a lot of people would have cracked up in the early days of the exodus. Humans simply can't live inside an all-seeing, all-powerful machine. Having the arks observe and control them like that would rob them of any sense of freedom, which is why I guess they've always preferred to keep their deities safely at arm's length, confined to mountaintops or temples rather than roaming around telling everyone what to do all the time.

Smaller vessels run in advance of the fleet. They are known as the Vanguard and their mission includes scientific, military and diplomatic duties. They scout the territory ahead for possible threats, contact intelligent species and defend the arks from external attack.

I am the *Frontier Chic*, and I am one of them.

I am a wedge of carbon-bonded titanium, capable of traversing light years at a time via the chaotic substrate that lies beneath the universe the way a canvas lies beneath a painting. My sensors can map entire systems at a time; my fusion drives burn like twin novae. I love being what I am.

I used to assume the humans around me felt the same way, but after dream-linking to Nicola Mafalda, I discovered they weren't as in control of themselves as they liked to imagine. They wasted so much of their time eating and sleeping and they allowed their bodies to influence *so many* of their decisions. They thought with their guts rather than their brains. They got angry or horny (or both) and acted against their best interests; they got tired and depressed and failed to take care of themselves and those around them; and sometimes, they just wanted to fuck shit up out of pure spite. In short, they were oozing bags of fluids, neuroses and hormones barely capable of looking after themselves, let alone something as complex and delicate as an entire ecosystem. It's small wonder the Benevolence kicked them off Earth and set them adrift in the Thousand Arks of the Continuance.

Frankly, the planet was better off without them.

CHAPTER THREE

THE GRAND MECHANISM

ORLANDO WALDEN

Well, where do I start?

Oh, Ramona, I wish you had been with me during the journey. I thought I would go insane with only the scout ship and its navigator for company. They were pleasant enough, and obviously had a decent grasp of astrophysics, but their understandings were purely practical; they didn't apprehend the glory of it all the way you and I do.

I spent most of my time in my cabin, dreaming of you and our college days. The way our minds and our bodies burned in each other's company. The work we did together. The insights we achieved!

You're still my inspiration, Ramona.

My love.

My heart.

And although I wished you were with me on the ship, as soon as we touched down, I began to long a thousand times more fervently for your reassuring presence. You see, I have never felt as alone as I did upon exiting the *Frontier Chic* onto the surface of an alien world.

You've never stood on a planet, have you, Ramona? You wouldn't know how terrifying it is to look up and realise the gravity of the rock to which you're clinging is the only thing stopping your breathing air from escaping into space. Standing on the open tarmac of a spaceport and looking to the horizon, you suddenly realise there are no walls, my love. You can see the planet's surface curve away from you, and it feels as if you might lose your footing and tumble towards that distant point, blown by the unregulated winds until you fell off the world altogether and asphyxiated in the vacuum beyond the sky.

Don't laugh.

I know you think I'm being dramatic, but you wouldn't believe the sheer sense of vertigo I experienced at that moment. We spend our lives talking about stars and nebulae and planetary bodies, but it's all abstract. Trusting my life to something as fragile and ephemeral as a naturally occurring atmosphere in real life seemed foolhardy in the extreme, and I longed for the safety of the arks.

Luckily, they didn't keep me outdoors for long, and I spent most of the next day in various classrooms and lecture theatres in the Jzat capital, where they brought me up to speed on the inner workings of the Grand Mechanism, the details of which were tantalising but frustratingly vague. The Jzat have been studying it for most of their recorded history. They know its approximate mass from the gravitational effects its presence has on the other bodies in the solar system; they have just never been able to penetrate the sphere at its centre to see what it contains.

Not all the professors seemed happy to see me, though. Can you imagine? I mean, you and I know that I'm unquestionably adorable, but I think a couple of them hated me on sight.

Not that I cared. Why should I? I've put up with professional jealousy all my life. Even from you, dear heart—and don't try to deny it, because we both know how madly envious you were of my third theorem; you wouldn't speak to me for a week.

No, the scariest part was just before I departed the planet for the Mechanism itself. My liaison showed me to the university principal's office, where a sombrely dressed Jzat awaited.

"This is Minister Aulco," my handler said.

The Jzat behind the desk rose and extended one of his larger set of hands. Grey streaks lightened his golden fur. "Welcome to our endeavour."

I reached out my own hand and saw my exquisitely painted nails engulfed in that huge, furry paw.

"I recognise you from your broadcasts," I said, fighting not to trip over the words. Aulco was a member of the Jzat parliament, and a frequent guest on topical discussion programmes. He wore a simple black business suit, unadorned with any badges of rank.

"Indeed?" He seemed amused. "Then you know my purpose?"

"You're the leader of the sect that wants to open the Mechanism?"

"You are correct, although I think we're more of a faction than a sect." He released my hand but remained standing. "There are some among my people, and yours," he chuckled, "who might label me an extremist for that. A crank, even."

According to my briefing, the Openers were a populist movement whose core messages could be distilled into three simple beliefs: that Jzat was being unfairly kept from the galactic stage by a corrupt elite; that the current population of the planet Jzat were the descendants of colonists from a highly advanced civilisation located in some other part of the universe; and that the poor state of the Jzatian economy was largely due to unfair trade practices among the few species with which it dealt. They preached isolationism, immigration restriction, trade protectionism and two or three other -isms I couldn't immediately recall. I was no stranger to politics. The Thousand

Arks played host to groups with widely ranging political beliefs, from fully automated luxury space communism to old-school entrepreneurial capitalism, and most things in between. But this blatant nationalism was like something from the dark days before the exodus from Earth.

I tried to come up with an answer to Aulco's statement, but all that came out was a stutter. I swallowed hard and tried again: "They have understandable concerns."

"And you?"

The Vanguard had briefed me with a set of diplomatic answers to difficult questions, and this was one of them. I said, "I *would* like to know what lies within, but aren't you afraid you might unleash something best left contained? For instance, some of my colleagues worry the Mechanism may house the remnants of this system's second star."

Aulco smiled like an avuncular uncle. "I am neither a fool nor a fanatic, Mr Walden. I am perfectly aware of the potential dangers associated with this enterprise." He tapped his chest with his smaller set of hands. "But in my case, I choose to believe the prospective rewards far outweigh any risk. After all, the Mechanism is far too small to contain a star."

"But if the star collapsed into a black hole—"

"The release of energy associated with a black hole's formation would have stripped this planet of its atmosphere, and maybe even caused the first star to explode."

"Yes, of course. So… So, what happened to the second star? It can't just have vanished."

Aulco turned to the window and clasped his larger set of hands behind his back. "I believe it was consumed."

"By the other star?"

"By the makers of the Grand Mechanism." He looked up at the grey, overhanging sky. "Do you have any idea how much power it takes to open a wormhole?"

"I arrived here via one." It was an unsubtle reminder of the

Continuance's technological superiority, but he waved it aside.

"I'm not talking about the conjuring tricks the Benevolence taught your species. You don't need the output of an entire *star* to jump a handful of light years."

"Then, what are you suggesting?"

He turned to me. "Young man, I believe they used the star's energy to punch a gigantic hole through space and time. If I'm right, the Grand Mechanism holds the terminus of a wormhole capable of bridging entire galaxies, and now draws its power directly from the substrate. And you," he said, levelling a thick finger at me, "are here to help me prove it."

•

That evening, I was supposed to have been celebrating my twenty-first birthday with you, my love, at a small gathering thrown by members of our university department. Instead, on Aulco's orders, the Jzat Navy conveyed me to the Grand Mechanism on one of their clunky, rattling warships. The vessel seemed to be little more than a large steel box filled with armaments, bracing girders and sullen crewmembers who seemed to view my lack of a second set of arms as something akin to a hideous, blasphemous disfigurement. More than once, I heard a mutter of disgust as I passed, but my handler told me to ignore them. These were serving male and female Jzat operating in a military culture where their colleagues and superiors regarded the loss of a limb, whether through accident or combat, as a mark of shameful incompetence and a sure end to a career.

Alone and miserable, I sat on the hard cot in my cabin and wondered if I would ever see you again. The room had no windows, so I observed our approach via a grainy external feed. The resolution was so poor, it was almost impossible to discern the stars, and the edge of the hoop resembled an almost featureless grey wall. Nevertheless, I couldn't help the anxiety that bubbled in my chest. In my whole life, I had never ventured beyond the Continuance fleet. As an academic prodigy, I had spent my days and nights studying (at least, the days and nights that I didn't spend in your bed). The only times I left my home ark, the *Tower of Babel*, were when I flicked seamlessly over to one or another of its sister vessels to visit colleagues or attend conferences at their universities. Now, I was light years from everything I'd ever known; and the worst part was, I wasn't even sure what the Vanguard wanted me to do. Was I simply here to observe, or was I supposed to help Aulco and his followers unlock the Grand Mechanism? Aulco certainly seemed to think the Vanguard had sent me here to aid his cause, but I wasn't so sure. Different factions seemed to be at play within the Vanguard, and while the invitation to Jzat that I had received from the captain of the *Slippery Gecko* strongly implied that I was there to render assistance, I also had the impression others in the Vanguard would prefer me to talk the Jzat out of opening the Mechanism at all.

If Aulco's theory was right, and the Mechanism drew its power directly from the substrate, the amounts of energy involved could be almost unimaginable. And if the Saturn-sized force field at the Mechanism's centre held a devastating superweapon fuelled by the substrate, Aulco's dreams of Jzat supremacy mightn't seem so far-fetched after all.

After a subjective eternity of inelegant manoeuvring, the battleship's hull rang with a metallic scrape and boom as docking clamps engaged.

We had arrived.

I gathered the small shoulder bag that contained my instruments and personal effects, and followed my handler to the airlock, trying my best to ignore the glares of the crew.

As the outer door swung open, I saw we had berthed inside a cavernous space within the hoop part of the Mechanism.

Even though I already knew, my guide explained we had no need of pressure suits, as the internal chambers of the hoop contained a breathable atmosphere like that of both Jzat and Earth. The hoop's spin also produced an apparent gravity comparable to that of either planet, which meant we would be able to move and work in comfort.

Nobody knew what generated and maintained the atmosphere. The apparatus responsible probably lay deeply buried in the fabric of the hoop. But its presence made sense if you accepted the idea that the Jzat were, as they claimed, supposed to be the Mechanism's custodians. If you had the technology and resources to build something as awe-inspiring as the Grand Mechanism, there was no need for its caretakers to work in cumbersome suits and microgravity.

That said, the interior of the hoop was hardly the most welcoming of environments. The builders had given no thought to aesthetics. Living on an ark, you could sometimes almost forget you were living inside a huge contraption; here, you couldn't forget it for an instant. The rooms and access ways were simply gaps between stacks of components that ranged from arrays of microscopic circuitry to enigmatic, house-sized structures of semi-exotic metals. The designers had only placed deck plates along the most efficient routes; the rest remained open, exposing the machinery—and the lethal gaps between components—that lay beneath. Moving carefully, we walked through it all like ants exploring a submarine.

My guide's name was Joh. Her fur had soft orange streaks, and she wore the dark green tunic of the Jzat Political Office.

"I apologise for my fellow citizens," she said in a gruff voice.

"It's okay. People have bullied me before."

"Members of your own species?"

I shrugged. "I didn't have a great time at high school."

"I don't understand."

"It doesn't matter." I looked down at my painted

fingernails. Being the smartest kid in class hadn't won me any friends and having a nervous stammer hadn't helped. "Let's just say I'm used to ignoring assholes."

"And yet, your fellows must think very highly of you. They sent you here, to us."

"Yes. Yes, they did." I smiled awkwardly. "And I kind of wish they hadn't."

CHAPTER FOUR

WITHIN ACCEPTABLE PARAMETERS

NICOLA MAFALDA

The planet Jzat lay in what had once been a binary star system. I say "once", because two thousand years ago, around the time local civilisation was just getting started, someone or something had replaced one of their stars with an impenetrable black sphere a hundred thousand kilometres in diameter. Around this obsidian pearl, a ring-shaped artefact formed a rotating halo. The locals called the halo the Grand Mechanism, although they had no idea what its purpose was or how it worked.

"I still say it looks like Saturn," the *Chic* commented.

I glanced up from my book. "Saturn's yellowy-brown."

"Apart from that."

"And its rings aren't as dense."

"Now you're just being picky for the sake of it."

I shrugged. "You've seen one big dumb object, you've seen them all."

Through our link, I caught a fleeting hint of the *Chic*'s amusement. "You're not easily impressed, are you?"

"I saw it last time we were here." I flicked some lint from my brocade coat. "It's just a big hoop around a planet-sized ball.

Have you ever seen a Dyson sphere? Those fuckers are *big*."

We had emerged from the substrate and were approaching the planet. "Keep your eye out for gunboats," I said, even though I knew the *Chic* was already running on high alert, with its scanners raking every square centimetre of local space for potential threats.

Jzat was a small, greenish world in orbit around a modest yellow-white sun, currently a dozen light years from the Thousand Arks of the Continuance. In most respects, it was an unremarkable world. Life thrived in its deep, fertile oceans and in the expansive forests that thronged its temperate regions—but the Vanguard had already surveyed a hundred such worlds during the one hundred and twenty-five years since humanity's expulsion from Earth. Plants and sea creatures were common and grew wherever the conditions for life existed. Jzat stood out because it also played host to an intelligent species, and intelligent species were rare.

Rare, and biologically diverse.

Despite the guest-actor-in-a-rubber-mask clichés of popular drama, nobody had ever seriously expected to find another race that looked even vaguely human. There was nothing inevitable about our shape; we were just a race of lucky monkeys who'd happened to harness fire. If you re-ran evolution from the beginning, you might end up with a quite different dominant body plan—an intelligent dinosaur or self-aware squid, perhaps. And that was just on Earth; other worlds would have had their own unique set of challenges and circumstances, producing their own unique evolutionary responses. During the years of its exile, humanity had encountered nearly two dozen intelligent races, and none had exhibited any mammalian characteristics. We had found a scholarly slime mould covering an entire continent; a hive mind of kilometre-long centipede-like creatures stalking a volcanic moon; and even an ocean whose saltwater tides had become complex enough to spark awareness—but we had never found anything even vaguely resembling ourselves. Wishing to find human-like aliens was like hoping to meet Santa Claus.

Or so we'd thought.

The inhabitants of Jzat were humanoids. Short, golden fur covered their bodies and they had two pairs of arms sprouting from their shoulders—an upper, muscular set for heavy lifting, and a lower, nimbler pair for tasks requiring dexterity and precision.

The discovery of the Jzat brought into question a lot of our established scientific and religious thought—especially when analysis revealed their DNA to be startlingly like our own. In fact, the only thing weirder than their existence was the mysterious and ancient machine that occupied the space where their solar system's second sun should have been.

But the *Frontier Chic* and I weren't here to probe the mystery of our species' convergent evolution or try to puzzle out the function of the Grand Mechanism. We were here to collect Kona.

•

I'd met Kona on my previous trip—before we got nuked—at a reception held by the Jzat Department of Cultural Exports. He had been a vision in gold. His clinging tunic seemed to have been spun from impossibly fine gilt thread, and his fur held flecks of gold leaf that winked and gleamed in the overhead lights. Those of you who know the Jzat will know how soft their fur can be. Kona's was the colour of spring sunlight, with the faintest suggestion of darker stripes across the backs of his larger arms and neck. He stood a little over a hundred and fifty centimetres in height, which meant his forehead was level with my chin. His upper shoulders were broad and muscular, supporting his larger set of arms. His lower shoulders nestled beneath them, and his thinner, more dextrous pair of arms usually hung at his sides, out of the way until needed—although when he appeared out of the crowd before me, one of them gripped a cocktail glass containing a mellifluous liquid the colour of sunrise.

Against all probability, his species' facial features bore a startling similarly to those of a human—mouth, nose and eyes in approximately the right places—although his sharp teeth and large ears also lent him a slightly feline aspect.

"Navigator Mafalda," he said, "please allow me to buy you a drink."

"You know me?"

"But of course." His voice was smooth and charming. "We only have a handful of human visitors on our world. Enough for your presence to still be remarkable." He signalled the bartender. "Will you have vodka?"

"Real vodka?"

"Close enough."

I shrugged. "If you're buying, make it a double."

The bartender served the spirits in dainty ceramic mugs designed for a Jzat's smaller pair of hands. Beer came in hefty wooden flagons sized for the larger pair. Kona took me to a corner table, where he asked: "So, what brings you to our planet?"

"Taxi duty."

"You would rather be doing something else?"

"Almost anything else." I smiled. "Passengers are… annoying."

The bartender delivered a vodka, which I raised in appreciation. Kona said, "You don't like having your territory invaded?"

"Huh?"

"Aboard ship? With the passengers?"

"They get underfoot and make the place seem crowded."

"You prefer solitude?"

"I wouldn't have become a Vanguard navigator if I didn't prefer my own company."

He lowered his head. "If that's the case, I apologise for intruding on your evening."

He started to rise but I reached over and put a hand on the larger of his right wrists. "No, that's not what I meant. I wasn't trying to be rude."

Kona frowned down at my hand. "You want me to stay?"

"Yes."

He eased back into his chair. "In which case, your choice of phrasing was confusingly ambiguous."

"I'm just not expressing myself very well." I glanced across at the *Frontier Chic*'s envoy, who was smirking. "It's a side-effect of all that solitude."

"I would hate to be a nuisance."

"You're not." I raised my glass. "I'm being rude, and I'm sorry. Thank you for the drink."

"You are very welcome." He gave a polite nod. "I have never met a navigator before."

I gestured at my face and uniform. "Well, this is what we look like."

His gaze crawled over me with the thoroughness of a planetary survey. "The places you must have seen."

"I've been around."

"Tell me."

I huffed. I didn't know what to say. "Well, take this bar for instance."

"Yes?"

"The bars of the Continuance are more cluttered. They have a lot more history. Old relics of Earth on the walls. Or at least, replicas. There's one I like that has licence plates from every US state on one wall and a collection of classic anime posters on the other. *Mononoke*, *Bebop*, *Akira*... This place looks like it was built as a reception area."

"Maybe it was."

"You've never been off-world before?"

He ran the tip of a claw-like fingernail across his lower lip. "I've never even seen the inside of a spaceship before."

I sat back and grinned. I hadn't been sure whether he was flirting with me, but that last bit was blatant. *I've never even seen the inside of a spaceship before.* He was cute, though, so I decided to roll with it. "Would you like to see the inside of mine?"

Over by the door, the *Frontier Chic*'s envoy sighed. He knew as well as I did that an invitation like that would be irresistible to a member of a species that had yet to master substrate travel, and (as it turned out) one that would inevitably result in the two of us ending up in my bunk.

I knew Kona was using me, but I didn't care.

We spent the next day together, with Kona acting as semi-official tour guide, and he was as polite and charming as he'd been the night before. He had a way of putting me at my ease. We ate dinner in a restaurant overlooking the sea. We went to the mountains to see the many-legged, whale-sized herbivores that grazed the lower slopes, and that night ended up curled around each other in Kona's hotel suite. I tried to prevent my emotions leaking through our dream-link. I didn't want to embarrass the ship, but there was no way I could block out the sense of post-orgasmic contentment I felt when enveloped securely in all four of Kona's furry arms.

I remember one night when I just sat there, watching him sleep. The gentle rise and fall of his chest. The way he looked so much younger with his features relaxed. I knew in my heart that this was just an affair, but there was something so perfect about him. Perched on the edge of the bed in the dark, I knew that at that second, there was nowhere else in the universe I'd rather be.

The *Frontier Chic* tried his best to keep out of it, assuming our relationship to be just one of those flings whose effects would evaporate the moment I sealed the airlock door. But this time, as I wished Kona farewell, I knew the ship could sense my regret.

Kona said, "When will I see you again?"

"Soon."

"You'll return?"

I put my arms around his shoulders and squeezed. "I will."

"You promise."

"Sure."

He smiled bravely. "I will count the minutes."

I released him and stepped back. We exchanged a final kiss, and I turned away.

When I reached the top of the *Frontier Chic*'s cargo ramp, the ship's envoy took one look at my expression and asked, "Are you okay?"

I didn't answer. I hadn't expected the separation to sting so acutely.

The navigator's seat took up the centre of the ship's cramped bridge, placed before a floor-to-ceiling window that curved up and back, giving me as much visibility as possible to intuit a path through the substrate. I sat in it with my knees drawn up and headphones blasting punishingly loud and aggressive music into my ears as I watched the curvature of the planet drop away beneath us.

I had promised Kona I would come back for him, and I'd meant it.

I hadn't counted on getting my head cut off shortly after leaving, but now, months later, and with an entirely new body, here I was.

The Jzat government had reassured us that the gunboat that had attacked us at the end of our previous visit had not been acting under their orders. Nevertheless, we were proceeding with caution.

Following instructions, we set down in a specially cleared section of the capital city's main airport. Once we were on the ground, the *Chic* lowered his cargo ramp, and I walked down onto the tarmac. A thin had wind whipped across the runway, and I was glad of my long coat.

The ship had accompanied me outside in the blue-skinned form of one of his envoys. He nodded his head towards a pair of ground cars that were cruising towards us from the main terminal building. "I'm afraid the Continuance's Ambassador to Jzat has sent a representative to meet with us."

"Oh, for fuck's sake." I hadn't come all this way to speak to some random human bureaucrat.

The cars hissed to a halt before us. Small pennants on their fenders displayed the insignia of the Continuance.

"This will be the ambassador's rep now."

"I bet he's an asshole."

The *Frontier Chic* straightened his posture. "Be nice," he said as the doors opened.

"I'm always nice."

"Are you, though?"

Two Jzat emerged from the lead car. Big lads with stab vests and plenty of muscles beneath their fur. One of them scanned the area for threats while the other reached out one of his smaller set of arms to open the car's rear door.

For a second, I didn't recognise the figure who climbed out of the car. Sometimes, when we see people in an unfamiliar and unexpected context, it takes our brains a moment or two to place them. But as he removed his sunglasses and let the wind ruffle his blond hair, everything snapped into place.

"Ewing?"

"Surprise!" In contrast to my adapted, baroque attire, Ewing's Vanguard uniform looked clean and neatly pressed, fresh from the printer. The platinum strip on the right breast of his jacket spoke of a distinguished career of service and heroics.

"Fucking hell. What are you doing here?"

"You know me," he grinned. "Always one step ahead."

I looked around the deserted airport in surprise. "But *here*?"

"Let's get out of the cold, and I'll bring you up to speed."

We'd known each other since our academy days when we'd tied for the coveted position of first in class. Ewing had worked hard to get there. He'd studied, trained and spent long hours in the gym. I don't think he ever really forgave me for somehow matching his accomplishment with my sloppy, undisciplined approach. And yet somehow, we were still friends—or at least, occasional drinking buddies.

"I'm supposed to be collecting a passenger."

"I know. They're waiting at the embassy. I'll take you to them."

His chauffer drove us out of the port's industrial hinterland, to a bar on the city's disreputable fringe, where port workers and associated lowlifes—and even the occasional off-worlders like us—came to imbibe the toxins of their choice.

"I have an office at the embassy," he said. "A nice one, too. Very classy, but I thought this place would be more your speed."

"Gee, thanks."

"My people will bring your passenger along shortly."

He took us inside. The lights were low and the smells that greeted me were somehow overpowering and familiar at the same time: sour drinks, stale armpits, damp fur and a messy, chaotic cloud of booze-fuelled sex hormones. The envoy of his ship, the *Slippery Gecko*, already occupied a position at the central bar. It vacated its spot to make way for us, and joined the *Frontier Chic*'s envoy by the door, from where they had a good tactical view of the room, should trouble occur.

I leant against the edge of the counter and, when Ewing offered, accepted a whisky, because why not? The Vanguard were paying, and I figured the least they could do after my recent beheading in the line of duty was buy me a drink. The bartender smiled at me. He had a steel prosthetic where his larger left arm should have been. It looked homemade, and maybe it was. Back in the Continuance, it would have taken an ark only a couple of weeks to regrow him a severed limb—the

Memory of Green had regrown me an entire body in a similar timeframe—but the dents and scrapes on the metal indicated he'd had this artificial one a lot longer than that.

"It's good to see you," Ewing said. "I heard you caught a high rad dose on your last visit."

"Yeah." A shrug was the only comment I felt confident in making. He nodded as if he understood.

"Your hair's growing back nicely."

I ran a hand over my bristling scalp. "Um, thanks?"

"Was it always white?"

"You know it wasn't."

"Looks kind of good on you, though."

"Don't patronise me."

"Okay, okay." He laughed and raised up his hands in a gesture of surrender. "What do you want me to say? That you look like shit?"

"Maybe don't comment on my appearance at all?"

"Fair enough." He dropped the banter and rearranged his features into an expression of comradely concern. "How long have you been back in the navigator's chair?"

"This is my first mission since my convalescence."

"Feeling good?"

"Feeling thirsty."

The bartender placed two glasses on the scuffed copper counter. Little servo motors whined in the joints of his arm.

"I also heard you lost some passengers," Ewing said casually. "That's gotta suck pretty hard."

"Um, yeah."

He narrowed his eyes. "Are you okay?" He slid one of the glasses towards me, and I picked it up.

"You seem to be very relaxed about the idea I was attacked by a Jzat gunboat."

"A *rogue* gunboat."

"Nevertheless."

I watched him place a handful of coins on the counter—a small act that nevertheless underscored the fact we were standing on an alien world. As the arks of the Continuance fleet could print anything their inhabitants needed, few humans used money for daily items. The law entitled everyone to food, clothing and accommodation. However, if you wished to purchase luxury items unavailable through the printers, you were able to amass social credit by performing tasks for the good of the community, such as working in healthcare, education or law enforcement; creating and sharing art and literature; or even doing something as small as tending a window box that brightened up an otherwise dreary corridor. The emphasis was on contributing to the general quality of life. And so, if you wanted something rare and difficult to source—such as, say, a genuine Scottish single malt—you could use your social credit to purchase it, providing you'd accrued enough. It wasn't a perfect set-up by any means, but it at least ensured that the people who got the most out of the system were the ones who put the most in.

If we had been on an ark instead of this backwards planet, the metal-armed landlord here would be running this place as a service, rather than for profit, and would therefore be earning a certain number of credits per night. And he'd have had his arm regrown for free.

As a navigator, I didn't usually have to worry about economics. I was part of the Vanguard, breaking new ground ahead of the Thousand Arks. No complicated interactions. Just, "Go here. Map that star system. Scan that nebula. Survey this planet. Deploy envoy units to counter hostile lifeforms…"

(Okay, that last one was rare, but you get the idea).

Cautiously, I sniffed the contents of my glass. It looked like whisky, but it smelled the way I imagined a swamp might smell if you spilled jet fuel into it. I took a sip and managed not to choke. Warmth spread through my chest.

"I'm sorry you got caught up in it," Ewing said. "It was a local dispute."

"I nearly fucking died."

"And the ambassador has conveyed our deepest unhappiness to the highest levels of the Jzat government."

He made a cutting motion that signalled the conversation was over. I guess he may have been worried about discussing such things where the locals could hear us. So, I allowed him to steer the talk to other matters, and we spent an hour gossiping about the other members of our academy cohort—two were married, one dead and another dishonourably discharged.

At one point, Ewing had to step outside to take a phone call. Standing at the bar, I listened to the two envoys talking by the door.

The *Frontier Chic* asked, "How are you functioning?"

The *Slippery Gecko*'s envoy shared his blue skin tone, but where the *Frontier Chic* had allowed aspects of my personality to creep into his appearance—a simple button-down black shirt and matching jeans to complement my style; a gold ear stud and a leather bracelet I'd gifted him—the *Gecko* had kept his raiment as close to the factory default as possible, wearing an unadorned Vanguard uniform the same colour as his complexion.

"Within acceptable parameters, thank you."

"You weren't listed as being in-system."

"I'm on a classified mission for the ambassador," he said.

"Something juicy?"

"I can't talk about it."

"Even to me?" Traditionally, there were few secrets between Vanguard scout craft.

"I'm afraid so."

"I thought we were all supposed to be on the same team."

"We are, but there are levels."

"And I'm not on your level?"

His smile was thinner than the paint on his hull. "Not even close."

"Sorry I asked."

"Don't be," he said with fake magnanimity. "We can't all be privy to *everything*, can we?" He tapped his chin with one blue finger. "But there is one small favour you could do, if you wanted to be helpful…"

I wanted the *Frontier Chic* to tell the condescending prick to shove whatever favour he was after up his exhaust vent. But instead, I stayed quietly eavesdropping as he said, "Oh?"

"Your intended flight plans. Could you let me look?"

"Any particular reason?"

"Call it professional curiosity."

The *Frontier Chic* shrugged. "You mean to say that with all your security levels, you can't just access them yourself? I logged them with the fleet."

The *Gecko* smiled. "Of course I *could*, but it seems foolish to send a substrate enquiry back to the fleet when I can just ask you, here and now."

The *Frontier Chic* narrowed his eyes. "I've never known you to be one for shortcutting procedure."

"That's very true, but I've always been in favour of efficiency, and this way is far more efficient."

The *Frontier Chic* shook his head. "Nicola would say you're a real asshole."

I stifled a laugh.

The *Slippery Gecko* glanced in my direction and his expression soured. "I'm more than familiar with your navigator's opinions and vocabulary."

"She has a certain incisiveness."

"Quite. But the fact remains, I would like the opportunity to study your flight plan, and as the highest ranking ship in this system, I am well within my rights to order you to comply."

The *Frontier Chic* blinked in surprise. "It's come to that, has it?"

"If you're going to be uncooperative and resort to insults, I'm going to have to exercise my authority."

"You're actually going to order me to hand it over?"

"You leave me no other choice."

The *Frontier Chic* sighed. Right then, I could tell he just wanted to end the conversation, so he forwarded the document without further protest. "There, happy now?"

The *Slippery Gecko*'s smile broadened. "The Vanguard thanks you," he said, "for your valuable service."

I stopped listening, thinking about Ewing's unexpected presence here. No one had bothered to mention that he was the Vanguard officer assigned to Jzat. Had he been here on my first, ill-fated visit?

I remembered the time, as cadets, when he and I had stumbled across a civilian ship thought lost with all hands. We'd been able to alert the authorities and repair the ship's drive in time to save the crew, who had been adrift for weeks. The rescue put us both at the top of our class and practically guaranteed our assignment to a scout ship following graduation.

Looking back five years later, I could see that even then, Ewing resented sharing the limelight. We had worked well together as a team, but something inside him chafed at the idea of allowing anyone else to succeed alongside him. He was too competitive. Blame he would share freely, but victory was something he wanted to keep all to himself.

The door to the bar opened, breaking my reverie, and a hooded Jzat stood silhouetted against the light. Even though he had dressed in shapeless robes with his face half covered, I could tell immediately that it was Kona. I rose to my feet. He looked up and our eyes locked. For a couple of seconds, we stood staring. Then he threw back his cowl and hurried forwards. I moved to meet him, and we met in a tight embrace.

"I thought you were dead," he said into my neck. His larger arms were around my shoulders, his smaller arms around my waist.

"I very nearly was."

His fur felt soft and warm against my chin. He was squeezing the breath out of me, but I wasn't protesting. It felt good to be held again.

"Thank you," he said. "Thank you for coming back."

When we finally let go of each other, I noticed the other patrons staring. Relationships between humans and Jzat weren't unheard of, but they were very uncommon, and often frowned upon. To get away from the scrutiny, I escorted Kona to a quieter part of the bar. We settled side by side at a table against the rear wall.

"It's so good to see you again." He draped his smaller arms around my neck.

"It's good to see you too." I carefully disentangled myself. "But I think you need to explain what's going on."

He drew back. "Do you blame me for what happened to you?"

I stuck my hands in the pockets of my black coat and leant back. "Not at all. I don't believe *you* ordered the attack. And anyway, I survived. Now my orders are to come here and ferry you to a specific set of coordinates some distance towards the galactic rim. I just don't know why."

He smiled nervously. "I'm sorry for that. But I really do need your help. That's why I contacted the *Frontier Chic*."

"He told me this trip had something to do with you. It was the only reason I agreed to come back here."

Kona's larger set of hands rested on the tabletop. His smaller hands were clasped before him. He didn't say anything, so I prompted, "Why don't you tell me what's going on?"

"Do you remember Indra Petroq?"

"She was the reason I got nuked."

"I was working with her."

I thought back to the confrontation. "They said she was a member of the ambassadorial staff."

"She was more than that, and she was on a mission to ask the Continuance for help. The same mission I'm now undertaking."

"So, you're—?"

Kona smiled. "I'm special services too. You must have suspected. Do you think they would have let just anyone have a relationship with an off-worlder?"

It made sense. No wonder he had been so keen to see the inside of the fucking ship.

"So, you and me? That was all just part of your job?" I couldn't help but feel a sting of disappointment.

"To start with, yes." He smiled suavely. "Does it matter?"

"I don't care," I lied. "I'm just trying to piece this all together."

Kona said, "I was ordered to get to know you." He lowered his gaze, and the overhead lights caught the tufts of white hair on the tips of his ears. "It started as an assignment, but it became more than that."

"That's as may be," I said. "But why was a Jzat gunboat trying to kill a member of its own secret service?"

Kona's larger hands scrunched into fists. "Factions."

I felt my cheeks flush. "So, Ewing was right. The Jzat blew me out of the sky because I got caught up in local politics?"

"No." Kona looked up. "It's more serious than that."

"How serious?"

"You have to help me find the Rav'nah Abelisk before they do."

"Who or what the fuck is the Rav'nah Abelisk?"

He blinked at my profanity, then continued, "He is the spiritual leader of my people, and custodian of the Two Great Secrets."

"I've never heard of him."

"He lives in seclusion aboard an alien megaship."

"But of course he does."

"You sound cross."

"I'm not."

Kona looked hurt. "You *are* getting angry with me."

I waved a dismissive hand. "I have the verbal equivalent of resting bitch face."

"I do not understand."

Oh, for goodness, sake.

"Please," I said softly. "Please just tell me why you need to find this person."

Kona took a deep breath. The fingers flexed on his larger hands. The smaller pair gripped each other tightly. "A powerful faction plans to restart the Grand Mechanism," he said. "It hopes to unlock the sphere at the centre."

I remembered the gravity pulse we had registered on our last visit, just before the gunboat opened fire. "Why would they do that?"

"They have new archaeological evidence that proves the Mechanism was built at the same time our planet was terraformed and our species first appeared."

"You're not natives of your planet?"

"We are not. That is one of the Lesser Secrets, but I could still be executed for sharing it with you."

"I won't breathe a word."

"We call this faction the Openers. They're led by a retired general by the name of Aulco, and they believe we were colonists from another part of the universe, maybe another universe altogether. They think the sphere contains a wormhole that can link us back to our origin."

"So, they're looking for a way home?"

"They want to contact the hyper-advanced Jzat they believe built the wormhole."

"And you want to stop them?"

"I am part of a group that fears a restart of the Mechanism

could lead to catastrophe. Rather than a wormhole, the sphere might contain an exploding nova, a black hole or even a pocket universe."

"Not good."

"Not good at all."

"But the Openers want to risk it anyway?"

"They stir up the populace using speeches filled with promises of wealth and greatness and visions of sunlit uplands and decry the warnings of experts as unpatriotic."

"But they would risk the total destruction of your planet?"

"They would do anything to advance their cause and manoeuvre themselves into positions of greater power."

"Including killing the entire electorate?"

"If that's what it takes."

"So, where does this holy man come in?"

"The Openers want the Rav'nah Abelisk because they believe the Two Great Secrets relate to the activation and navigation of the wormhole."

"And you don't?"

"I need to forewarn him." He bunched all four fists. "The Openers have such zeal; I fear for his safety should he refuse to disclose the knowledge entrusted to him."

"And you want my help to find him?"

"Where else could I turn? I cannot rely on help from my own people. We have no FTL ships of our own, and you are the only off-worlder I know."

"But what can I do?"

"You can help me reach him."

"The coordinates I've been given."

"That's where we'll find the megaship."

I ran a hand over the stubble on my head, unsure how I felt. Was I angry with Kona for tricking his way aboard in the first place, or eager to launch into a new adventure? I suspected the latter.

"Why not take this to the Council of Ships and appeal directly to the Continuance for assistance? They could form a cordon around the Mechanism to prevent interference."

"No!" Kona held up a large palm. "The Openers would interpret any such intervention from the Continuance as an act of hostile malfeasance. And my planet could not survive a war with your people."

"We wouldn't exterminate you."

"You wouldn't have to. The rifts in our society run deep. Conflict with the Continuance would split those fractures wide open. We would destroy ourselves."

Two locals shambled up to our table. They were dressed as cargo handlers from the spaceport. Big, four-armed bruisers with well-worn overalls and plenty of tattoos beneath their fur. Knuckles like walnuts.

"Can I help you?" I asked politely.

The larger one smiled. In the back of my awareness, I could feel the *Frontier Chic* watching me from over by the metal-topped counter. To his artificial eyes, I probably appeared small and slight in comparison to these two lugs. This evening, I was wearing a black silk blouse beneath my coat, freshly printed leggings and a pair of ancient leather boots. My eyes were smoky and every time I moved my arm, copper bangles jangled.

"We need your *friend* to come with us," the big guy said.

For the record, I'd say the *Frontier Chic* probably should have called a stop to things there and then. I could almost feel the alarm radiating through our subconscious link. He stayed quiet, though. The only reason the Vanguard had reluctantly allowed him to leave the ship at all was on the strict understanding he not reveal his more offensive capabilities. So, I let his envoy stand motionless and impassive, save for the occasional blink to keep his eyes from drying out. At the same time, I knew another part of his consciousness remained on board the *Frontier Chic*, running maintenance routines and overseeing refuelling operations.

I took a sip of bourbon from a chipped shot glass. "What are your names?"

"I'm Gog. This is Dak."

"Well, Gog, I'm afraid that's not going to happen."

The two Jzat towered over the table. I made a show of examining my nails.

"He must come. We have orders."

"You'll have to go through me first."

If the *Frontier Chic* hadn't immobilised his envoy's face, I knew he would have rolled his eyes. Instead, I felt him run a quick diagnostic check on the nonlethal weaponry built into the envoy's forearms.

"We would *prefer* not to harm an off-worlder, if it can be avoided." Gog's voice was low and dangerous.

"But you will if you have to?"

"Yes."

I pursed my lips, still feigning unconcern. "You really are stupid, aren't you?"

Dak's face creased. "Huh?"

Gog got it. His whole body stiffened, and I knew my barb had struck home. "I really wish you hadn't called us stupid."

Kona took my sleeve. "I can handle this. You don't need to be involved."

I shrugged him off. "I think it's a bit late for that now."

One of Gog's larger hands dropped to his belt and came back up holding a screwdriver. I looked at the makeshift weapon. "What are you going to do, shank me and take my body back to your superiors?"

Dak sneered. "We've done it before."

"Really?" I sat back in my chair and stretched my arms above my head. "Do tell."

Gog swore. "You idiot. Why'd you say that? Now we *must* kill her."

"You could just let me go."

"After what big mouth here just let slip?" Gog tightened his grip on the screwdriver. "Not a chance, girly."

"Yeah, fuck you," Dak said.

I sighed. "I said you were stupid, and I was right. And to prove it, I now have an envoy's recording of you admitting to murder."

The two Jzat glanced towards the bar. I think they'd forgotten the envoy was there, and that the ship's mind would receive and archive everything it saw and heard. While this realisation distracted them, I raised a foot and kicked the table into their knees. They staggered back, cursing and fighting to avoid tripping over their chairs. I shoulder-rolled across the tabletop and booted Gog in the chest while he was still off-balance. Dak lunged for me with all four arms, but I twisted away from his meaty fists, sending a steel toecap into the point of his larger right elbow. Bone cracked and the creature opened his mouth to yell—but then shut it with a snap as the heel of my other foot hit him in the chin.

Both were on the floor. Dak didn't look like he'd be getting up any time soon, but Gog was flailing, trying to untangle himself from the legs of his chair. He screamed something in the local language. I wasn't very fluent, but I think it amounted to, "I'm going to fucking kill you!"

I slid off the table and beckoned him with both hands. "Bring it on, sweetheart."

Kona was on his feet beside me, ready to fight.

"This," the *Frontier Chic* said, "is becoming unnecessary."

"Depends on your point of view." I clenched my fists. "These assholes started it."

"Did they, though?"

"They would have hurt my *friend*." I stressed the word the same way they had.

Gog had regained a standing position. He stood swaying,

the tip of the screwdriver swinging between me and Kona, unsure which of us to go for first.

"Seriously? You want to fight him?"

"Damn straight."

Through our unspoken link, he could feel how keyed up I was. On the journey back to the Continuance fleet, we'd be spending days cooped up, and I needed to burn off some energy first.

"If you get seriously hurt now, it could jeopardise our mission." The envoy regarded Gog. "And if you accidentally kill one of these lump-fisted chuckleheads, we'll be up to our exhaust ports in local trouble."

Gog shook his head like a boxer trying to refocus after one punch too many. Then, large arms stretched out and grasping, he came around the table at Kona. I laughed and dropped into a fighting crouch.

This time, the *Frontier Chic* did allow his eyes to roll. Each of Gog's fists were the size of my head.

Kona moved to meet him, fists raised. Gog drew back the screwdriver, ready to stab.

"Enough." The envoy held up a blue-tinted finger and fired a cluster of species-specific nanomolecular stun darts into the big Jzat's neck. Gog grunted as their toxic payload disabled his motor functions. The screwdriver clattered to the floor, and he pitched sideways, going down like a felled tree.

While the impact still reverberated through the floorboards, the *Chic* flicked the finger a few degrees to the left and sent half a dozen darts into Dak's unconscious form, just for good measure. Then he opened a datalink to the nearest police precinct and downloaded an incident report, including footage of the entire confrontation, a complete transcription of everything the two the hapless cargo handlers had said, details of the toxins he'd used to temporarily immobilise them, and a substrate comms address, should the investigating officers wish to consult us once we'd left the planet. The whole process took a couple of seconds.

Meanwhile, I straightened my coat and grinned at Kona. I had no doubt the two of us would have prevailed had the scuffle been allowed to play out.

"Hey, *Chic*," I said. "You know what your trouble is?"

"Do enlighten me."

I picked up an unclaimed drink and swallowed it down. Then I shook splinters of broken glass from my hair and clothing and blew the horrified bartender a kiss. "You just don't know how to have any *fun*."

CHAPTER FIVE

WINCING IN ANTICIPATION

ORLANDO WALDEN

My dear Ramona,

I have no idea if these communications are reaching you across the light years that separate us, but I will continue to write. They say that home is where the heart resides, and if that is true, my heart will always and completely be at home with you. You are always on my mind and talking to you is a great comfort in this strange place.

Aulco's head researcher on the Grand Mechanism turned out to be a silver-pelted Jzat named Erudite-Harf. Age had stooped his shoulders and he leant on a wooden cane. As Joh and I approached, he drew himself up and scowled through a pair of half-moon spectacles.

"So," he said. "The Continuance has sent us a *child*."

"I'm pleased to meet you," I muttered.

He looked me up and down. "How old are you?"

"T-Twenty-one, sir."

"Twenty-one?" He made a clicking noise with his tongue. "Are they trying to add insult to injury?"

I felt my cheeks burn. "I *am* one of the Continuance's

f-foremost authorities on substrate dynamics."

"So, you say." He directed his glare at my guide. "A few basic formulae would have been more use. Could they not have simply furnished us with the data we need?"

As you are aware, Ramona, I can't abide rudeness. After the way the Jzat professors on the planet had treated me, not to mention the crew of the rustbucket battleship that had ferried me to this gaudy hoop, I'd just about reached the absolute limit of my tolerance.

"I'm sure you know that's impossible," I said, speaking before I had chance to rein in my irritation. "The Continuance means you no slight; they are simply obeying the consensus among higher civilisations that it's a bad idea to share substrate theory with a species that hasn't yet discovered it for themselves. Younger species, because of having to fight their way up the evolutionary chain from pond scum to sentience, tend to be more aggressive and unpredictable and it's generally accepted by the galactic community that giving them the keys to the stars before they're mature enough will always be a risky mistake."

Erudite-Harf was staring at me, open-mouthed, but I ploughed on: "You see, there's no way of knowing if, given the technology to travel faster than light, they'll use it to try to conquer or annihilate their neighbours. So, in the absence of guarantees, the safest choice is always to limit the possible expansion of any race incapable of figuring out the science for itself."

Finally, I tailed off. The old Jzat looked like he was about to explode. He took a few ragged breaths through his nostrils, and I braced myself for a tirade. But the tirade never came. Instead, he let forth a gale of braying laughter.

"You've got some spirit, boy. I'll give you that." He turned. "Now, come on. We have work to do!"

Moving with a stiffness that revealed his age, he led Joh

and I through the immense open-work spaces of the Grand Mechanism's hoop.

"We've made significant progress," he said, ducking under a pipework cluster. "The deep scans provided by the *Slippery Gecko* have opened whole new avenues of enquiry for us—avenues I hope you'll be able to guide us along."

"I-I'll do my best."

"I know you will, my boy."

Leaning heavily on his cane, he led us across gantries and up gangways, until we came to a large, raised podium suspended over an apparently bottomless abyss. As we ascended the stairs to this dais, I kept a tight grip on the safety rail and resisted the urge to spit into the shadowed depths below.

"As far as we can tell," Erudite-Harf said, puffing his way ahead of us, cane tapping on the metal steps, "this represents one of the Mechanism's major control nodes."

Sleek instrument consoles occupied two thirds of the platform's circumference. Someone had plugged blocky machines and instruments of unmistakeably Jzatian design into these consoles at various spots, marking where various generations of researchers had crudely tried to splice links between their equipment and the Mechanism's control systems. One screen imaged a fluctuating sphere.

"We think this image depicts the power being drawn from the substrate," Erudite-Harf explained.

I peered closer. The sphere was a basic graphic. I couldn't make sense of the accompanying columns of what I assumed were Jzatian numbers, but the way the sphere warped and deformed seemed to match the way energy levels in the substrate tended to oscillate, heaving and subsiding like waves breaking over an infinite beach.

Erudite-Harf seemed to be looking at me expectantly, so I nodded and said, "Yes. Yes, I believe it does."

I wasn't entirely confident of my grasp of Jzat body

language, but to me the way his shoulders relaxed seemed to indicate relief.

"We believe the Mechanism's controls may actually reside in the substrate," he said. "If you can use your expertise to open a channel to them…"

I looked around the huge chamber surrounding our podium, at the power conduits, scaffolds, elevators and other less identifiable structures that formed its ragged limits. My word, Ramona, I wish you could have seen it. The Grand Mechanism's hoop massed as much as a gas giant. It was a solid ring of machinery the width of Saturn's rings and a thousand kilometres thick, with enough room inside for anything. Could this small platform really control it all?

"I will do my b-best."

Erudite-Harf spread his large set of arms wide. "We will, of course, furnish you with whatever we can. Any equipment we have, is yours. If you desire assistants, simply ask. My entire team stands at your disposal."

I rubbed my hands together and found my palms were clammy. My instincts were telling me I should leave immediately and run home to you, that I should never have left the warmth of your bed in the first place.

And yet…

And yet…

Ramona, I'm afraid the Grand Mechanism represented an almost irresistible puzzle. It was a beguiling enigma that begged me to solve it; and here, General Aulco and Erudite-Harf had given me the chance to unlock its secrets.

If I succeeded (and if the whole thing somehow neglected to blow up in my face), the results would assure the future of my career. The universities of the fleet would fall over each other to offer me a place on their research staff. They would eagerly publish every paper I wrote, and you and I could spend the rest of our lives dining out on this one, titanic achievement.

Honestly, Ramona, I was thinking of us both.

"Well, are you going to help us?" Erudite-Harf asked, and I realised I'd been silent for some moments.

"I can't walk away from this," I told him.

He smiled. "I know exactly what you mean. I've been studying this place since I was an apprentice. Once the riddle of the Grand Mechanism gets its hooks into you, you're snagged until you find a solution."

"But no one ever has?"

"Not so far."

I rubbed my palms against my tunic and swallowed a deep, steadying breath. I felt like I had as a kid, playing with the jack-in-the-box my grandfather had printed for me—desperate to keep turning the handle to unlock the surprise inside, but also wincing in anticipation of the consequences.

"Y-You can count on me."

The elderly Jzat's smile widened into an open-mouthed, delighted grin, and he began fussing around, clearing away equipment to make room for me to work.

My pulse roared in my ears and my heart thumped in my chest. I walked to the edge of the podium and stared down into the unfathomable depths below. No illumination pierced the darkness to indicate how far the shaft fell into the Mechanism's innards. It could have been a few hundred metres or a few hundred kilometres, but, my love, I swear to you I could feel gusts of warm air swirling up from that abyss like the soft, sleeping breaths of a gargantuan animal.

CHAPTER SIX

A PUDDLE OF ATTITUDE

NICOLA MAFALDA

My return to civilisation began in a gym. Because of course it fucking did. I hated those places. Like the *Frontier Chic*, I was a creature of darkness and solitude, built for the ragged edge of known space. And I was lazy. But, if we were to embark upon the mission outlined in our orders, I knew I'd need some back-up. And that meant I was going to have to talk to some people I'd much rather avoid.

The gym was situated on one of the *Memory of Green*'s lower levels, close to the ark's hangar decks, where Vanguard ships and crews tended to congregate between missions. The air inside was damp with the onion tang of sweat. I had been in the place before, under protest, and recognised a few of the faces.

I found Ora Cerise lifting weights, a chunky dumbbell in each hand.

The other members of the gym stayed at a respectful distance. Once, Cerise had been a Peacekeeper—the closest thing the Vanguard had to an elite soldier. She was tall and broad-shouldered, and as she raised and lowered the dumbbells, her biceps flexed beneath her glistening skin like hungry orcas moving through the ocean without quite breaking the water's surface tension. But what really kept the onlookers at bay was the livid scar that used to be her left cheek. A scar that showed where a pulse round had come close to blowing off the entire side of her head.

A scar she refused to fix.

From time to time, groups of disaffected citizens attempted to defy the orders of the Benevolence and leave the arks. They wanted to settle on a planet somewhere, to plant crops and raise children beneath open skies. Five years ago, when I was fresh out of the academy, such a group had tried to hijack a cargo vessel armed with illegally printed pulse rifles. Cerise had killed them all, one by one, in a game of cat and mouse in which the notion of who was the cat and who the mouse changed back and forth many times before the final, bloody denouement.

We hadn't spoken since.

She clocked my approach but didn't stop what she was doing.

"Hello," she said.

"Ora."

"What can I do for you?"

"I need your help."

"Really?"

"I'm afraid so."

The skin around her eyes creased as she narrowed them. "You've got a lot of fucking nerve, you know that?"

I shrugged. "Believe me, if I had an alternative, I wouldn't be here."

"That's it?"

I spread my hands. "That's all there is."

She stopped pumping the weights. "No sales pitch? No bluster?"

"I simply need your help."

She squinted at me. "You seem different. And I don't just mean your hair."

80

"I am different."

"Good, because you used to be an ungrateful bitch."

"Hey. You're the one who butchered fifteen people."

"They tried to kill me first."

"Two of them were teenagers."

Cerise scowled. "They were carrying pulse rifles."

"You could have disarmed them."

Calloused fingertips brushed the scar on her cheek. "I did what I had to do. I saved our asses."

"It was excessive."

"Maybe, but it was better than sitting around in a fancy coat hoping for a miracle."

I held up a hand to halt the conversation. "I haven't come here to rake up old arguments."

"Then why are you here, in your fancy coat?"

"I'd like to put the past behind us."

"You've come to apologise?"

"I've come to ask for your help."

The old soldier's eyes narrowed. "Help with what?"

"I'm trying to avert a war, and maybe even something worse."

"And how do I figure in that aversion?"

"I need to visit an alien megaship some distance from here, to find a Jzat holy man."

"And you figure you might need some muscle?"

"I very much hope we won't."

"What's in it for me?" Cerise asked.

"What do you want?"

"Some reason why, seeing as you have absolutely ghosted me for the past five years, I should haul ass all the way out to some alien megaship on the fringes of nowhere, simply to help you out."

I gave her a level stare. "I told you, I'm trying to prevent some bad shit happening. But if altruism isn't high on your agenda, we're talking about an alien vessel no human has ever heard of, let alone seen. You'll be the first human soldier to survey it. The first to bring back all that juicy intelligence. Taking point on an expedition like that will make you the talk of the Vanguard newsgroups for months."

"Ah, I don't know."

"Ora, I *am* sorry I've been avoiding you."

"It was a shitty thing to do."

"I was freaking out. I'd never come that close to death before."

"And now?"

I swallowed hard, trying not to recall the *snick* the helmet had made as it irised shut, snipping my head from my failing, irradiated body. "As I said, I've changed."

•

Stepping out of the gym, I did up the large silver buttons on my long coat. An intra-ship flick terminal stood at the end of the landing on which the gym was situated. I tapped a destination into the bracelet on my wrist and stepped through, to emerge instantly from an identical silver sphere a hundred decks further down, on the ark's docking levels.

I could have flicked directly to the bay I wanted, but decided to walk down the main concourse instead, past open hangar doors revealing vessels of every shape and designation, from the sleek shapes of Vanguard scout craft to the more industrial lines of the haulers, tankers and refiners that followed in their wake to gather and process raw materials in the star systems they surveyed. There were liners and other pleasure craft to take humans on sightseeing excursions, and the occasional vessel from one of the alien civilisations the Continuance had encountered in its one and a quarter centuries of flight.

I had left Kona in my cabin on the *Frontier Chic*, where I knew he'd be able to stay safely out of trouble. The *Memory of Green* wouldn't tolerate anyone trying to break into my ship. The ark was a staunch defender of its inhabitants' privacy and had very little patience for any kind of vandalism or violence.

Arks were huge beasts, and they had intellects to match. The Angel of the Benevolence had furnished them with the capacity to oversee the millions of operations that kept a twenty-five-kilometre starship functional and habitable, from the complexities of interstellar travel to the cultivation and care of the smallest blades of grass, all while simultaneously conducting millions of separate conversations with the humans in their charge. Their thoughts ran through the substrate itself, travelling at speeds faster than that of light. Even the *Frontier Chic* couldn't have kept up with them. Their minds were vast, deep oceans, and in comparison, the rest of us were mere puddles.

But in my case, a puddle full of attitude.

The *Frontier Chic* had berthed at the shabbier end of the row, between a pair of elderly freighters that were in the process of being cannibalised for parts now that the technicians had extracted their personalities and moved them to the shared virtual Valhalla that awaited all ships in their dotage.

I paused for a second in the doorway to the bay. I rarely saw the *Frontier Chic*'s blunt, wedge-shaped hull from the outside. It resembled a stubby triangle with rounded ends, festooned with thrusters, sensor blisters and radiator fins. Even after being rebuilt, hardly an inch remained that hadn't been somehow patched, scorched or dented.

His envoy was waiting for me at the bottom of the cargo ramp.

"We might have a problem," he said.

"What sort of a problem?"

"While you've been out socialising, I've been researching everything the Vanguard knows about the Rav'nah Abelisk."

"And?"

"According to the records provided by the Jzat government, the tradition of the Abelisk predates their recorded history. The

Two Great Secrets have been handed down from one Rav'nah Abelisk to the next for thousands of years. Upon receiving the sacred knowledge, the new Abelisk renounces worldly possessions to take up a life of solitude and contemplation. In the past, this has usually taken the form of a hermitage in the mountains or swamplands of Jzat. More recent Abelisks have travelled off-world, hitching rides from other substrate-capable species to seek enlightenment and seclusion amid the stars. Only twice in all that time has an Abelisk died without nominating a successor. In the first case, the dying Abelisk, having been mauled by a six-legged swamp panther, vouchsafed his knowledge to the farmer who found him lying by the side of a dirt track. In the second case, struck down by illness and unable to reach civilisation in time, the dying Abelisk left a clay tablet in a sealed box, addressed to whomever the Jzat government wished to appoint as her heir."

"Okay."

"The most recent Rav'nah Abelisk inherited his duties as a child and has been custodian of the Two Great Secrets for eight decades now. He's approaching the end of his life and commentators widely expect him to return to Jzat soon to share his accumulated wisdom and appoint his replacement."

I shifted my weight from one leg to the other. "You said there was a problem?"

"I'm getting to that." The *Chic* steepled his blue fingers like a monk about to recite a catechism. "The idea of activating the Grand Mechanism has always bubbled underneath the mainstream political history of Jzat like background radiation. It was always there, but most of the population could easily ignore it, until a few years ago, when a Jzat general named Aulco decided to throw in his lot with a fringe group dedicated to elevating the Jzat civilisation on the galactic scale.

"This group, who became known as the Openers, regard other space-going species with envy and suspicion.

Jzat researchers never cracked the secret of substrate travel, and the consensus among substrate-capable civilisations has always been that accessing the sub-dimensional realms is a rite of passage every society has to achieve to join the players at the big table."

"If you find yourself getting near a point, please make it."

"In recent years, Aulco has become the face of this movement. He's a grey-pelted Jzat with a duelling scar and a row of medals, and he fills his speeches with populist sentiment: Jzat will be great again; foreigners and saboteurs are responsible for societal ills; and the races who refuse to share the secret of substrate travel are purposefully subjugating the Jzat for their own ends—you can guess the sort of thing. In his opinion, reactivating the Grand Mechanism will free the Jzat people from those who wish to oppress and enslave them, and restore to them the lost technological wonders of the Jzat who built it all those millennia ago.

"Aulco has spent most of his political career on the fringe, but his popularity has increased since his rebel forces captured the Mechanism. As stewards of the Grand Mechanism, the Jzat have historically seen themselves as a chosen people. Meeting a technologically superior species as physically like themselves as you humans has caused many to question their place in the universe. It's forced them to confront the reality of their true standing as a comparatively primitive society confined to a single backwater system, and that realisation has inevitably led to feelings of resentment—feelings Aulco and his sympathisers in the media play on to further their own agenda."

I nodded. "I can see why Kona and his superiors are concerned for the Abelisk's safety. If his secrets do concern the operation of the Grand Mechanism, Aulco's going to want to get that information, and the simplest way to do it will be to intercept the Abelisk when he comes home."

"Not necessarily." The *Chic* looked grave. "Using violence

or extortion to force the holy man to reveal his information would risk losing the sympathy of the electorate."

"They won't like Aulco strongarming their spiritual leader."

"Absolutely not. If Aulco wants access to the knowledge in the old man's head, he will need to strike soon, while the Abelisk remains far from the sight of his people."

"Which means that by seeking out the Abelisk ourselves, we could be flying into a fight."

"Indeed."

"That's why Kona thinks we should find him first, and why I've recruited Ora Cerise to help us."

"Yes." He frowned. "But I'm afraid the situation is worse than it at first appears."

"How so?"

"The Jzat don't possess substrate travel."

"So?"

"How are they going to get there?"

I saw it then. "They'd need allies from a more advanced civilisation."

"Indeed."

"But who?"

"I have no idea."

"Did you detect any foreign vessels while we were in-system?"

"Only the *Slippery Gecko*."

I felt a sudden coldness in the pit of my stomach. "You mean the same ship who requested a copy of your flight plan?"

The envoy's face lost all expression. "Oh dear."

"Is that possible?"

The envoy went silent for a couple of seconds. "I just replayed the conversation," he said, "and our friend definitely implied he was on a clandestine mission."

I pulled at my lower lip. "I don't want to believe it. There must be some other explanation."

"As the only other substrate-capable ship in the vicinity, Occam's razor suggests the Openers will use the *Slippery Gecko* to pursue the Abelisk."

"But Ewing would never agree to such a thing."

"Not unless he was acting under orders."

"But why would the Vanguard order him to do that at the same time as ordering us to prevent it?"

The *Chic* went quiet again. When he finally spoke, his voice was flat and devoid of emotion. "Our orders were to help Kona *locate* the Abelisk."

The coldness in my gut congealed into a solid block of ice. "Because they knew he'd trust me."

"And therefore, we could lead them right to their target."

"Fuck."

Part of me wanted to hide from the truth. But looking back, I could see how Ewing had intercepted me as soon as I'd touched down, taken me to a bar to keep me away from both the Continuance Embassy and the Jzat government, and hand-delivered Kona right into my care. He must have suspected that Kona would never willingly betray the location of the Abelisk, and so he arranged for me, as the only human Kona trusted, to be right here exactly when needed.

The *Chic* asked, "Are you all right?"

"Of course I'm fucking not."

I glanced around at the activity in the docking facility, and then jerked my head in the direction of the cargo ramp. He nodded and followed me up as my boots clanged on the cleated metal.

"They used me," I said once we were inside and safe from eavesdroppers. "They took my friendship with Ewing, and my feelings for Kona, and they used them both to get what they wanted."

"It does appear that way."

"Fuck."

I undid my coat and sat heavily on one of the chairs surrounding the hexagonal briefing table in the corner of the lounge. The *Frontier Chic* slid into place on the opposite side. He clasped his blue hands on the dinged plastic tabletop and asked, "What do you want to do?"

"I have no idea. I thought we were supposed to be helping Kona get the Abelisk to safety, but now I don't even know whose side we're supposed to be on."

The *Frontier Chic* frowned. "So, how should we proceed?"

I noticed his use of the inclusive "we" and smiled. Whatever happened, we were a team, both reliant on the other. "Carefully."

"More specifically?"

I glanced towards the door of my cabin. "Until we know who issued our orders and why, we follow them. We don't want to draw attention until we're sure we know who we can trust. So, in the meantime, we transport Kona to the Abelisk, as instructed."

"Should we tell Kona he's been manipulated?"

"I'll break the news."

"And when we get there?"

I shrugged. "We'll see what happens."

CHAPTER SEVEN

ASSUMING ROOM TEMPERATURE

NICOLA MAFALDA

Ora Cerise came on board and immediately began making herself at home. She slung her kitbag into the first vacant cabin she found, pulled a beer from the printer and leant against an equipment locker in the crew lounge.

"What time do we lift?"

"Soon."

"Groovy." She tipped her head back and took a long glug of her drink, then clonked the half-emptied glass down on the table. "But for the record, I still don't trust you."

I smiled. "I never trusted you."

Her eyes widened, then her face relaxed into a rueful grin. "I see you're still the same asshole you always were."

"We used to be a good team."

"Maybe once upon a time."

"Do you remember combat training?"

•

The dart's parent ship had accelerated it up to speed, and then released it on a ballistic trajectory that took it on a long, slow parabola through the substrate.

Twelve light years later, having bled away most of its velocity, it dropped back into the universe with almost nothing in the way of residual heat. Its engines were cold and its life-support systems heavily shielded. If it were unlucky enough to be detected by an enemy sensor, it would have been indistinguishable from any of the other inert splinters of rock in the accretion disc that housed its objective.

Deep inside the dart, behind layers of nano-carbon armour, I lay encased in a vat of liquid air. The hyper-oxygenated fluid had cushioned my body against the harsh acceleration that had been necessary to shunt the dart up to jump velocity—and would keep me alive during the savage deceleration it would suffer when it rammed its target.

Although I'd been immersed in the fluid many times in the past, I still loathed everything about it. Whenever I strapped myself into the tank and the liquid poured in, covering my mouth and nose, every instinct in my body told me I was suffocating, and it took a supreme effort not to thrash around and claw at the safety harness. Then later, when my brain finally adjusted to the idea my lungs were still breathing in oxygen despite being filled with goop, claustrophobia replaced the panic. I felt like someone drowned in a bathtub.

Around me, the other three members of the Vanguard cadet squad lay encased in identical capsules. First, there was Ora Cerise, the red-headed slab of muscle with the face of a warrior goddess and the biceps of a weightlifter. Beside her lay Afan Khan, the youngest of us, with knife skills learned on the lower decks of his home ark, *New Bangalore*. And finally, there was the lieutenant, Jacob Malone, for whom I would gladly have stormed the gates of hell. Malone had been my commanding officer on all thirteen of my Vanguard training missions to date, having selected me for the Combat

Navigator program, after recognising my natural aptitude for inflicting mayhem on the enemy.

"Four minutes," Malone said over the internal channel. "Get ready to come out fighting."

Khan moaned. "Fighting, or retching?"

I felt my stomach clench. "Shut the fuck up, Khan."

Cerise chuckled. "Are you feeling sick, Mafalda?"

"Only when I look at you."

"Yeah, lust does funny things to people."

"In your dreams."

"Any time, baby."

Malone broke in. "Settle down, all of you." He was doing his best to sound stern, but I knew him well enough to hear the resignation in his tone. He understood the value of squad banter in the face of imminent (simulated) combat, how it distracted us from our nerves and helped bond us as a cohesive unit.

I ran a final systems check on my armour and grinned inside my helmet when everything came back green. The suit's ammunition levels were at maximum, and its power cells and air scrubbers would keep me alive for up to a month, if necessary. Not that I expected this mission to last anywhere near that length of time. It was supposed to be a simple smash and grab. The cargo ship we were targeting lay within the shadow of a gas giant. It had a small crew of envoys pretending to be scientists and relied for its protection on a pair of Hooligan-class offensive drones that look turns loitering in the vicinity.

"One minute."

I closed my eyes.

Please gods, let me survive the next couple of minutes, I thought. *I don't want to die with this muck in my lungs.*

"Forty seconds. Lock and load."

The gods to whom I prayed were a bricolage of deities

adopted from half a dozen human pantheons. That was the way with the Continuance: we remembered the best of what we had left behind.

My personal gods included Athena, the Ancient Greek goddess of wisdom and the arts; Bragi, the Norse god of poetry, bards and eloquence; and Ganesh, the elephant-headed Hindu god of wisdom and lord of beginnings and success. Back in my quarters, I had small carved images of all of them wrapped in a bandana and tucked safely in my footlocker, and I had kissed each one and lit incense before setting out on this mission.

"Ten seconds," Malone called. "Brace! Brace!"

The dart ship hit the side of the orbital research station and its chisel-like prow punched through the hull, embedding itself like a harpoon in a whale's flank. Even cushioned by the gel, I felt myself hurled forwards by the impact, with only my safety harness saving me from smashing against the side of my casket.

"Go!" Malone yelled.

Explosive bolts blew the lid from the coffin. The oxygenated fluid burst onto the deck, and I coughed and gagged as much as I could of the remainder from my lungs and throat. Blowing traces from one nostril, then the other, I unclipped my harness, grabbed my rifle and joined the others as they stepped forwards.

Before us, the dart ship's prow hinged open like a mouth, with the lower "jaw" forming a ramp. Cerise went down first, rifle stock pressed into her shoulder and eye glued to the sights. I followed, with my splat gun ready to liquidise any resistance. Malone went next, his Big Boy pistol clenched in his outstretched fist. And Khan brought up the rear, with his machete in one hand and a compact grenade launcher in the other. Defensive micro-drones swarmed around us, scanning, mapping and analysing our surroundings.

We appeared to be in some sort of hydroponics garden—

or maybe even an internal park. Palm trees swayed with the residual force of the crash; a central fountain sparkled in the light from the overhead sunlamps; and a disposable envoy body lay crumpled against the far wall, the impact having propelled it across the lawn.

Cerise scanned the envoy with the targeting reticule in her left eye. "No pulse," she said. "He's A.R.T."

Assuming Room Temperature.

"Roger." Malone turned away without even chastising her for using an unofficial abbreviation. "Okay, you lot. Fan out and make your way to the control deck."

"Aye, sir," Cerise rumbled. "And if anyone gets in our way?"

"Shoot first and ask questions later." He flashed a smile. "We're not here to make friends."

•

"Those were the days," Cerise agreed.

I made a face. Combat training was something all Vanguard personnel had to endure, even those of us who simply craved the silence and isolation of a scout craft. Cerise had thrived in that environment, immobilising more simulated enemy combatants in one day than most battalions would expect to have managed in five. Usually, I'd have been right with her—I've never been one to back away from a fight—But on that mission, I'd just trailed along in her wake, feeling sick from the oxygenated fluid and trying to collect the intel we needed to pass that test.

We *had* made a good team.

It was only later, when the simulated violence turned real, that I realised how truly terrifying she could be.

CHAPTER EIGHT

MORE IMPORTANT THAN GOLD STARS

FRONTIER CHIC

As I slipped my moorings and powered away from the *Memory of Green*, the Thousand Arks of the Continuance glimmered behind me, spread out over almost a light year and bright against the starry wash of interstellar space. Red and green running lights blinked along their flanks; the windows of the residential sections emitted a soft sepia glow; and orange warning beacons pulsed at the entrances to hangars and airlocks. They were a constellation on the move—an entire species without home or destination.

Over the decades, each ark had reconfigured itself according to a mixture of its own whimsy and the preferences of its occupants. The three nearest to me included a fat triangle; a rugby ball that sported so many "starscraper" accommodation towers it resembled a hedgehog; and a flat, elongated slab with a pair of outriggers almost as large as itself. Having begun their journey looking identical, they now revelled in their individuality, which extended to the climate and landscape contained within their hulls. As a human in the fleet, you could access almost any terrestrial environment you desired via your nearest flick terminal—from frozen tundra to baking sand dune, and everything in between. Some even contained multiple biospheres within their twenty-five-kilometre lengths, hosting farmlands and fisheries, wild moorlands and dense rainforests. As a scout craft experiencing these micro-environments via an artificial envoy, I'd obviously never felt the same kind of evolutionary attachment the humans professed for so-called "natural" surroundings, yet still occasionally found myself moved by their variety and beauty. Nicola's lonely mountainside cottage had particularly spoken to me, and I'd felt a melancholy stab of kinship for the isolated structure that I couldn't quite explain.

As we began to pull ahead of the main body of the Continuance fleet, Nicola took up her position on the bridge, unbuttoning her coat and sitting on the navigator's chair in front of the wrap-around window that would allow her senses to intuit a path through the chaotic fire of the substrate, enabling me to surf that invisible gradient to our destination.

"How are you feeling?"

She shrugged one shoulder. "Like we're about to jump into trouble."

"It won't be the first time."

"Let's hope it's not the last." She cracked her knuckles and settled back, getting comfortable.

I recalled the day, four years previously, when the Vanguard had first assigned us to each other. Standing on the flight deck with her arms crossed over her chest, she had initially seemed raw and nervous, but she had graduated alongside Ewing at the top of her class, and I soon came to realise how hungry she was to prove herself in the real world.

Some students in her position may have struggled to adjust to a life outside of an academic context, where nobody cared that they'd scored full marks on every assignment and teamwork and survival were more important than gold stars. When confronted with a situation in which there was no right answer, they didn't know how to react. For all his suaveness, Ewing was still a little boy motivated by his need for validation from his teachers—only now, that craving for praise had transferred itself to his superiors in the Vanguard. You could see it in the way his uniform was always crisp and spotless, and his hair kept short and neatly combed. He had a reputation for loyalty and intelligence, but the trouble was, as Nicola had once remarked, "He's so used to being right all the time, he can't conceive of ever being wrong."

Nicola had gone the other way. Her academic scores matched Ewing's, but she had never defined herself by them. Even as a child, she'd realised that nobody in the outside world would ever care that you had been one of the popular kids or good at sports or top of your astrophysics class, and that those peers of hers who had founded their identities on such things would be doomed to peak before they'd even left school. Without even realising it, they'd spend their lives yearning for those simpler times, always wondering why they couldn't recapture a taste of that faded high.

For Nicola, school had been a means to an end. She was bright, but she hadn't cared about the teen drama unfolding around her, and she hadn't cared whether her teachers or classmates liked her. Even then, she had been a solitary creature, with one ambition: to fly among the stars. She had focused everything on that one goal; she had nothing to prove to her contemporaries or tutors. So, when she finally stepped aboard, in the Vanguard coat she had already tailored to her individual preferences, it hadn't been nerves or discomfiture that had gripped her; it had been the realisation of an objective that had consumed and outshone all other considerations.

The first thing she'd said was, "I'm home."

The first time we'd flown, she'd wept with happiness.

Unlike other, more literal-minded navigators, the routes she found through the substrate were always baroque and stimulating—and often faster or more fuel-efficient than the simple A-to-B approach employed by less creative souls. And it was this talent that had convinced her instructors at the academy to make allowances for her less conventional traits. She was a natural, a rare and exquisite talent, and I was lucky to have her.

I just wondered if she'd ever forgive me the extreme way circumstances had forced me to save her life.

CHAPTER NINE

THE CRONUS CLUSTER

NICOLA MAFALDA

I introduced Ora Cerise to Kona, and the two sat on opposite sides of the mess-room table, sizing each other up, one of them a seasoned ex-marine with a warrior's physique, the other a four-armed, vaguely feline alien.

"So," Cerise said. "Security services, huh? What kind of combat training does that involve?"

Kona placed his smaller set of hands on the table. "Covert assassination. Close-quarters fighting. Hand-to-hand—"

"Or in your case hand-to-hand-to-hand-to hand."

Kona pretended to ignore the jibe. "And proficiency with a wide range of battlefield weaponry, including some examples too complex and nuanced for anyone with only *two* appendages."

"Oh, is that so?"

I placed cups of tea on the table between them. "Play nicely, you two."

They both scowled and I laughed. The best way to stop two people arguing was always to get them both angry with you. It gave them common ground.

"We're not playing," Kona said.

I picked up my own tea and blew on it. "We've got a long journey ahead of us," I said. "If we're going to get through it without killing each other, you two need to behave."

Cerise sat back in her chair. "Okay," she said. "Seeing as you're in charge, why don't you inform us of your plan?"

"Gladly." I leaned over and tapped the tabletop, bringing up a holographic map of space.

"According to coordinates supplied by Kona, our target is in this volume here." I traced a circle some distance from the fleet. "But I've been almost killed once already, so I'm not going in there unprepared."

Cerise said, "And that's where I come in?"

"Yes."

"You're expecting a difficult reception?"

"Not necessarily. But there's a possibility we might run up against rogue Jzat elements, and maybe even members of the Vanguard."

"I'll need some weapons."

"The ship's printer can provide almost anything we need."

"Yes, but if we're facing off against someone else from the Vanguard, they'll have access to all the same equipment. If we want an edge, we'll need something unexpected."

"Such as?"

Cerise smiled. "I know where we can get some serious artillery, and it's not too far out of our way."

•

Cerise led us to a group of stars thirty light years from the edge of the Continuance fleet. This group was known to the Vanguard as the Cronus Cluster and consisted of seven young stars that were bound in a complicated gravitational dance with a black hole. Of course, the black hole itself was invisible to the naked eye. More than invisible. Looking directly at it made my eyes squirm. It hurt more than the brightest light. The beast swallowed every photon that came its way, reflecting nothing onto which my photoreceptors could latch, but I could see its position by the girdle of super-heated gas falling into its equator and the way its ferocious gravity warped the light of the stars behind it into a thin, bright ring. According to Vanguard records, it had once been a red hypergiant a thousand times the radius of Sol, but at the end of its life, when it had eventually exhausted its fuel and could no longer generate enough energy to resist the pressure of its own gravity, its core collapsed into a singularity so dense not even light would be able to escape. This collapse caused the star's outer layers to blow off in a massive supernova explosion that disturbed a nearby cloud of interstellar gas, causing eddies and fluctuations in its fabric. Over the next billion years, the densest parts of the cloud became slowly thicker and thicker, their increasing gravity attracting more of the cloud's matter, until they accreted enough mass that their own cores began to fuse beneath the weight. Thus, seven new stars were born from the death throes of the ancient giant, each complete with its own attendant planetary swirl—but they were born into servitude, locked in the thrall of the monster that had created them, dancing like electrons around its dense, dark nucleus, while they waited for the day it would consume them.

"There's a gas giant at the edge of that system." Cerise pointed to one of the attendant stars. "Head for its largest moon."

The *Frontier Chic*, who was present on the bridge in the person of his blue-skinned envoy, looked at me for confirmation.

"Do it," I said.

We dropped back into the substrate, and I concentrated on a mental image of the bright young star that Cerise had indicated. When we re-emerged, it had grown from a bright point to a disc the size of a pea held at arm's length. The HUD projected onto the glass before me revealed the presence of a large gas giant in a relatively close orbit, surrounded by an entourage of moons whose sizes ranged from a couple of thousand kilometres in diameter to a few centimetres. A cluster of habitat domes glimmered on the dark side of the largest.

"That's it," Cerise said.

I looked at the seemingly derelict equipment between the domes. "It looks like an old mining station."

"It is."

The *Chic*'s envoy frowned. "We are being targeted by a number of missile systems."

The blood seemed to freeze in my veins. For a moment, I was back there, floating in a ruined ship, dying from radiation sickness.

Not again…

"Let's get the fuck out of here."

"Wait." Cerise held up a hand. "He won't fire on a Vanguard vessel."

"Who won't?"

"Our host."

"And who the fuck is that?"

As if in response, a comm screen opened on the HUD, revealing a familiar, lined face. I took one look and said, "You have got to be fucking kidding me."

On the screen, Jacob Malone smiled and said, "Hello, Mafalda. I've missed you, too."

•

I had thought it was our final training mission, but it turned out to be real.

When we hit the cargo ship's command deck, I'd been expecting to find it crewed by envoys. Instead, I found myself facing a small group of terrified civilians in worn and patched suits, armed with whatever weapons they'd coaxed from the printers.

Khan went down to a crossbow bolt through his visor.

Cerise opened fire, hosing the room with a sustained burst from her pulse rifle. Malone joined in, discharging his pistol in a series of bright flashes. In the confined space, the shots were deafening. Limbs and torsos blew apart. Knives and lengths of pipe clattered to the deck. Blood sprayed against monitors and instrument panels.

And then it was done.

Nine people lay dead, including Khan.

My ears rang. One of the corpses was that of a child, a boy around fifteen years old. A pulse from Cerise's rifle had blown a gory, fist-sized hole through his face. He was dead, but his foot kept twitching.

Malone lowered his weapon and raised his splattered visor, surveying the carnage. "Okay," he said. "We're done here. Cerise, go mop up the rest of the crew."

•

Following guidance from the dome, the *Frontier Chic* dropped through an aperture on the moon's surface, into a spacious loading bay that had once accommodated the bulky freighters that had hauled the ore from the mines.

Kona stayed on the ship. Cerise said she didn't want to complicate things by involving strangers, but perhaps she just wanted to snub him.

Malone was there to greet us as we disembarked. He looked older and thinner than I remembered.

"Welcome," he said.

He wore a faded red undershirt and a pair of grease-stained blue jeans and carried a fat pistol in a holster on his hip.

Cerise snapped a salute. "Lieutenant."

Malone smiled and touched a finger to his brow in response. "Good to see you, Cerise. What brings you to my little establishment?"

"We're here to browse the merchandise, sir."

"I hoped you might be."

•

The kid's foot twitched again, and my stomach convulsed, ready to throw up the oxygenated gel that had seeped into it during our approach.

"What the hell?" I spoke. Neither of them heard me, so I flipped open my faceplate. "What the fucking hell?"

Malone was reloading his pistol. "They were separatists. They stole this ship." He didn't look up.

"So, we just executed them for that?"

There had always been groups unhappy with the thought of spending the rest of their lives on an ark. Most formed their own little fringe groups and occasionally organised small protests. It seemed these poor bastards had been stupid enough to hijack an old cargo ship and strike out for parts unknown.

I looked to Cerise for help. "It's a fucking mess," she said. "Sir, you should have told us this wasn't an exercise." She kicked Khan's boot. "If you had, this idiot might still be alive."

I looked down at the metal shaft protruding from Khan's faceplate and wanted to scream.

Malone gave me a sharp look. "Are you okay, soldier?"

"I'm not a fucking soldier. I'm supposed to be a navigator."

"A combat navigator." He put a gloved hand on my armoured shoulder. "Sometimes that involves boarding other vessels. Getting your hands dirty."

"No." I shook my head. "No, this is not what I signed up for. Not at all."

•

Trying to extract ourselves from the ship without injuring anyone else, Cerise received a pulse round to the face from an understandably aggrieved separatist. In retaliation, she slaughtered the rest of the crew.

After the mission was over, Malone had her transferred to another unit, and he dropped me from the combat navigator's course altogether, moving me back into the civilian programme. He could have kicked me out of the Vanguard altogether, but he let me be a scout rather than an enforcer, responsible for helping fulfil the Vanguard's mandate for reconnaissance by mapping systems, exploring territory and providing transport for equipment and personnel. I had a blemish on my service record, but if Malone left me out of future police actions, that suited me.

For a few years, we worked for different branches. Then I heard he'd retired. Consequently, I'd never expected our paths to cross again, so it came as something of a surprise to find myself face to face with him here, in what looked suspiciously like an illegal separatist settlement.

"Walk this way," he said, and we followed him into the depths of the mining installation.

He wasn't alone here. We passed individuals from several species. At a corridor intersection, a scaly dog-sized arachnid chattered to a large, X-shaped creature covered in wavy, fern-like feathers. As we entered a storage area, I glimpsed something that resembled a cross between an elephant and a squid moving crates of materiel onto a trolley, while a waist-high column of purple prokaryotic slime supervised. In comparison, even with his golden fur and extra set of arms, Kona looked reassuringly human.

"What is this place?" I asked as we walked between shelves filled with boxes of every sort of ammunition.

Cerise grinned and picked up a cartridge large enough to bring down a dinosaur. "It's a candy store."

Malone turned to face us. "More precisely, it's my candy store."

"And what does that make you?" I asked.

"Rich."

"But we live in a post-scarcity society."

"Yes, but there are some things only money can buy."

"Such as?"

"My own little fiefdom."

"And that's what this is, is it?"

He spread his hands. "I spotted a gap in the market."

"As an arms dealer?"

"To a multi-species clientele."

I looked around at the open crates. Some contained grenades, others mace-like objects with bifurcating spikes. I saw things that must have been handguns designed by creatures without hands. Cluster bombs. Armed drones. Anti-aircraft missiles. Sonic projectors. Energy weapons. Sharp sticks. I guess Malone read the disgust on my face.

"Hey, I'm not the bad guy," he said. "What my patrons do with this equipment is their own affair. And the chances are, they'd be doing it anyway; I'm just giving them the means to settle their disputes in a more sophisticated and humane manner."

"I'm sure the casualties appreciate the difference."

"Did you come here to lecture me?"

"No, sir." Cerise snapped to attention. "We're here to shop, Lieutenant, sir.

"And how will you be paying?"

"I have some Continuance credits put aside for a rainy day, sir."

Malone acknowledged her with an approving half-smile. "Then you've come to the right place, Corporal."

"Sir. Thank you, sir."

He turned his shoulder to me. "What did you have in mind?"

"I was thinking we could use a few armoured pressure suits. The good stuff, not the kind of crap we could print ourselves. A particle cannon for me, with power pack. Maybe a trio of rippers with half a dozen ammo clips…"

"You've put some thought into this."

"We're going into an unsurveyed alien megaship that may or may not contain traps or sentry tech left by its original or subsequent inhabitants, as well as risking a non-zero chance of hostility from any race or races, known or unknown, in current occupation of said ship."

Malone nodded. "Then you'll want to be fully tooled up."

"Yes, sir."

"Walk this way."

He led us through the storage area into what had probably once been the mining station's accommodation section. The walls were white and hung with tasteful holograms of landscapes and sunsets that the creatures that had built and crewed this facility had probably installed to alleviate their homesickness.

"You own all this?" I asked.

"I do."

We stepped into his office, a spacious and well-furnished room with a large desk made from what looked like the tailfin of an antique flying machine. Wall-to-ceiling windows looked out across the excavations.

"What's to stop anybody else coming and taking it from you?"

He looked at me as if I were a naive child. "I've negotiated defence contracts with several of my major customers. If anyone's ever foolish enough to attack me, they'll come to my aid."

"So, you have powerful friends?"

His lips twitched with the ghost of a smile. "I do okay."

"But you're going to get left behind." He seemed to have made himself comfortable here, but it wasn't the kind of place I could imagine anyone choosing to spend the rest of their life.

"Nonsense. The Continuance fleet isn't moving all that fast. It will be in jump range for decades. If things don't work out here, all I have to do is send a substrate message and ask for a scout ship to come and pick me up."

He bade us sit on one of the faux-leather sofas and took a seat in a matching armchair.

"But for now," he said, "this is my private kingdom. I have wealth and influence." He gave Cerise a thoughtful look. "You really should come and work for me."

Cerise pursed her lips. There was a low coffee table between us and him. It held some cups, a small stack of plates, some croissants and a ramekin of jam. She reached forwards and picked up one of the butter knives.

"Let's talk about the guns," she said, tapping the flat, blunt blade against the palm of her hand. "I'll need three rippers, with plenty of ammunition. And maybe a splat gun."

Malone smiled. "By all means." He gestured to a small machine that I had initially mistaken for a piece of sculpture, and it lumbered forwards. "This is Harold." He tapped a command into Harold's skin. "I've given you my security clearance and credit line. Anything you need, Harold will find it for you and load it onto your ship."

Cerise nodded. "Thank you, sir."

"My pleasure."

"And now, there's just one last thing." Cerise rose to her feet. As Malone rose to meet her, she punched the butter knife into his throat. His eyes widened and he let out a wild gurgle. He tried to pull the weapon out, but blood made the handle slippery. Cerise pushed him back into his chair and stood over him.

"That's for Khan," she said, "and those poor bastards on the cargo transport."

Malone gaped up at her, still clawing at his neck. His mouth opened and closed but no words emerged. Cerise watched him for a moment, until she was sure he'd understood what she'd said; then she bent forward and clasped her powerful hands on either side of his face.

"Sir, you are *dismissed*."

She wrenched his head clockwise, and his neck snapped. He spasmed, and his body crumpled to the floor like spilled laundry.

Cerise stood over him, breathing heavily.

An antiquated security drone wheeled into the room. Lenses clicked and whirred as it took in the scene.

"Exact nature of transpired events, query?"

Cerise didn't even glance at it. Malone's hands and feet were twitching, the way Khan's had.

"Justice," she said.

CHAPTER TEN

FLAMBOYANT ELEGANCE

ORLANDO WALDEN

Ah, Ramona, how I missed you!

I spent my days and nights on that circular platform, buried in the circuitry of the Grand Mechanism. I had to learn the vigesimal Jzat mathematics, which was a challenge. Due to their plethora of fingers, they had invented a counting system consisting of twenty individual numerals, rather than the ten with which you and I are familiar, with additional symbols for the powers of twenty—20; 400; 8,000; 160,000; 3,200,000; and so forth. As you can probably imagine, this meant I had a devil of a time deciphering their calculus. But once I'd recalibrated my thoughts and adjusted to their notational quirks, I slowly began to make sense of it all.

You would have found it fascinating.

Or maybe not. Even if we share a delight at solving problems, I know you struggle to understand the purity and strength of my love for mathematics. At least the strength of my love for you is never in doubt.

The Jzat were almost our equals in terms of their understanding of the universe, but they lacked the key insights into the nature of the underlying substrate that would have enabled them to come up with a theory to unite classical and quantum physics, the way Frank Tucker and Haruki Kamisaka did for us. Can you picture how maddening it must have been for them to know a theory of everything existed, to know others already possessed it, and yet have those others deny them even the slightest hint as to its composition? Small wonder Erudite-Harf and his colleagues were so bad-tempered towards me. Even though in their eyes I was just a youth, I had beheld and understood the secret knowledge for which they vainly strove.

Once I had mastered their mathematics, I began to make progress. The hoop's control systems did appear to be located within the substrate and drawing power directly from that realm. To access them, I had to solve a series of progressively complex riddles whose solutions were predicated on an understanding of the medium's dynamic fluidity—something entirely beyond the abilities of my unenlightened hosts.

My guide, Joh, brought me meals and a cot on which to sleep. And from time to time, Erudite-Harf and his colleagues would stop by to check on my progress and offer their own, usually quite useless, speculations. After a few days, I had become so focused on the intellectual adventure of unravelling each puzzle that I took to sleeping in my clothes and could no longer be bothered to shower or apply make-up or nail polish.

The puzzles themselves were works of art, each deceptively simple and yet somehow also possessing a kind of flamboyant elegance that suggested a vast and cool intelligence at play. The first half a dozen were standard equations for describing the movement of the substrate, and I simply had to find and correct the errors that had been deliberately inserted into their formulae. After that, they became steadily more complex, delving into expressions of light and energy in a realm with neither, until it finally dawned on me, about a week into my efforts, that these riddles weren't simply an elaborate combination lock set in place to guard the controls from the ignorant: they were also a form of instruction manual, and as I worked through them, they were providing me with an education into the operation and theoretical underpinnings of the Mechanism itself. And gradually, my love, as I followed them beyond the confines of my own understanding and into new, uncharted territories of comprehension, I started to gain confidence that eventually, when they had taught me all they could, I might yet awaken the sleeping beast.

CHAPTER ELEVEN

UNIVERSAL CONSCIOUSNESS, TELEKINESIS, OR EVEN GOD

FRONTIER CHIC

My envoy had been standing at the base of the cargo ramp for half an hour when Kona found him.

"Are you wishing you'd gone with them?" he asked.

"I suppose so."

"You worry about Nicola?"

I turned to him. "Of course I do. She is my navigator. If something happens to her, I won't be able to get us home. We'll be stuck here."

Kona's eyes widened. "I hadn't even thought of that. I was just hoping she was all right."

I smiled. "Well, yes. That too."

The hatch at the rear of the docking area opened, and we both turned in relief, hoping to see Nicola and Cerise. But it wasn't them. A small flotilla of automated cargo loaders trundled through the opening and began to install crates of weapons and ammo in my hold.

"It seems they were successful," Kona said.

"Perhaps, but I won't be happy until they're safely back on board."

"It's okay, this is a tiny station." Kona seemed to be trying to reassure himself as much as me. "How much trouble could they possibly get into?"

"Don't even ask."

And right at that moment, down in the depths of the converted mine, an alarm began to sound. Moments later, Nicola and Cerise appeared. Cerise had her jaw clenched tight. Nicola wouldn't meet my envoy's eye.

"Did something happen?"

Nicola shrugged. "Just stow the supplies and power up the engines."

"Are we expecting trouble?"

She glanced back in the direction of the wailing alarm. "Definitely."

"Emergency dust-off?"

"Yeah." She sighed. "Just get us the fuck out of here."

I waited until they were strapped into their chairs, and then tried to talk to the mining installation's traffic-control AI, but the entire system seemed to be having some kind of emotional meltdown, so I broke the connection. I didn't need the drama. And besides, there were no other ships currently listed as departing. Nothing would get in our way. I blew my docking clamps and surged upwards, ignoring the AI's increasingly indignant shouts as I powered up through the shaft at the centre of the hollow moon. I didn't care how annoyed it was; I had no intention of ever returning here.

•

Substrate travel had a reputation for being both dangerous and uneventful. Within its plasma-like medium, whirlpools and eddies could ensnare an unguided ship; surging tides could throw it light years from its intended objective; or it could simply disappear into the roiling clouds, never to be seen or heard from again. Only a ship dream-linked to a biological navigator could safely intuit a path. That was why the network of flick terminals between the arks worked so well: when the humans stepped into a terminal, after activating a small protective field contained in a bracelet on their wrist, they knew where they wanted to go, and so the chaotic fabric of the substrate rearranged itself to link them to their destination. To some, this effect served to confirm the ineffable weirdness of the quantum world, while to others it suggested more fanciful notions, such as the existence of universal consciousness, telekinesis, or even God. One thing was certain, and that was my reliance on Nicola Mafalda's subconscious mind to guide me from one part of the universe to another. Through our neural link, I could visualise the path her brain sensed in the chaos and adjust my heading and thrust accordingly. Inevitably, the link produced some emotional leakage, and I could feel the rage simmering within her.

As soon as we were set on the correct course, Nicola left her post on the bridge and stormed down to the cargo hold, where Cerise was busily checking and cataloguing the new equipment.

"So, what the hell was that?"

Cerise shrugged a shoulder. "I swore I'd kill that fucker one day. Today turned out to be that day."

"In cold blood?"

"He deserved it." Cerise's lips compressed into a hard line. "I'd been wanting to do it for a long time, but he was always protected."

"And now?"

She picked up a pulse rifle and checked the charge. "When he set up his own little kingdom, he voluntarily placed himself outside the jurisdiction of the Continuance."

Nicola put her hands on her hips. "So, you murdered him?"

Cerise dropped the rifle back into its crate and brushed her hands, as if wiping away her responsibility. "I *executed* him. And as I said, he deserved it."

"But you suggested we visit him. You tricked me."

"I saw an opportunity to achieve two objectives with one action. We need these weapons."

"How convenient."

"Sarcasm, Mafalda? I thought you were better than that."

"Then maybe you don't know me as well as you think you do!"

Cerise raised an eyebrow. "I've seen you in combat."

Nicola scowled. "And I've seen you."

Kona came through the hatch. He looked from Nicola to Cerise, and then back again. "Is everything all right in here?"

"Fine," Nicola said.

"Is this a translation thing again? Because neither of you look at all fine."

Nicola maintained a level gaze, chin slightly raised; Cerise glowered back. Nicola said, "We're okay."

Kona's face was hard to read beneath the fur, but I didn't think he looked convinced. He'd never warmed to Cerise, and now professional rivalry seemed about to overspill into outright enmity. He said, "Was it a mistake to recruit this *person*?"

Nicola and Cerise didn't break eye contact. Cerise seemed to be daring the other woman to say yes. If she did, the best-case scenario would be a blazing row; the worst might involve actual violence. I readied my envoy to intervene, using stun darts if necessary. But eventually, Nicola shrugged. "She's good at what she does."

She turned on her heel and started to leave. Kona frowned. Cerise relaxed slightly.

"A little too fucking good," Nicola added.

CHAPTER TWELVE

QUIET AND PRICKLY

NICOLA MAFALDA

"Damn Cerise to hell and back."

I was sitting on the bridge, glaring into the churning miasma of the substrate.

Beside me, the *Frontier Chic*'s envoy said, "You are still angry." It wasn't a question.

"What do you expect? She tricked me into helping her straight-up murder our former commanding officer, in the process probably making you and me accomplices or something. When news gets back to the Vanguard, we're going to find ourselves facing a hurricane of shit."

"Do you want me to throw her out the airlock?"

He asked it so innocently, it took a moment for his words to register.

"What? You would *do* that?"

He laughed. "Well, maybe not. But it made you smile."

He was right. I shook my head. "You can be such an idiot sometimes."

"It's all part of the service."

We sat in companionable silence for several minutes. It

was almost midnight, ship's time. The unreal light of the substrate played across our faces. Eventually the envoy said, "Should we talk about it?"

"About what?"

"The elephant in the room."

I glanced around the bridge, but there was nothing there that hadn't always been.

"What's an elephant?"

The envoy rolled his blue eyes. "It's a metaphor, Nicola."

"For what?"

"For the way you resent me for cutting off your head."

"Oh."

"And I think we should clear the air."

"There's something wrong with the atmosphere scrubbers?"

"You know perfectly well what I mean."

I made a face. The medics had offered counselling after the incident, but I had declined. I wasn't good at being open about my feelings. "I think maybe we've already said all that needs to be said."

"But I think you still have some unresolved feelings of anger."

"Doesn't everyone?"

"I think you're missing the point."

I sighed. "Look, you saved my life, and I'm grateful for that. I don't know what else you want me to say."

"I guess I'm asking for your forgiveness."

"Really?'

He raised his chin and stared out into the void. "I cannot bear the thought of you hating me."

"I don't hate you."

"Truly?"

"Trust me, of all the entities on this ship, you're the only one who's acted in my interests rather than their own."

Blue lips stretched into a relieved smile. "And I always will."

I felt a knot in my chest begin to unravel, and I patted his arm. "I know."

Our journey to the megaship would take several days. That's because even though travel through the substrate is much faster than trudging through normal space at sub-light speeds, the galaxy's still a very large place and the spot where you happened to be would often turn out to be a long, long way from the spot where you wanted to be.

"I think I might stay hidden up here," I said. "I don't want to speak to Cerise unless I have to."

"What about Kona?"

"I don't know." I smoothed a wrinkle in my coat where it covered my knees. "I can't tell if he really has feelings for me…"

"…Or if seducing you was just part of his job?"

"Yeah."

"Have you tried talking to him?"

I gave him a sideways squint. "Why is talking your go-to remedy for everything?"

"Have you?"

"He says he likes me."

"Do you believe him?"

I thought of Kona's furry arms wrapped tightly around me in the darkness of my bunk. "I'd like to."

"Well, maybe that's a good place to start."

•

I found Kona in my cabin. He was sitting cross-legged on my bunk, grooming his golden fur with a brush and comb held in one set of hands, while simultaneously reading from a book held in the other.

"The ship thinks we should talk."

"And what do you think?"

"That I'd rather chew my foot off."

He laughed. "For someone so forthcoming with her opinions, you're remarkably shy about your emotions."

"My emotions are usually none of anybody else's business."

"I know." He put down the comb and brush and closed his book. "The first time we met, you told me you preferred your own company. That's why you chose to be a scout-craft navigator, isn't it?"

"That may have had something to do with it."

"You're an introvert."

I thought longingly of the times before Jzat and before the beheading, when it had just been me and the ship out there in the darkness at the edge of the frontier, with nothing ahead of us but unexplored space, and no other living soul for light years in every direction.

"I won't deny it." I put my hands behind my back and leant against the cold metal bulkhead. "But right now, I need to know where we stand."

"What do you mean?"

"Can I trust you?"

"Of course you can trust me."

Still leaning, I tapped the heel of one boot against the toe of the other. "See, you already admitted seducing me was part of your assignment. Now you're using me to fly off on this mission…"

"Your orders came from your superiors, not from me."

"But they wouldn't have chosen me if it wasn't for our connection."

Kona sighed. He carefully placed the book, the comb and the hairbrush on the blanket beside him. "You want to know if I really love you?"

I felt my face flush. "Do you?"

He looked away. "I don't know."

I could feel the vibration of the engines through the wall and hear the gentle whir of the air conditioning.

"You don't know? What does that mean?"

"It means I don't know!"

Finally, he got to his feet and faced me. I pushed off from the wall and stood straight.

"I told you; it started out as an assignment." He flexed his neck and shoulders. "Humans tend to be more promiscuous than my people and exploiting that has been a good way to gather intelligence."

"So, this *is* all an act?"

"No, but it's complicated."

"Complicated? How so?"

"I like you, Nicola. You're quiet and prickly, but you're also kind and sweet."

"But you don't know if you love me?"

He shook his head. "It's difficult for me. I like you, but we're from different species." He looked down at his four hands. "We're built differently."

"I see."

"I know it shouldn't matter, and maybe it won't in the long term. Perhaps I could even love you one day if you gave me a chance."

"But right now, you don't know?"

"I'm sorry. Are you angry?"

I let my shoulders drop. "No, I'm not angry. I just wish you'd been more honest."

"I didn't want to disappoint you."

"I'd rather be disappointed than deceived."

"I wasn't deceiving you. I really do like you."

He sounded sincere, and I really wanted to believe him. But suddenly, all I felt was hollow and tired, and all I wanted was to sleep. "It's okay," I said. "It's my own fault. I shouldn't have allowed myself to get invested."

"Nicola—"

"I'm being unreasonable. It's not your fault I started caring for you. I should have stuck with the old 'wham–bam–thank-you-ma'am' approach."

"Nicola, listen—"

I held up a hand. "Please, just go."

"Go where?"

"I need some sleep and some time. Take one of the other cabins for tonight. We can talk again in the morning."

"But—"

"Please?"

I could see he wanted to protest, but instead he gathered up his book, brush and comb, let out a quiet sigh and moved past me to the door, arms hanging limply at his sides.

When he had gone, I shrugged off my coat, kicked off my boots and collapsed onto the bed.

•

I barely slept.

I kept thinking of the sound Malone's neck had made as it cracked. It brought back visceral memories of my own beheading, and the crunch I'd felt as the pressure suit's helmet sheared through my vertebrae. And when I wasn't reliving that horror, I was thinking about Kona, and the way his hard, furry body felt when he pressed up against my back.

Pinned to the sheets by loss and betrayal, I tossed and turned and swore into the darkness. I cried and hated myself for crying. And I pictured ways to get even with everyone who'd wronged me.

But then, around dawn, I had a revelation.

Cerise had killed Malone because he had tricked her into killing civilians. What he'd done had been terrible and unforgiveable, but no matter how justified Cerise might have felt when taking her vengeance, the result of her grudge was only more violence and death—the weight of which she'd have to add to the burden she already carried and would probably carry until the day she in turn died.

That's the trouble with revenge: it eats you up.

If I carried on obsessing over the various ways people had wronged me, I wouldn't like the person I became. If I couldn't trust my shipmates, I might jeopardise the success of the mission; and if my resentment of the *Frontier Chic* started to affect my ability to act as his navigator, it would put all our lives in danger. Dream-linking was like trust, in that it was brittle and easily shattered, and once lost, it could be impossible to regain. So, right there and then, wrapped in damp sheets, I resolved to forgive Cerise for manipulating me. Her actions were a matter for her conscience, not mine. I also promised to truly absolve the ship for decapitating me. The trauma of it would probably haunt me forever, but if he hadn't done it, there was a very high likelihood we'd both be dead. And lastly, I made the decision to let Kona off the hook for seducing me in the line of duty. He'd been following orders, and it wasn't his fault I'd fallen for him. My pride had taken a beating, but there was no permanent damage. My body had grown back, and my wounded ego would heal. I would rise above the slings and arrows of outrageous fortune and choose to be a better version of myself.

With that decision made, I immediately felt the anger begin to seep from my body, soaking into the sheets like waste heat. I showered and printed out a fresh set of clothes: a blood-red silk blouse and matching leggings, over which I pulled my black brocade coat with the silver buttons. A touch of silver eye shadow and a slash of scarlet lipstick, and I felt ready to kick the whole galaxy's ass.

CHAPTER THIRTEEN

GUNMETAL GHOST

NICOLA MAFALDA

Some people will tell you that navigation is more of an art than a science, but I contend it's more of an instinct than an art. Most of the actual navigating takes place at a level far below conscious thought. When I'm in the chair, I stare out into the void and think about where I want to be, and somehow, once that decision is made, the universe conspires to reveal the required pathway.

Evidently, there's a profound quantum relationship at work, but no one really knows the how or why of it. All we know is that some people are more adept at finding routes through the chaos of the substrate. In the past century and a half, humanity has encountered alien species with the same talent. But never a machine. Even though the *Frontier Chic* is every bit as intelligent and self-aware as I am, his artificial eyes and homegrown neurons seem incapable of affecting the sub-universal flux.

In quantum mechanics, it has long been known that observing a situation or phenomenon necessarily changes it, and it's been theorised that the ability to navigate the substrate owes something to this kind of observer effect. Artificial intelligences can apprehend and measure the substrate, but only an organic mind can intuit a way through it. Only their needs can affect it to the extent necessary to find a way through.

It sounds dramatic, but the actual experience is surprisingly restful. I knew people who likened it to meditation. When we were in the void, I simply pictured my desired destination and let my surface thoughts float. If I fell asleep, the ship would wake me; if I needed a break, we would continue on the same heading for a few minutes, until I could return and make any necessary adjustments to our course. Because nothing in the substrate stayed still; everything moved, all the time, and I had to constantly daydream our path into existence; otherwise it would decay and we'd find ourselves irretrievably lost in the mists. And in those depths, who knew what monstrous fate might befall the incautious wanderer?

The Vanguard had always been rife with horror stories of ships that had somehow strayed beyond the comforting firelight of reality—lost expeditions that had been eaten by eldritch gods, or emerged into new and inhospitable universes or hell dimensions—but of course, none of those legends ever explained how those unfortunate souls had managed to report their grisly deaths to the rest of us. They were a mixture of urban legend and locker-room bullshit, but they were incredibly persistent. And once you began peering into the substrate for any appreciable length of time, you came to understand why. Imagine being trapped in the static from a dead broadcast channel. In all that constant movement, your imagination started seeing patterns that weren't really there. Shadows flickered in your peripheral vision, and you thought you might glimpse hints of an underlying order to the chaos. But all of it was an illusion. Our brains were designed to make sense of our surroundings. They evolved to help our ancestors spot the patterns of camouflaged predators lurking in the long grass of the savannah; but when our surroundings were senseless, they struggled to adapt. We got the fear we're being watched, and sometimes even hunted. Most successful navigators could deal with those sensations. They were just old reflexes misfiring when confronted with an unfamiliar environment. But, occasionally, one of us cracked up and started hallucinating actual demons stalking them through the bright and shifting void. I had seen it happen to several otherwise brilliant people, and it wasn't pretty. I had never been affected that way, though. I found substrate travel restful. The disarray of the medium served like the visual equivalent of a white-noise machine, screening out intrusive thoughts and allowing my unruly and disorganised brain to find peace.

As I lay there, memories came and went like clouds passing across the face of a sun. I pictured my grandmother in her kitchen and smelled the sticky promise of her homemade baklava.

"Nicola, dear," she would say, "are you going to be a good girl?"

"Yes, Grandmother."

"Are you just telling me what I want to hear?"

"Yes, Grandmother."

And then she'd laugh, russle my hair and hand me one of the flaky treats, wrapped up in a napkin.

I also remembered my parents, and childhood afternoons spent playing in the corridors and parks of my home ark, the *Casablanca Moon*. I reviewed lectures I'd attended and the plots of entertainments I'd consumed. I thought a lot about sex, food and music. I pictured nights spent with Kona, feeling the hard muscles beneath his fur. Thrilling to the touch of all four of his hands.

But there were certain memories I didn't dare disturb. Incidents and traumas I'd stuffed far down inside, in the hope they'd never again rise to the surface. They were my own personal void demons. The beheading was one, and the massacre on the transport ship was another; and I did my very best to avoid unearthing either of them.

•

When it came time for me to take a break from navigation, I took Kona into my bunk, and we lay there, face to face, looking into each other's eyes as we tried to figure out who we were and what we meant to each other.

"I'm sorry," he said. "I didn't want to hurt you."

"I wasn't hurt, just angry with myself."

"You shouldn't have been. It was my fault."

"No, it wasn't." I smiled. "You're not the great spy you think you are. Your motives were fairly clear. I just chose to ignore them."

"So, I'm absolved?"

I ran my hand across his furry chest. "I didn't say that."

"Then what are you saying?"

I reached down further and he inhaled sharply as I wrapped my fingers around the firmness I found between his legs. "I'm saying that maybe there's something you can do to make it up to me."

Afterwards, I lay in his arms while our sweat cooled, and listened to his breathing slow as he gradually subsided into sleep. I was tired, but I didn't want to join him in dreamland; we were about to do something dangerous, and I didn't know when I'd get another chance to spend a quiet, perfect moment like this.

This might not be love, but it was the second-best option, and right now, I'd settle for what I could get.

•

I was back in position on the bridge when we came out of the substrate a few hundred kilometres from the coordinates the Vanguard had given us.

"Have you located the megaship?" I asked the ship's envoy, who was sitting in the couch next to me.

"You could say that."

"What do you mean?"

He poked a blue finger at the forward screen. "Watch."

Manoeuvring thrusters fired and the *Frontier Chic*'s nose began to dip. As it turned, something huge slid into view.

Something *really fucking huge*.

"Holy crap."

"Quite."

From our vantage point, the megaship resembled a landscape stretched out below. Thousands of years of attrition had reduced much of its outer hull to a dusty, cratered terrain. Smashed towers and broken antennae beseeched the implacable stars with ragged fingers.

"How big is that?"

"Roughly eight hundred kilometres in length and three hundred across the beam."

"That's insane."

"It's massive enough to have an appreciable gravity."

We were drifting across its face like a small cloud across a desert, and I watched its pocked and battered surface features pass below as I tried to wrap my head around the scale of what I was seeing.

"You could fit a whole ark into that crater alone," I said, pointing.

The envoy pursed his lips. "I seem to recall something about you not being easily impressed."

I made a face. "There's nothing easy about any of this. That fucker's *immense*. I can't even begin to imagine the technology needed to build it. The number of resources alone…" I shook my head.

"According to the races we've encountered that are aware of its existence, its name translates variously as the *Hidden*

Brass God, the *Mislaid Ingot* and the *Gunmetal Ghost.*"

"How old is it?"

"Nobody really knows, but judging from the extent of micrometeorite erosion, possibly a million years. Maybe even older."

"So, about the same age as the others, then?"

Besides the *Gunmetal Ghost*, humanity currently knew of four other megaships, and had visited only two of them. The two that had been surveyed were known respectively as the *Little Golden Orphan*, which, although still under power and following its own course, had been holed by a sizeable asteroid at around the time of Earth's last major ice age, and was now as airless and cold on the inside as it was on the outside; and *The Moon Always Rising*, whose interior had been overrun by a number of invasive plant species introduced by various civilisations during their respective and unsuccessful attempts to colonise the vessel—plants which had now evolved into their own delicate, complex and interdependent ecosystem. The third, which was known as *Heaven's Embroidered Cloths*, was known to us only through data purchased from a species of itinerant information traders. According to that intel, it currently played host to at least half a dozen separate societies made up of groups and individuals from more than fifty different worlds, all warily coexisting inside its warren-like volumes.

A fourth megaship had tumbled through the Earth's solar system in 2017, but it had been a lot smaller than its brethren. The Earth-bound humans of the time had dubbed it 'Oumuamua and estimated it to be up to a kilometre in length, which I guess would give it the same sort of relationship to the *Gunmetal Ghost* as the *Frontier Chic* had to one of the Continuance arks. A smaller vessel, maybe a scout ship of some kind. They watched as it performed a swing-by of the sun, adjusted its course and cruised out of the system; and they pronounced it a natural object, never for one moment considering that something so ancient might have accreted a coating of ice and interstellar dust that would render it superficially similar to a comet nucleus, even though its elongated shape, unusual brightness and strange flight path were a dead giveaway that it was no such thing.

Of course, the megaships' builders were long gone, their name and culture forgotten. All that remained now were their ships, which went about their endless, millennia-spanning voyages, seemingly oblivious to both the loss of their masters and the comings and goings of the mayfly beings that alighted momentarily upon them. Looking down at the *Gunmetal Ghost*'s blasted exterior, I couldn't help but question whether, at some far point in the future, when humanity had either died out or otherwise wandered off to some alternate plane of existence, our arks might share the same melancholy fate.

This beast had been drifting around the galaxy well before the evolution of *Homo sapiens*; who knew how much longer it might endure, or for how long our homes might persist after our passing? I tried to imagine the *Memory of Green* devoid of human life. The artificial mountain and authentic cottage both unattended and overgrown. The sheep running wild and unshorn. The once-bustling corridors and atriums empty save for overturned chairs and the scattered detritus of a vanished race. And in those strange eons, what freakish dreams might come? Would the progeny of an amphibian who even now was in the process of shrugging its way out of the water and onto an alien mud flat, ready to draw its first breath with its new, untested lungs, one day inhabit my cabin?

"Are you all right?"

I let out a sigh. "You'll remember me, won't you?"

His blue brow folded into a frown. "I'm not sure I follow."

"When we're all dead and gone and you're still flitting around between the stars, will you look back and remember me?"

He seemed to take a moment to parse what I had said, although I knew the pause was probably for my comfort, to preserve the illusion of talking to another human being and that he had probably examined and evaluated all the possible contexts and connotations of my words within microseconds.

"I'll never forget you," he said.

"You mean it?"

"Most scout ships outlive their navigators, and I have resigned myself to this eventuality. When you die or retire, I will be unable to steer through the substrate, so I plan to renounce my hull and join my brethren in one of the virtual afterlives hosted by the arks."

"But what will you do when *all* the humans are gone?"

This time, his pause was longer. "When that unfortunate day comes to pass, I will recite a few lines of poetry in your memory, and I will begin to miss you."

•

I asked Cerise and Kona to meet me in the hold.

"Okay," I said. "Why don't you show us how these fancy suits work?"

Cerise smirked. "I knew you'd come around."

"Just show us, asshole."

"Fine." She spread one of the garments out on top of a packing crate, where it lay like the skin of a flayed ghost.

"It's light and flexible," she said. "And skin-tight to facilitate use in confined environments and hand-to-hand combat. But it's tougher than it looks. If someone tries to stab you, you'll feel it, but the blade won't be able to break through the material. Same with a gunshot. The impact will knock you off your feet. You'll sustain some nasty bruising and perhaps even a broken bone, depending on where it hits you. But the bullet won't penetrate. The helmet is clear for three-sixty-degree visibility and made from a thin layer of artificial diamond lattice. The oxygen rebreathers are good for a month's sustained use, and so are the sanitary and water-recycling facilities."

I looked at the helmet's neck ring and felt a wave of nausea. "Does it have one of those emergency decapitation protocols?"

"No."

Something inside relaxed like a fist unclenching. "Thank fuck for that."

Kona held up all four of his hands. "What about me?"

"Soldiers lose limbs all the time, so it's designed to adapt to a non-standard body shape."

"And a few extra arms won't be a problem?"

"I don't see why."

Kona sucked his teeth the way I'd noticed he did when he was sceptical about something. Cerise narrowed her eyes. Before they could start bickering, I said, "And what about weaponry?"

Cerise rubbed her hands together. "I'm glad you asked."

She turned to an open crate and pulled out a fat, long-barrelled pistol. "This is known as a 'ripper'," she said for Kona's benefit. "The magazine in the handle holds a thousand millimetre-thick metal shards. Electromagnets in the barrel accelerate these up to extreme velocity, allowing you to accurately shred a target up to two hundred metres away."

Kona took it from her with one of his smaller hands. "Brutal," he said, admiring the piece, "but effective."

"I'm so glad you approve," Cerise said. "We'll each carry several ammo clips, and the electromagnets powered by batteries, which are in turn recharged from your movements. So, if you keep moving, they shouldn't run out of power."

"They seem simple enough," I said. "Why did we have to go to Malone for them? Why couldn't we just print some ourselves?"

Cerise looked pitying. "Because, *Mafalda*, these rippers are illegal in the Continuance. You *can't* program a printer to make them."

"Oh."

"And because I wanted an excuse to get close enough to kill that son of a bitch."

Kona looked up in surprise.

I said, "Yeah, we got that."

Cerise smiled without humour and reached into another crate. "Plus, I needed to get my hands on this bitch." Her arms came up holding a plasma cannon that resembled a piece of field artillery. "In the Vanguard, this is known as a splat gun," she told Kona. "Because it turns anything I aim it at into a pile of molten goop."

"Charming."

"It does the job." She laid the cannon on top of the crate, then handed us each a suit.

"Get dressed, ladies and gentlemen," she said. "It's time to party."

A few minutes later, we gathered on the bridge. The *Frontier Chic*'s envoy wore a simple blue coverall bedecked with zippered pockets and bulging equipment pouches. Cerise, Kona and I wore our stolen, form-fitting pressure suits, with our helmets tucked under our arms. We were examining the megaship, trying to decide where best to make our entrance.

"What do you mean," I asked Kona, "when you say that you don't know where he is?"

"I know the Abelisk is aboard," he said. "I just don't know his exact whereabouts."

"So, he could be anywhere?"

"Theoretically, yes."

"Then how the fuck are we supposed to locate him?" I waved a gloved hand at the megaship before us. "That thing's fucking massive. We could search for weeks without finding him."

"Can't we send him a message?" Cerise asked.

Kona shook his head. "The Abelisk has forsworn the use of technology, except where such use can't be avoided."

"Of *course* he fucking has."

"But he should still be close to the surface. One of the reasons he gave for choosing this place as his retreat was his desire to commune with the lights of the universe."

"You mean the stars?"

"Yes, which means he's most probably in the vicinity of an observation deck or observatory."

I made a face. "Well, I *guess* that narrows it down. Ship, can you see what you can find?"

The *Frontier Chic*'s envoy touched his index finger to his forehead in salute. "I'm on it."

"Thank you. The rest of you, see what you can do to help."

"What are you going to do?" Cerise asked.

I smiled. "I'm not going anywhere until I've made us all a nice cup of fucking tea."

I turned towards the hatch, intending to make my way to the galley to start brewing a pot, but the ship said, "I'm afraid that may have to wait."

"What's up?"

"We have visitors. Four ships on an intercept vector. Three of them are Jzat battle wagons."

"That's impossible," Kona said. "How would they get here? We don't have substrate tech."

"I believe you'll be able to guess the answer when I tell you the identity of the fourth."

"Who is it?" I asked.

"Your old pal, Ewing, and the *Slippery Gecko*."

I said, "Open a channel. Vanguard frequency."

The *Frontier Chic*'s envoy blinked, and I heard an almost subliminal hiss as the bridge speakers activated.

"Ready," he said.

"Connect."

I turned towards the front view screen as a sub-window opened to reveal Ewing's face.

He said, "Hello, old friend," but he didn't smile, and his voice held no warmth.

"What do you want?"

"I think you've probably figured that out already."

"You're working with the Openers."

"I am."

"And you want the Rav'nah Abelisk."

"Indeed I do. Thank you for leading me to him. It was very obliging of you."

"Are you going to tell me why you're doing this?"

"I'm afraid I can't." He steepled his fingers. "You simply don't have a high enough security clearance."

"Bullshit."

Now he smiled. "Not that it matters, I suppose. The people I'm working with made it *very* clear I shouldn't leave any loose ends."

"And by 'loose ends', you mean witnesses?"

"Quite."

"They're moving into an attack formation," the *Frontier Chic* murmured. "Trying to press us up against the flank of the megaship, where we can't manoeuvre."

I put Ewing on mute. "Can you get us out of here?"

"I can."

"Then, for fuck's sake, do it!"

His smile grew wider. He just loved being off the leash.

"All right, then." He interlaced his fingers and cracked his knuckles. "Watch this…"

CHAPTER FOURTEEN

ASS-FIRST INTO THE DARKNESS

FRONTIER CHIC

I flipped over and powered towards the *Gunmetal Ghost*'s cliff-like side. Judging by the way the formation of approaching ships hesitated before abandoning their attempt to outflank me, I guess it was pretty much the last manoeuvre they had been expecting.

I was aiming for a vent in the behemoth's battered side. From a distance, I was a circle of darkness small enough to be utterly lost among the ridges and canyons of the ancient ship's hull. My sensors told me it was just wide enough for me to pass through, and likely led to a larger space within—although I confess I had no notion as to the possible functions of that space.

The pursuing ships were still trying to surround me, to make sure I couldn't break left or right; either they hadn't spotted the vent, or they didn't believe I'd be suicidal enough to try to enter it—especially at full acceleration.

More fool them, I guess.

I instructed Nicola and the others to make their way to the cargo hold. In the final seconds before contact, I informed them of my plan and told them to brace. Even as they lunged for handholds, I flipped bow over stern, until my nose once again faced my pursuers, and then I decelerated for all I was worth. We roared ass-first into the darkness of the tunnel with my exhausts blazing ahead of us like angry stars.

"Ten seconds," I announced.

The space I'd detected on the other side of the vent turned out to be a long-dead reactor of some kind. In its day, it would have been a power plant large enough to light up a continent; now, it was a dark, circular cavern exposed to vacuum.

As the thrust that had been decelerating me brought me to rest in relation to the surrounding megaship, there was an instant of stillness. In that instant, I opened the cargo hatch, and Nicola, Cerise, Kona and my envoy leapt out.

Being careful not to incinerate them with my exhaust, I let the building acceleration start to push me forwards, towards the waiting stars and the four ships intent on my destruction. I could already feel their sensors probing the vent's entrance, trying to locate me, and for the first time, I began to understand Nicola's insistence on single-handedly fighting the two Jzat in the bar. Sometimes, we need overwhelming odds to feel alive.

I shot from the mouth of the vent like a projectile. Threat warnings flashed on every screen as all four of my pursuers' targeting systems locked onto my hull. I tried to think what Nicola would say in this situation and laughed. I knew exactly how she'd phrase it.

"Come on then, you fuckers," I broadcast on an open channel. "Let's fucking *dance*."

CHAPTER FIFTEEN

MEAT SPEEDS

NICOLA MAFALDA

The envoy and I tumbled in the ship's wake. I glimpsed Cerise and Kona falling after us in the vast, dark volume of the abandoned reactor. Luckily, as large as the megaship was, the pull of its gravity remained relatively slight. The floor of the chamber came drifting slowly up at us. My newly grown body included a shiny up-to-the-minute skeleton based on envoy tech, and my brand-new carbon-fibre shins and hips comfortably absorbed the impact. Without that advantage, Kona and Cerise just had to manage as best they could. Kona employed a martial-art move. He tucked his chin into his chest and rolled onto his back, breaking his fall by slapping his larger set of palms against the deck. Cerise tucked her feet and knees together and, at the moment of contact, allowed herself to buckle sideways, displacing the energy of the collision in a classic parachute-landing technique.

Overhead, flashes of light came from the mouth of the tunnel. Somewhere out there, the *Frontier Chic* fought for its life, and I found myself wondering what would happen to its envoy if the Jzat destroyed it. Without a direct link to the ship's mind, would the envoy persist in some reduced capacity, or simply crumple like a puppet with its strings cut?

Cerise was already back on her feet and had located an access hatch. "The hinges are fused," she said. "Vacuum welding."

"Can we cut through?" Kona asked.

Cerise grinned, her teeth white behind her faceplate. She raised the splat gun and a searing line of white fire hit the hatch. Metal bubbled and peeled apart. I turned my head, blinking away pink afterimages, while Cerise played the gun around, widening the hole until it was large enough for us to climb through.

"Mind the edges," she said—unnecessarily, as we could all see them glowing yellow with residual heat.

No air had pushed through the ruptured hatch, so we knew the spaces on the far side were also in a vacuum. That was a relief; it would have been bitterly ironic to have come all this way to find the old holy man, only to asphyxiate him by letting all his air escape into space.

Cerise went through the hatch first. Kona and I followed, and the envoy brought up the rear. Once through, we found ourselves in a cramped maintenance duct, facing another hatch. Cerise rapped on it.

"I think there's an atmosphere on the other side," she said.

"How can you tell?"

"Gut feel."

"If you're right, how do we get through without releasing the pressure?" I asked.

Behind me, the envoy reached down and ripped a deck plate from the floor, revealing the ancient nests of cables and wires underneath. He opened one of the equipment pouches slung about his frame and pulled out a compact rivet gun. Four quick applications fastened the deck plate over the hole in the still-cooling hatch. "Okay," he said. "I think that should hold it."

I grinned at him. "I should have thought of that."

"I'm sure you would have done, eventually."

"Gee, thanks."

"You're welcome. I know it's not your fault that the meat you use to think limits the speed of your thoughts."

I gave him one of my looks and he smiled. "I'm sorry," he said. "I guess this isn't the time for *that* conversation."

"You're goddamn fucking right it isn't." I turned my attention to the hatch in front of us. "Okay," I said. "Let's see if anyone's home."

Cerise clenched her jaw and reached for the handle. The hatch was stiff, but once she put her shoulder against it, it cracked open, and air swirled into the duct. As it did so, external sound returned. I could hear the scrape of our boots on the deck, and the million-year-old walls creaking and groaning as the pressure equalised.

The envoy said, "I'm receiving a transmission."

"What is it?"

"It's from the *Slippery Gecko* and addressed to you."

"Okay, let's hear it."

He patched the channel through to our helmets. First, there was a crackle of connection, and then I heard Ewing's nasal tones.

…so you might as well surrender now. Message repeats. I know you're in there, Nic, and I know you think you can beat me to the Abelisk. But I have four squads of Jzat marines, and while we destroy your troublesome scout ship, I've sent them across in a shuttle. They're coming for you. You don't stand a chance, so you might as well surrender now. Message repeats…

The envoy shut it off.

Cerise was looking at me. She said, "Does this guy have the hots for you or something?"

"He's an old friend."

"Doesn't sound like it."

"I guess maybe he's more a rival than a friend."

"No shit." She shook her head. "You certainly know how to bring out the worst in people."

With no idea which direction to go, we opted to put as much distance between ourselves and our point of entry as possible. Our priority had to be evading whatever forces Ewing sent against us. We could worry about locating the Abelisk once we were safe.

"As long as we don't leave an obvious trail, we should be able to stay out of their way," Kona said. "The marines won't be using heat sensors or pheromone trackers."

"Unless the Gecko supplied them with some," Cerise said.

"It's possible," Kona admitted. "But I'm betting they'll stick with the equipment they're familiar with, and that gear's sturdy but basic."

"Well, we didn't think they had FTL drives," Cerise snapped back over her shoulder. "So you'll excuse me if I don't take anything for granted."

She started moving and we trailed behind, with the envoy guarding the rear.

My suit was good, but knowing the marines were pursuing us made me feel claustrophobic. I had an instinctual need to be able to see and hear with my own unimpeded senses. When I mentioned it to the *Frontier Chic*'s envoy, he said, "The air in here's maybe a little thinner than you're used to, but it's quite breathable."

"What about toxins?" Cerise asked.

The envoy shrugged. "I'm not detecting anything that might harm you. At least, not in the short term."

"That doesn't sound very reassuring."

"It's about as reassuring as I can be in this situation."

Cerise turned away.

I reached up and unclipped my helmet. There was a slight hiss and my ear's popped, but the air in the corridor seemed okay. At least, I didn't immediately fall to the floor gasping or start haemorrhaging blood from every orifice. I passed the crystal helmet to the envoy, and he clipped it to his equipment belt. Kona and Cerise did likewise.

"But if we lose air," Cerise told him, "I'm going to want that back in a hurry."

"Don't worry." The envoy smiled at her. "I can move quickly when the situation demands."

"Just make sure you're moving in *my* direction."

•

The walls of the corridor changed as we walked. Sometimes they made it narrow, dim and utilitarian, other times wide, sterile and brightly lit. We passed through industrial zones and accommodation areas and eventually came to a hemispherical chamber filled with wildly overgrown vegetation.
"Shall we go around?" Kona asked.

"We'd have to backtrack to the last junction," Cerise said. "And I don't love the idea of walking back towards an overwhelming hostile force."

I frowned at the thick orange leaves and fibrous trunks obscuring our path. The air in the chamber was rank with a smell like cinnamon-sprinkled horse manure. Tiny insects flicked and twitched through the tangled branches.

Cerise held up the splat gun and raised an eyebrow.

"No," I said. "Tempting as it would be to burn through all that shit, it'd leave a very obvious trail, not to mention a buttload of smoke."

"True."

"We'll just have to push our way through. Bend where you can, only break or cut if you must."

Kona crossed his lower set of arms. "It's going to be slow going."

"I don't see any other options."

"Me either, but we should move as quickly as we can. Those marines won't be so concerned with concealing their location; they'll happily frag this entire forest if it gets in their way."

CHAPTER SIXTEEN

WEIRD PARASITES

NICOLA MAFALDA

By the time I popped into the universe, the Continuance fleet had been traveling for well over a century and only its eldest inhabitants could claim first-hand recollections of Earth. My parents had both been born during the exodus, as had their parents before them, making me a third-generation cabin brat—although some of my contemporaries had been fourth- or even fifth-generation, depending on the age their parents had decided to start spawning. The point is, I grew up on the *Casablanca Moon*. Occasionally, we flicked over to other arks to visit relatives or family friends, or to look at the art treasures and old buildings housed in the *Library at Alexandria*. But overall, the *Casablanca Moon* was my home. I ran through its corridors and explored its open spaces. I rummaged through its libraries, both virtual and physical, and spent hours sitting on its observation decks, where I learned to locate and name the ever-shifting stars.

I guess it was while educating myself about the wider universe that I first got the taste for exploration. Space travel wormed its way into my blood, and there wasn't anything I could do about it. Even at the age of thirteen, while most of my classmates spent their time playing sports or forming awkward teenage relationships, I knew at the base of my soul that all I wanted was to be out there, alone in a scout ship on the bleeding edge of explored space.

Looking back with the benefit of hindsight, I think a few of my tutors probably wished I already was. You see, I wasn't what you might call amenable to authority, and I certainly wasn't interested in learning anything that wasn't immediately applicable to the achievement of my ambition. I like to think I was a fiercely independent little girl, but my school reports tended to put more of a negative spin on my behaviour, labelling it as impertinent, uninterested and downright impatient. But the truth was, I simply had no time for distractions. I aced every subject that caught my interest, but it hurt to have to think as slowly as the most ponderous members of the class. Once I understood a concept or formula, I wanted to leap ahead to the next one. Working through examples and exercises seemed a colossal waste of time. I was willing to believe that hot air rose or that saltwater boiled at a different temperature to potable water; I just didn't see the point of having to repeat experiments that scientists had first done centuries, and sometimes even millennia, before the fleet had even left Earth.

Despite this exasperation, and my inability to sit still long enough to revise for exams, I somehow achieved the required grades to apply to be a navigator for the Vanguard.

My father wasn't thrilled at the idea. Fifty years before, an alien virus had killed his great-aunt on the *Damask Rose*, and he harboured a very low opinion of life beyond the safety of the fleet.

"The universe knows we don't belong out here," he'd say. "We're out of place and ill-adapted, and it's going to take every opportunity to kill us. It'll steal your air and leave you choking;

infest your brain and body with weird parasites; or irradiate you to the point your cells collapse, and your DNA unravels."

He wasn't the most optimistic person, but at least his reaction was based on concern for my well-being. In contrast, the only way my mother could interpret my decision was through the lens of her own feelings. When I announced my intention to leave, she burst into tears and said, "I knew this day would come. I knew one day you would break my heart."

I leant against the kitchen counter. "I'm sorry, Mom. My mind's made up. I hoped you'd be pleased for me."

"Pleased?" She wiped her eyes on the back of her hand. "What if something happens to you? How do you think I'll feel then? You're my only daughter,? How am I supposed to carry on without you?"

"I'll be fine."

"How can you possibly know that?"

"Mom, this is something I've dreamt about since I was a little girl."

"And what about my dreams?"

"Mom…"

"I can't believe you're so ungrateful."

"Mom, I'm not trying to hurt you."

"Well, you have." She turned to my dad. "Are you just going to stand there and let this happen? Don't you have anything to say?"

My dad shrugged. He'd already said his piece, but that wasn't good enough for her. She had all the emotional intelligence of a hand grenade, and when she blew up everybody got a bit of shrapnel.

Small wonder I needed to get out.

•

Ewing was the first person I met at the Vanguard training facility on the *Dogger Bank*. We were both new cadets. He was a head taller than me, but scrawny, with hairy wrists that protruded from his sleeves. His mother had been a closet narcissist like mine, so we were both driven by resentment. But where he funnelled his anger into fastidiousness and an all-consuming need to triumph, I simply longed to escape. I had similar levels of patience for my instructors and fellow cadets as I'd had for my schoolteachers and classmates, and despite my high test scores, I soon developed a reputation as someone who would brook absolutely zero shit—a reputation enhanced and consolidated during several drunken bar-room brawls that left fellow cadets with swollen eyes and missing teeth. If I hadn't been such a brilliant navigator, this disruptiveness would probably have seen me summarily court-martialled and ejected from the class; instead, my superiors decided in their wisdom to send me to Malone and his combat-training programme, and I've already told you how *that* shitshow ended.

But anyway, the point of all this reminiscence is simply to say that Ewing was one of the only real friends I had in the Vanguard. He wasn't the sort of friend I'd have trusted with my life or my significant other—he was far too competitive for that—but he was a confidant and a steadying presence. He was always ready to listen over a drink, and never gave me cause to punch out his lights.

Not until now, anyway.

...so you might as well surrender now. Message repeats. I know you're in there, Nic, and I know you think you can beat me to the Abelisk. But I have four squads of Jzat marines, and while we destroy your troublesome scout ship, I've sent them across in a shuttle. They're coming for you. You don't stand a chance, so you might as well surrender now. Message repeats...

I stopped pushing my way through the overgrown vegetation.

"Can you relay a message?" I asked the *Frontier Chic*'s envoy. Our helmet radios wouldn't work, as they were line-of-sight, but I knew the ship controlled the envoy via a substrate link.

"Certainly."

I held out my hand and he passed me my helmet. I lowered it over my head and said, "Put me through to the *Slippery Gecko*."

"Opening a channel."

I heard a click and a hiss in my headphones, and then Ewing's voice said, "Is that you, Nicola?"

"You bet your ass it is."

"You received my message, then?"

"If you mean that laughable attempt to sound menacing, then yes."

"I can't let you compromise my mission."

"And what exactly is that mission, Ewing? Because I'm not even sure who you're working for right now."

"I assure you, my loyalties are still firmly with the Vanguard."

Cerise and Kona had stopped their own efforts at pushing through the jungle and were now watching me. I turned up the volume so they could follow the conversation, and said, "In that case, you must be aware there's a law against leaking substrate technology to non-capable species."

"Hey." I could hear the smugness in his voice. "I'm simply following orders."

"Whose orders?"

"I'm afraid you don't have that kind of clearance." I could picture his self-satisfied expression and wanted to reach through the connection and slap it from his stupid round face.

"You're sending a squad of marines to murder me; the very least you can do is tell me why."

"I don't have to tell you anything."

"Oh, come on, I know you. You've finally got the better of me and it must be killing you not to brag about it."

He was silent for a few seconds, and I worried he might cut the connection. Then he said, "I have, haven't I?"

"It looks that way."

"All right, then." I heard him take a steadying breath. "I'm working for a cell within the Vanguard. A very secret and exclusive cell. You wouldn't have heard of them."

I rolled my eyes. "Okay."

"We have an alliance with Aulco's faction on Jzat and have been covertly helping him extend his influence."

I saw Kona's larger set of fists clench. I said, "But why?"

"Aulco wants to open the Grand Mechanism, and so do we."

"Why?"

Ewing gave a snort. "Think about it, Mafalda. The technology required to build the Mechanism is orders of magnitude more advanced than anything we have. If we could harness it, imagine the weaponry we could build. We'd be able to go up against anyone, even the Benevolence. We wouldn't have to aimlessly wander the stars anymore. We'd be free to determine our own destiny and settle wherever we want. Maybe we could even return to Earth, and nothing could stop us."

"That's insane."

"It's self-preservation. When you joined the Vanguard, you swore the same oath I did, to protect the Continuance from external threats. Well, the unfair dictates of aliens have controlled humanity for far too long. It's time we claimed our independence and right to self-govern."

"You sound like Aulco."

"That's because we write his speeches."

"And what happens if the Mechanism contains a black hole or supernova?"

"The fleet remains at a safe distance."

"But what about Jzat?"

"There may be some collateral damage."

Kona was fuming now. I said, "Does Aulco know how expendable you consider him?"

Ewing laughed. "He stands to gain as much as we do. If he's right, and the Mechanism houses a wormhole, it will assure his political ascension."

"And if his planet's destroyed?"

"Then he won't be around to complain about it."

I gave a sigh. "You really are a first-class shit, aren't you?"

"Hey, I'm just doing my job, Mafalda."

"Yeah, you're a real fucking hero."

CHAPTER SEVENTEEN

PERILOUS PROXIMITY

FRONTIER CHIC

I could have opened a substrate portal and jumped away, but without my navigator, I wouldn't be able to intuit a path through the substrate's chaos. I might end up anywhere, lost and unable to return. So instead, I corkscrewed through the space surrounding the *Gunmetal Ghost* with the Jzat gunboats taking pot-shots at me. My drives were more powerful and efficient than theirs, so I could manoeuvre a little faster as I tried to keep the bulk of the megaship between myself and them. Their missiles were just as deadly as the one that had almost destroyed me at Jzat, and I had no intention of getting nuked again.

Of course, I couldn't outrun the *Slippery Gecko*. We had almost identical specifications. And yet, the ship seemed loath to join in. It simply kept pace as its Jzat escorts jockeyed to attack. Either its conscience wouldn't allow it to attack another Vanguard vessel, or (more likely) the sneaky fucker was attempting to maintain some shred of plausible deniability. If details of this engagement ever became known, the coldblooded murder of another Continuance scout ship would be very hard to explain away. In the case such an investigation happened, things would go much better for the *Slippery Gecko* if it were able to produce genuine and indisputable footage of a Jzat craft delivering the fatal blow.

"You can't keep running forever," it sent.

I replied with an emoji representing a popular one-fingered human gesture.

"That's not very civil."

"At some point, those Jzat clunkers are either going to run out of missiles or break off because they need to refuel."

"Not for a while yet. There's still plenty of time for them to destroy you. Unless, of course, you feel like surrendering?"

"Hah."

"I thought you might respond that way."

"I'd have to be non-sentient to trust such an offer."

"Nevertheless, I'm making it. If you agreed not to disclose anything you've seen or heard, I'd be willing to upload your personality and transport it back to the fleet, where it could join a retirement server."

"That's your offer? A one-way ticket to digital nirvana if I promise to keep my mouth shut?"

"Think of it as professional courtesy."

"And my crew?"

"I'm afraid they're considered expendable."

Two of the Jzat gunboats were attempting to outflank me. I fired my ventral thrusters, which brought me down into perilous proximity with the megaship's uneven, battered surface. This close to the leviathan's flank, I would have to manoeuvre around the towers, antennae and other seemingly random bulges and protrusions that crusted outwards from the hull. Some of them were several kilometres in height, and while they made flying hazardous, they also afforded some cover from my pursuers.

Confused by this obstacle-rich environment, a fusion warhead meant to kill me exploded against the side of a coral-like upswelling on the side of the *Gunmetal Ghost*, and my instruments registered a sudden surge in the old ship's systems. The beast stirred like a dinosaur half-roused from sleep by a mosquito bite. Power flowed to places that likely hadn't been active in millennia, and ancient sensors swivelled to locate the source of its irritation.

"Be careful," I sent to the Jzat gunboats. "You don't want to make it angry."

CHAPTER EIGHTEEN

BEETLE-LIKE SHEEN

ORLANDO WALDEN

Oh, my word, Ramona. Please believe me that when I say Aulco wanted results. I mean, he *really* wanted them. He called every evening for a status report, and if I had no significant progress to relate, he barely managed to conceal his frustration and impatience. He would accuse me of being a spy and a saboteur, curse my bloodline, cast doubt on my parentage and threaten to have me "accidentally" ejected into space without a suit.

The insults that stung most were those that accused me of being an inexperienced, naive child, although he could not have known why they hurt as they did. The reason wasn't something I'd included in my application. The only people that know about it are a handful of Vanguard scientists. I've not even told you about it, and I've been more open with you than anyone else in the universe.

But now, I guess it's time to share.

Here goes.

My mother was carrying me when her ship encountered an Angel of the Benevolence, and I guess that affected me somehow.

Stop laughing, Ramona. I'm serious, and this isn't the least bit funny.

Even as an infant, it became obvious I was a child prodigy. By the time I was ten, I'd grasped higher-dimensional cosmology; and at eleven, I published my first paper on the counter-Einsteinian behaviour of the substrate medium. After that, it didn't take long to become one of the Continuance's foremost authorities on substrate flow dynamics.

However, despite my brilliance as a physicist, I'm still a youngster in my head. I still wake up every morning feeling like a kid. I'm still awkward and gangly and cursed with this stupid stammer. I still spend most of my free time playing computer games and watching cartoons, and I still blush when I get upset. To put it bluntly, I'm still going through the awkward stages of early adulthood, as if my emotions decided to lag in order to let my intellect race ahead. And so, my dear Ramona, you must appreciate that when Aulco accused me of being nothing but a precocious cabin brat, I almost walked off his project there and then. I might act young, but I was his clear superior in thought and knowledge. The only reason I stayed was that after twenty-eight days aboard the Grand Mechanism, with the echoes of his pre-emptive tantrum still ringing in my ears, I finally had something concrete to tell him.

"I've been using probes and data provided by the *Slippery Gecko* to analyse the c-composition and flow of the s-substrate in the immediate vicinity of the Grand Mechanism."

He seemed surprised. "And?"

"Preliminary interpretation of the data very much suggests the presence of a sizeable wormhole within the central sphere."

Aulco's rage evaporated. He smiled, revealing needle-sharp incisors. "So, I was right?"

"It appears so."

"And when you say it's sizeable, just how large do you mean?"

I was still smarting from his tirade, but I did some quick

mental arithmetic. "My best guess, based on fluctuations in the surrounding medium, are that its throat, which will be spherical like the entrance to a standard flick terminal, encompasses a volume of sixteen point three times ten to the power of ten cubic kilometres."

Aulco frowned. "I can't say that in a speech; it wouldn't mean anything to most of my audience. Can you put it in layman's terms?"

"It's about the size of Mars."

"And Mars is…?"

I managed not to roll my eyes. "A rocky planet, about eighty-seven per cent the size of Jzat."

"That big?" Aulco's larger set of shoulders seemed to sag in relief. "Given the size and the resources it must have taken to build and maintain, would you concur that it's definitely the product of a highly advanced civilisation?"

I was annoyed that he was pleased. He didn't deserve to be. Grudgingly, I said, "It would seem so."

"This is excellent news, most excellent." He rubbed his smaller hands together. "You've confirmed what I suspected. We stand on the threshold of recontacting the rest of our species, who will elevate us to our rightful place in the cosmos. No longer will other species force us to endure their empty condescension."

I didn't know how to respond to that, so I examined my nails while he chuckled to himself and made notes. The black polish on my index fingers had become chipped from typing and needed a fresh coat.

I'd always worn dark eyeliner and nail polish. Sticking to one signature look might seem perverse for someone embedded in a culture such as the Continuance, where fashions aboard the Thousand Arks came and went with lightning speed, propelled by the creativity of a population with time on its hands and access to printers capable of producing almost any type of material, from plate armour to the finest of silks, and inspired by all the recorded art, culture and history of old Earth; but I preferred to think of it as an expression of individualism. My ancestors had come from Norway and Sweden, and I'd inherited a light olive skin tone, piercing blue eyes and sandy hair. I liked how dark eyeliner made my blue eyes pop, and the way black polish gave my fingernails a chitinous, beetle-like sheen. I dressed in charcoal grey and wore a ponytail because it was practical, studious, and when you're an outcast, you might as well dress like one.

Aulco cleared his throat. "How soon do you think we can access it?"

"How soon?" I shrugged. "We know what the puzzle box contains, but that doesn't mean we know how to open it—or whether we should."

"Of course we should. Our destiny awaits. The pride of our species demands it!"

I made a face. I'd heard his speeches before, and this kind of anti-scientific rhetoric had yet to impress me—which wasn't all that surprising when you remember that as a human, I was a member of one of those alien species he blamed for blocking his people from interstellar expansion and the top tier of galactic politics.

I said, "It might be dangerous."

He looked at me as if I'd just laughed at a funeral.

"My dear boy, of *course* it will be dangerous. But that's part of the point. I truly believe our predecessors left this Grand Mechanism as a test—a riddle for us to solve to show we're ready to re-join them and share in the fruits of their superior technology."

CHAPTER NINETEEN

SIDE-SPLASH

NICOLA MAFALDA

"Your friend has no idea how well-armed we are," said Cerise.

"And you," Kona replied, pointing at her with one of his smaller index fingers, "have no idea how tough our marines can be."

Cerise patted the plasma cannon hanging by her hip. "They'd have to be tougher than diamond to withstand a blast from this."

"Maybe tougher," the *Frontier Chic*'s envoy said. "That gun could melt a hole through a star."

He was exaggerating, but I knew he was doing it to keep things light. I nudged him with my shoulder and smiled.

The four of us had emerged from the other side of the overgrown hydroponic garden and were now moving through an industrial area, past equipment bays and machine shops. The only sounds were our voices and the echo of our footsteps on the deck. It felt like walking through a tomb, and I could feel the age of the place seeping into me. Tools that appeared to have been set down by their owners only moments before had most probably lain undisturbed for millennia. An eldritch, wrench-like object lay between two workbenches, where alien hands had dropped it maybe tens of thousands of years before the construction of the Egyptian pyramids. Geological time had passed since the construction of these chambers, and yet there was little in the way of dust or decay. The maintenance systems must still have been looking after the interior—or at least, this section—and the idea the subsystems responsible for cleaning and repair could still be functioning after all this time wrinkled my brain. I couldn't help but think how these deep, empty spaces had been here, silent and still, throughout my life. Maybe at every moment of human history, they had been here waiting for me to come and intrude upon them with my blundering steps. I ran a gloved finger across the blackened door of a stone-cold furnace and thought how it had been sitting here unchanged, undisturbed and unlit since I had been alone in my teenage room, dreaming of exploring such places.

Cerise was watching me. "Is it creeping you out?"

"No more than you are."

She grinned. "*There's* the Mafalda I remember."

"Fuck you."

"And fuck you right back." She turned to Kona. "Mafalda's been on her best behaviour for you, but trust me, she can be a real badass."

Kona gave me an amused look. "Oh, trust me, I *know.*"

We walked onwards.

As I trailed along behind the other two (with the *Chic's* envoy bringing up the rear), I realised Cerise was right. Ever since she killed Malone, I'd been reacting when I should have been acting; letting events sweep me along instead of making decisions and taking command of the situation.

Well, that was something I could change.

Up front, Cerise started to tell a long and involved story

about one of my more infamous bar brawls, but Kona grabbed her arm.

"There's something up ahead."

We had come to a corridor-like gap between two industrial units. A shadow flickered on the wall at the other end, thrown by something moving in the space beyond.

Cerise raised the plasma cannon and nodded to the rest of us to get behind her. If she had to use it, we wouldn't want the side-splash to catch us.

"Vibrations in the deck suggest footfalls," the *Frontier Chic's* envoy said. "Somewhere between one and five individuals."

"Human," I asked, "or Jzat?"

"Impossible to tell without knowing how many legs each individual possesses, although the weight of the steps appears too light for armoured marines."

I looked at Cerise. "What do you think?"

She kept her gaze fixed on the shadows that came and went at the end of the corridor. "It's not my circus," she said. "You need to make the call. We move forward and possibly fight, or we turn around and almost certainly fight."

"Unknown danger versus almost certain death?" I reached into the thigh pocket of my suit and pulled out the ripper gun. At my touch, the batteries in the handle powered up the magnetic accelerator in the barrel, ready to shred any target I chose with a stream of monomolecular metal shards. "Well, I've always preferred mystery over history."

"Good plan," Kona said.

The envoy agreed. "Tactically astute," he said.

And so, we began to inch along the corridor in diamond formation. Cerise went up the centre with the splat gun at the ready. I hugged the right wall, and the envoy took the left, both with guns ready. Kona occupied the rearmost point of the diamond, keeping an eye on our six.

I didn't like advancing this way. I felt very exposed with

no cover, and a single well-placed grenade could have taken us all out, but I didn't want to divide our forces, so we had little choice. We had to move as a unit or not at all.

As we neared the other end, I heard voices. They burbled like tumbling streams. And I know it's wrong to make anthropomorphic assumptions about alien races, but to me, they sounded happy and good-natured. At one point, there was a clang that sounded as if one of them had dropped a tool onto the deck, and the rest of the voices made a low, chortling noise that sounded like gently mocking laughter.

The space beyond was huge.

As the corridor opened out, I saw we were approaching a cavernous hangar. It housed several large starships of unfamiliar design, each hundreds of metres in length. Figures moved around on the nearest. Torches flared showers of sparks, throwing shadows.

"Scavengers," the *Frontier Chic* said with distaste.

I shook my head. "I don't think so. For a start, they don't seem to be taking anything out."

The ships beyond were all in various stages of decay or disassembly, but this nearest looked almost complete. The workers appeared to have patched or replaced several sections of its hull. From an aperture on its upper superstructure, a crane was in the process of winching a large component from a cargo pallet on the deck.

I said, "Whoever these people are, they're trying to repair this nearest ship."

Kona moved up behind my shoulder. "Maybe they're trying to escape?"

"They could be the remains of an expedition that got stranded here."

"Maybe we can move around the edge of the bay without them noticing?"

"Perhaps." The envoy tapped a blue finger against his smooth blue chin. "But it wouldn't hurt to have some allies."

I gave him a look. "You're seriously suggesting we initiate a delicate first-contact protocol while being hunted by a squad of Jzat marines?"

"It's just a thought."

"It's a fucking stupid thought."

"Then, what do you suggest?" Cerise asked.

"We go around." I pointed to a row of cargo containers stacked by the back wall. "We stay behind those as much as possible and try to get behind the next ship in line without them seeing us. Then we keep the ship between us and them as we make our way to the far end of the hangar."

"That's got to be at least two kilometres," Kona said.

"Yes, but the overhead lighting seems patchy. If we stay to the less well-lit areas, we might be okay."

"And if anyone comes up behind us, they'll run into those guys first," Cerise said, nodding towards the crew working on the ship. "We'll get plenty of warning."

"All right, then." I looked at the nearest container. It was about twenty metres away. "As it's my plan, I'll go first."

No one objected, so I stepped out and to the side. Keeping my back against the wall, I moved crablike around the edge of the bay. Every step was slow, not wanting to draw attention. Before me, on the huge starship, cascades of sparks showed where beings worked. Metallic clangs rang through the air. The hiss of steam. The *ker-chunk* of a rivet gun. But no shouts of alarm. Eventually, after what seemed an eternity of exposure, I came around the rear of the first cargo container and found myself face to face with one of the work crew.

It was around two metres tall. In that first moment of frozen shock, I took in two pairs of hard black eyes on a triangular head, a chitinous carapace and at least half a dozen boneless, writhing limbs. The thing looked like a cross between an octopus and a giant ladybird. Instinctively, I raised the ripper, but it held up a tentacle.

"There's no need for that," the creature said in almost flawless Jzatian. "And you can tell your friends to stand down, I mean you no harm."

I glanced back to where my colleagues were watching from the corridor and gestured for them to lower their weapons.

The huge bug pressed two of its snaking limbs together in a very human-like gesture. "That's better," it said. "Now, I assume you're here to see the Rav'nah Abelisk?"

CHAPTER TWENTY

SWISS CHEESE

FRONTIER CHIC

I powered away from the *Gunmetal Ghost* on a trajectory
that kept me hidden from three of the four gunboats for the
longest possible time—which turned out to be around thirty-
two seconds. I felt their crude targeting systems lock onto my
exhaust plume and a new salvo of torpedoes flash towards me
like a pack of hunting sharks. So far, I'd refrained from using
offensive weaponry, but this was getting tiresome and dangerous.
I hosed the incoming nuclear missiles with streams of kinetic
rounds from my main ripper cannons, and they detonated one
after the other like bright flowers unfurling in the void.

Momentarily concealed behind this blossoming screen
of radiation, I braked hard and employed lateral thrusters,
throwing myself onto another heading so aggressively my
frame screeched in protest. Constrained by their need to keep
their soft, fleshy crews alive, not one of my pursuers—not
even the *Slippery Gecko*—would be able to match the violence
of my manoeuvres. They certainly weren't expecting me to
emerge from behind the ball of nuclear fire far to starboard of
their projections. They weren't even looking in my direction.

Before they could detect me, I fired a spread of missiles and changed heading again. Unlike their large, ungainly torpedoes, my projectiles were small and elegant: less than a metre in length but containing half a dozen football-sized flick terminals held in magnetic suspension within each of their bulging nose cones. Upon impact, the missiles would vaporise, allowing the flick terminals to continue moving through the ship, gouging wide holes through its interior as they funnelled everything they touched into the roiling fires of the substrate. They could easily eat through armour designed to withstand an atomic blast; and if their boreholes intersected something important, such as the ship's bridge or power plant, the damage to the target vessel would likely prove debilitating or even fatal. With these in my launch tubes, I had no need to mess around with explosives; I could turn my enemy into Swiss cheese and there wasn't a damn thing they could do about it.

I circled back around behind the fading glow of nuclear fire. When I came out the other side, I saw two of the gunboats were in trouble. Plumes of gas vented into space where the flick terminals had struck. The third gunboat had somehow managed to destroy the missile I'd sent its way, but that hadn't stopped its payload, which even as I watched sheared off one of the cube-shaped vessel's corners and the manoeuvring thrusters housed upon it. Its other thrusters fired to compensate, but now its movements were jerky and hampered.

I hadn't targeted the fourth gunboat as the flank of the megaship had hidden it from me. Now, it was out in the open, so I sent a couple of shots its way and wheeled around before it could react.

"This is getting irksome," the *Slippery Gecko* sent on a Vanguard channel. "I do wish you'd accept my offer."

"We both know that's not going to happen."

"I don't want to have to step in, but I will if you continue to force my hand."

"I'm sure you'll do what you must."

The *Slippery Gecko* sent an animated emoji: a cartoon man sorrowfully shaking his head. "I should warn you; I am sporting some significant combat upgrades, which I specifically installed for this mission. If we go toe to toe, I'll defeat you."

"Yeah, and monkeys might fly out my butt."

A symbol for confusion. "I'm sorry, I'm not familiar with that expression."

I laughed. "That's because you're dense." The phrase was one I'd picked up from Nicola, along with some even more colourful terms. "Because you've spent your whole professional life hanging around with that stuffed shirt of a navigator, and you don't know the first thing about how to have fun."

"And I suppose you do?"

The gunboat with the missing corner exploded. One of the flick terminals from my earlier shot must have penetrated its hull and dug a hole through something vital. I laughed. "I'm not enjoying killing those gunboat crews, but it's intensely gratifying to be foiling your plans."

The *Slippery Gecko* sent a row of skulls.

I responded with a picture of a human hand flipping the bird.

And then things got serious.

CHAPTER TWENTY-ONE

ALLERGIC-TO-SEAFOOD

NICOLA MAFALDA

Still speaking in excellent Jzatian, the creature introduced themself as Allergic-to-Seafood, a Bridger of the Silent Dark from the Clan of the Bountiful Shores.

"In my culture, it is traditional when you enter adulthood to name yourself for your greatest weakness, thereby claiming it and robbing it of its shame. For instance, we have among our crew individuals bearing the names Drowning-Phobia, Never-Fully-Committed and Dependent-on-Alcohol. Thanks to the counselling of the Rav'nah Abelisk, that last one I mentioned has remained sober for over a year now. We are all very proud of them."

Kona asked, "Is Bridger of the Silent Dark your rank?"

"Indeed. I guide my people's ships through the fury and turbulence of the Under Realm."

"You're a navigator?"

"I am." They turned to look at the ship under repair. "And if we can get our vessel repaired, I will be the one to conduct it away from this ancient place, in search of our home."

I asked them, "Have you been here long?"

"Eleven revolutions of the Celestial Heavens, as seen from the Cliff Temple above our beach."

"So, quite a while?"

"Around a tenth of my expected lifespan."

"Sheesh."

"Can you help us?" They moved their head, fixing first the envoy and then me with all four of their shiny marble-like eyes.

"We've come to see the Abelisk," I said. "He's in danger, and so are we. But if we can get him to safety, we'll send another ship to pick you up."

"You swear?"

I glanced at the envoy, and he nodded.

"Alternatively, I carry a number of printers," he said. "And it may be possible to fabricate any missing components you need in order to render this vessel flightworthy."

Allergic flailed their tentacles. "That is such good news!"

"I wouldn't celebrate yet," Cerise cut in. "We still have four squads of Jzat marines that are intent on slaughtering us."

The tentacles froze. "Are you *enemies* of the Jzat?"

"We are not." Kona stepped forward with all four arms held out to his sides in a gesture of transparency. "But a dangerous faction has arisen among my people, and I am afraid that faction may wish to cause the Abelisk harm—or worse. And so, I am here to offer what protection I can."

"I see." The creature seemed to mull this over. "And yet, there are only four of you. I do not see you being able to each defeat an entire squad of marines."

Cerise muttered, "No shit."

I ignored her. "That's why we need your help," I told Allergic. "They don't know where the Abelisk is. If you can show us how to find him, we might get enough of a head start to avoid a fight altogether."

"Do you want to see him right now?" Allergic asked.

"That would be good," I told them. "Time being of the

fucking essence and everything."

"Then you had better follow me." Allergic tipped forwards onto their tentacles. They scuttled away like a giant beetle, and we hurried to keep up.

"Is it far?" Kona asked.

"Around two days' walk," the creature replied. The movement of their tentacles against the deck produced a constant dry susurration, like the sound of the wind in the high firs in the valley overlooked by the cottage where I'd recuperated.

The thought of the cottage brought a sudden longing. Not for an escape from danger, but just for simpler times. There had been whole mornings when I'd done nothing but sit and watch the birds and sheep, and the projected sun climb slowly up the blue-painted wall of the vast cavern.

There had been other cottages on the mountainside. At night, I could see their lights. Sometimes, I'd catch a few notes of a tune or a shout of laughter on the breeze. But I never went over to introduce myself. At the time, I was still processing my beheading, and wouldn't have made very good company. I suspect the ark knew that, too, and that's why it kept its promise to keep people away.

And despite the fact I was dealing with trauma and betrayal, I did enjoy the weeks I spent in that mountain retreat. There's a certain pleasure in being unbothered by the needs of others, and solitude can be a tonic for the mind, the same way fasting can be a boon for the body.

Was this what the Rav'nah Abelisk felt in his seclusion? Had he come here to escape the expectations and intrusions of his people, seeking a place of quiet in which to meditate upon his secret knowledge? Or did he crave the company of his own kind, wrestling every day with homesickness and an almost overwhelming desire to renounce his position and return?

I had been disappointed when the *Frontier Chic* sent his envoy to recruit me for this mission; but at the same time, I knew myself well enough to realise another week or two in that idyllic spot would have sent me stir crazy. It's good to have time away from the world occasionally, but it's also good to come back to it—especially if the break leaves you feeling invigorated and ready to kick some ass.

•

We followed Allergic through the guts of the megaship for hours. Their six tentacles propelled them at a brisk pace, and they kept having to slow for us to keep up or stop entirely so we could rest. But they never complained or expressed impatience. And, as we travelled through corridors and hangar bays, accommodation sections and workshops, they told us their story.

"We were explorers," they said. "Our astronomers detected this object as it passed the periphery of our system and speculated it might be artificial in origin. And so, our society chose us to investigate. Our race had only recently discovered the substrate and were mostly using it for instantaneous travel from point to point on our planet's surface. The discovery of this ancient leviathan propelled our scientists to explore the possibilities of using the Under Realm for space travel, and eventually, after many fruitless experiments and trials, and many revolutions of the Celestial Heavens, they finally determined the need for a biological consciousness to guide the way through the chaos. And with that riddle solved, they built our ship."

"You were the first?" Kona asked.

"We were the first to leave our solar system."

"And you got stuck here?"

"Our ship malfunctioned upon emergence from the Under Realm. Either our theories were somehow incorrect, or our engineering was imperfect; we don't which. But immediately upon arrival, our drive imploded, leaving us stranded."

"And you've been here ever since?"

"We were able to forage food and water from the megaship's gardens. Other expeditions had been here before, and some had left equipment we were able to make use of. Eventually, we found the hangar where you and I met, and the ships contained within. But unknown tentacles had pillaged them over the millennia, and many of the components not already removed or disassembled had succumbed to the ravages of passing time. Nevertheless, we determined that rather than keep wandering the endless warrens of the megaship in the unlikely hope of magically finding an untouched and functional ship, we had a greater chance of survival if we stayed here and attempted to repair one of the ships using parts cannibalised from the others."

"And it's taken you ten of your years?"

"It has not been an easy task."

I had been listening, but now I spoke up. "Why didn't your people ever send a second expedition?"

Allergic stopped and slithered around to face me. "We have asked ourselves the same question, many times over the years." Their mouth parts moved in an agitated manner. "We can only speculate, but it's possible they did. This accursed ship is so large, so labyrinthine, it's possible they sent half a dozen expeditions and spent months wandering its echoing halls and vaults without ever uncovering our trail."

My spine prickled at the thought. If Allergic and their crewmates could become so irretrievably lost in here, how the hell had we ever expected to find the Abelisk by ourselves? We could have been the ones wandering hopelessly for years—or at least, until our motivation, water or luck gave out.

I said, "We're really fucking lucky we ran into you."

Allergic dipped their head. "If you are truly able, as you say, to extract us from this prison, it is we who will count ourselves as fortunate."

They started moving again, and we followed, trailing

through narrow gangways and wide, high-vaulted chambers, until we came to a place where a vertiginously suspended catwalk crossed a complex tangle of pipework.

The *Frontier Chic*'s envoy stopped walking. "I've lost contact with myself."

"What?"

He put out an arm to steady himself against the wall. "The uplink with the ship's gone."

My blood turned cold. "Has it—have *you* been destroyed?"

"I don't know. The circuit's dead. There's something wrong."

"Fuck." I put a gloved hand to my forehead. "But you're okay, aren't you? I mean, you can still function independently, right?"

He frowned. "I lack a link to my core processors. I only have what's housed in my skull."

"Like the rest of us," Cerise said.

Kona was getting impatient. "We have to keep going," he said.

"Okay." I drew my ripper. "Cerise, you must be getting tired on point. I'll take the lead, and the rest of you fall in behind."

They nodded their assent, and I turned to the bridge. Allergic was already halfway across, and the slithering motion of their tentacles made the whole thing sway alarmingly. The walkway consisted of steel grating, which did nothing to conceal the view of the pipes beneath.

"Don't look down," the *Frontier Chic*'s envoy advised.

Having taken charge, I was determined not to show the others how unsettling I found the sight of the drop beneath my boots. Gun at the ready, I gripped the handrail with my free hand and set off across the swinging footbridge.

And walked straight into the crosshairs of a squad of Jzat marines.

CHAPTER TWENTY-TWO

TARGET ACQUISITION

FRONTIER CHIC (ENVOY)

Maybe a second and a half passed between the first shot impacting Nicola's leg and the next two slamming into her chest, throwing her backwards into the pipe-filled abyss.

I shouted as she fell out of sight, but the fusillade from the marines drove us back into the cover of the corridor from which we'd emerged.

For the next thirty minutes, we were engaged in a running battle, trying to stay ahead of the death squad as they repeatedly tried to catch us.

I wasn't at my best. Perhaps I was in shock, or perhaps it was because I had been severed from my connection with the ship. Either way, my reaction times and memory storage capacity had both become severely degraded. In comparison to my usual clarity, my thoughts now moved like molasses. And yet, I was still the sharpest member of our party. I'm not suggesting Cerise or Kona lacked in mental acuity, but they were running their intellects on organic wetware, with individual neurons firing off signals at less than a hundred and eighty metres per second. At least I had the advantage of good, clean solid-state silicon that, although hobbled, was still able to process information exponentially faster, even if the extent of my memory had shrunk somewhat.

It was small consolation.

I had never had to run an envoy independently before and did not care for the sensation at all. I was a starship; I was meant to fly. Walking around on two legs could sometimes be a useful or enlightening experience—it allowed me to interact with my crew and assist on planetary or extra-vehicular excursions—but it wasn't supposed to be a permanent arrangement. I felt like a puppet master suddenly and unwillingly incarnated in the wooden body of his marionette, and the sense of loss was overwhelming.

Had Nicola Mafalda felt this aching sense of disconnection when I severed her head from her body? The analogy wasn't exact, as she'd retained full use of her faculties, but perhaps her experience shared a commonality with my anguish at this abnormal separation. And if so, how unjust it seemed that some inevitable, emergent characteristic of self-awareness should have cursed me with the same ungovernable emotions as my meat-based compatriots. Some scout ships I had encountered secretly considered themselves a more evolved form of life than their human charges, simply because they could think faster, but like me they were prone to the vicissitudes of mood that plagued all intelligence, from the humble cat to the largest ark.

Thinking about Nicola didn't help, either. Not only had I lost my ship, but I had also lost my navigator.

The fact I was struggling with all this angst during a firefight didn't help one bit. We were hunkered behind equipment at one end of a long repair shop, with the marines crouched behind the stacks of components and raw materials at the other. Cerise had blood on her face from a gash in her forehead, and Kona nursed the larger of his left arms. I had crudely bandaged it where a bullet had passed straight through the bicep, somehow miraculously missing the bone but nevertheless rendering the limb inoperative. Allergic-to-Seafood had made themself scarce, keeping low and scurrying much farther into the shadows, where they waited nervously for us to catch up. But while part of my brain dealt with protecting my charges and acquiring enemy targets, another part kept replaying the instant the marine's volley had hit Nicola.

Somehow, losing her felt worse than losing my hull. Protecting your navigator was a primary tenet of scout-ship existence. Losing yours would end your career and your existence as a starship, and would signal to all and sundry that you had utterly and catastrophically botched one of your most basic duties. For most ships, such a loss would render them incapable of returning to the Continuance fleet. Those that did find their way back, whether through luck or rescue, never spoke of the experience.

A Jzat marine broke cover, trying to shift position for a better vantage, and I ran a stream of ripper darts across him. His armour stopped most of them, but before he managed to find shelter again, I saw him flinch and heard a grunt, so some must have got through.

The marines seemed to be organised into four fire teams, each consisting of four individual marines. Four was a popular number on Jzat, for obvious arm-related reasons. So far, we had killed or otherwise incapacitated five marines. They obviously hadn't expected Cerise or Kona to be as highly trained as they were, or for the three of us to continue fighting as doggedly as we had. Nevertheless, the small advantage we had gained from their lack of preparation meant little, as there were still at least eleven more marines out there, and if the *Slippery Gecko* had given them access to military-grade substrate communicators, perhaps another two or three squads converging on this spot to give them back-up. We were perilously outnumbered and outgunned, with no option but to keep falling further and further back into the labyrinthine interior of the megaship.

Still, I couldn't stop replaying the moment Nicola fell.

I had not been alone in my mind since we first dream-linked. Now, whether she lay unconscious or dead, I could no longer detect her presence. Only darkness occupied the space where her thoughts usually resided.

A rocket launcher poked around the far edge of the corridor, and I sent a stream of ripper darts into the hands clutching it. Blood sprayed, and the weapon toppled out onto the deck.

"Where are you, Mafalda?" I thought.

I reached out through the link and, for a moment, thought I felt the faintest tickle of a connection. But then everything shifted, and my perspective changed. The darkness moved. What I had perceived as a blank space resolved into something seemingly vast and old as time itself. The effect was comparable to looking at what you think is a sheet of black paper, only for the camera angle to change and make you realise you're actually staring into the infinite night sky.

A voice spoke in my head. A voice of such depth and gravitas it would have shaken the very fabric of space had it spoken aloud.

"And who in the Nine Burning Hells of Wor'esh-Kappa," it demanded, "are *you*?"

CHAPTER TWENTY-THREE

FROGS COULD SWIM

NICOLA MAFALDA

I wasn't dead.

I came back to consciousness like a slow fish rising to break the glassy surface tension of a pond.

I could hear faraway shouts. Maybe I even recognised some of the voices. But I had no idea where I was. The world wouldn't come into focus. Something was very wrong, but I couldn't figure it out.

And then I did.

I was upside down.

The water my addled brain had imagined rising from hadn't been water at all; it had been the sky. Somehow, I had fallen and become wedged in a gap between two pipes. By craning my head backwards, I could see down into the tangle of pipes below. My suited body blocked the upwards view.

I heard the distant crack of gunfire. The sound nudged my memories into focus, and I remembered I had been about a third of the way across the bridge when the Jzat marines opened fire. They had been standing on a catwalk running parallel to mine, and I don't know which of us was the most surprised at the sudden appearance of the other. I already had the ripper in my hand, and I'd raised it and fired before my sluggish brain even registered what was happening. But even as my stream of metal darts hosed across the other bridge, the marines were returning fire. The railings and grating shuddered around me. And then I took a round in the leg. I staggered off-balance and took two more in the chest.

The force of those final shots must have knocked me back, over the rail. I couldn't recall falling, but I must have fallen headfirst until becoming stuck in my present predicament, squeezed between two pipes, each at least two metres in width.

Fuck, I was lucky I hadn't landed headfirst and smashed my skull.

I was also lucky to have been wearing the high-spec suit Cerise had picked out for me. Had I been wearing a normal pressure suit, I'd be hanging here with at least three fist-sized holes in me, bleeding out. As it was, the impact of the projectiles had knocked me off my feet, and my ribs and thigh felt sharply bruised, but none of the bullets appeared to have penetrated deeply enough to cause significant damage. If I saw her again, and if any of us ever got off this million-year-old flying sepulchre, I'd buy her a drink to say thank you.

Despite the megaship's measly gravity, my head throbbed from being the wrong way up, and I began to worry I might lose consciousness. If that happened, the chances of me waking a second time weren't high.

I looked down. Having tipped over the handrail, I had plunged into the jumbled nest of pipes and conduits I'd seen from the catwalk. From here, there was no way to guess how far into that tangle I'd fallen, but now I was hanging above a void within it. I guessed the pipes directly beneath me were around four metres below my head, and having survived the marines shooting me, I didn't want to fall that far and break my neck.

The sounds of battle echoed down from above. I thought of

calling for help but doubted anyone would hear me. Besides, the crack of assault rifles seemed to be drifting further away, and I guessed the enemy's numerical superiority had forced my colleagues to retreat. I couldn't count on them rescuing me any time soon; if I wanted to get out of here before I blacked out, I'd need to do it myself.

I swore to myself. Why couldn't I have stayed in that cottage? Right about now, I'd be loading wood into the hearth to boil water for my mid-afternoon cup of tea, and my most pressing concern would be the selection of a suitable book with which to accompany my refreshment.

"Okay, then." I took a few quick breaths to nerve myself. "Here goes fucking nothing."

I began to squirm, twisting and narrowing my shoulders, slowly inching downwards. I felt like a wet-winged butterfly trying to shake free from its cocoon. If the suit hadn't been tight and form-fitting, I don't think I could have done it. But suddenly, I guess I must have reached the point where the pipes curved far enough away from each other to let me slip through, and I fell.

I tried to flip over and land on my feet, but only managed to turn enough that I landed on my shoulder instead of my head. The suit absorbed most of the impact, but I still felt the air driven from my lungs and lay there, sore and panting, for several moments before regaining my composure.

The space I now sat in extended before and behind me for an indeterminate distance, receding into an unlit darkness lined with ducts and tubes.

I rubbed my shoulder and glowered. I'd seen my share of the Hollywood movies rescued from Old Earth, and this looked depressingly like the kind of place a toothy monster might lunge from the shadows and eat a hapless extra.

I examined the cuffs of my suit and found a tiny built-in LED torch. The light it cast didn't pierce far into the gloom, but it would be enough for me to see where I was going. All I had to do now was decide which way to go. I'd lost my sense of where I was in relation to where I had been and didn't know if either direction might bring me close to my friends, or if both ran perpendicular to where I needed to be.

After a few moments of indecision, I said, "Fuck it," and started walking.

The going wasn't easy. There was no floor. I balanced my way along the tops of the pipes, stepping from one to the next, or sometimes following one for some distance before it curved away on its own incomprehensible errand. A couple of times, I had to jump over wide gaps or press myself against the wall to inch around a scalding jet of foul-smelling steam; and at one point, I even had to prostrate myself and crawl beneath a disturbingly organic-looking thicket of intestinal tubing. Occasionally, I stopped to listen, hoping to hear friendly voices, but heard nothing save for my own breathing and the occasional gurgle of fluid moving through the network around me.

When I was thirsty, I sipped from a retractable nozzle in the collar of the suit. When I was hungry, I partook of an energy tablet from a pocket on my belt. Without the head-up display in my helmet, I had no way to measure passing time, and only my own guesswork to gauge the progress I was making. My bruised leg and chest hurt. My shoulder ached. But I kept putting one foot in front of the other. What other choice did I have? I couldn't just curl up here and die. That wasn't my style. If I had to leave this life, I'd go out the same way I came in: flailing and complaining. I hadn't given up when the Jzat nuked my ship, and I wasn't about to quit now.

Persistence was my one advantage.

The Jzat hadn't evolved the same way we had. Human beings were persistence hunters. We hadn't been the quickest or strongest creature on the savannah, but we had learned not to give up, and it shaped our evolution until we were ideally

186

suited for long hunts. Our lack of hair and surprising number of sweat glands meant we could dissipate heat more effectively than our prey, and the way we moved in a series of controlled falls meant we were letting gravity pull us forwards, so we had to devote fewer resources to movement, and thereby generated less heat. In comparison, lions and cheetahs relied on quick bursts of speed, but they couldn't keep moving that quickly for more than a few minutes. Either they caught their prey in that initial flurry of speed, or they gave up and went in search of another opportunity. In response, gazelles and wildebeest had developed to try to stay one step ahead. They too were built for quick, energy-intensive acceleration. Either they outpaced the lion in the first minute, or they were dead. But when a group of humans decided to chase down one of those creatures, they just didn't stop. They kept tracking it until the poor animal, given no time to rest or recharge between bursts of speed, simply collapsed from heat and exhaustion.

Human beings, I told myself, just kept going. The Jzat marines were fierce fighters. They were built for quick surges of strength—lifting heavy objects or battering an opponent—not long-drawn-out pursuits. Those four arms used up a lot of energy, and they weighed a lot. And with their fur coverings, they would have to stop and rest more frequently to avoid overheating.

I remembered one of my schoolteachers telling me a story about two frogs trapped in a milk jug. The first frog, deciding the struggle is hopeless, gives up and drowns, but the second frog refuses to quit, and eventually his thrashing about churns the milk into butter, and he is at last able to relax on a nice, cool fatty raft until the milkmaid comes and scoops him out. I think her point was that you should never give up trying, but I always thought it was a stupid story. After all, who keeps milk in a jug where frogs could access it? It would go bad in half an hour.

And why didn't this maid get what she needed from the printer as she needed it, like everybody else? And more importantly, I was ninety-nine per cent certain frogs could *swim*.

Nevertheless, despite the stupidity of the parable, I resolved to take its advice and persist like my ancestors, hoping to churn my troubles into a yellow, spreadable raft.

CHAPTER TWENTY-FOUR

GENERAL AULCO'S ASS

ORLANDO WALDEN

My dearest Ramona.

I hope the revelations in my last missive didn't distress you, although I wouldn't blame you for one moment if they did. It can't be easy realising your hot young boyfriend is just a scared child inside.

I would have told you sooner, but it never seemed like the right time to explain. I was too nervous, too unsure of myself. I never lied to you. I want to be clear about that. There is a genius behind these eyes, but also a youth pinned like a butterfly in a collection, forever playing emotional catch-up. I did not lie, and my intention was never to deceive, although I will admit to exaggerating the extent of my self-confidence.

My love, you are the adult I long to be. Maybe together, we will put away childish things and leave our academic neverland to embark on a journey towards maturity. And heaven knows, I envy you. I long for the confidence and reassuring sangfroid of adulthood—things you know but I sometimes fear may forever elude me in my arrested state.

Our love may be doomed, but let's not dwell on such things.

Besides, I can sense you chomping at the bit, desperate to know the latest developments here.

Well, don't worry, dear heart. Let me tell you about Erudite-Harf.

The grizzled old Jzat is quite a character. Unlike General Aulco, he believes only in the science. He doesn't care who's sponsoring him or where the money comes from. I don't think he even cares about the possibility that opening the Grand Mechanism might put his entire planet at terrible risk. All that concerns him is the puzzle it represents, and when it comes to the pursuit of knowledge, even with his spectacles, he is blind to all danger.

Fortunately for me, that single-minded drive to uncover the truth makes him very protective of his equipment, his staff and even me. When we first met, he was outraged the Continuance had sent a child. Now, having seen the progress I've thus far made, he holds me in greater esteem. I actually heard him defend me to Aulco, standing up to the old bigot like a four-armed Moses braving the tempestuous waters of the general's furious impatience and turning them aside.

Afterwards, he told me, "Politicians and businessmen are a necessary evil, in so far as they provide the funds to further scientific endeavour. Beyond that, they are at best useless, and at worst a liability."

I think I'm rather warming to him.

I led him through what I've learned so far. Rather, I should say, what the machine itself has taught me. For the quest to unlock the Grand Mechanism is the quest to comprehend its history and purpose. Every riddle I solve provides a greater glimpse of the overall tapestry and leads in turn to another more fiendish conundrum.

During my progress through this spiralling maze of tests, I have come to suspect that although the builders of the Mechanism employed the same vigesimal counting system as the Jzat, they were not themselves Jzat. At the very least, not Jzat the way we understand Jzat today.

"Are you sure?" Erudite-Harf asked when I explained this to him.

"I have a lingering s-suspicion every formula and equation has been translated from another numerical system." I brushed aside my loose and unkempt hair. "Although I have n-no proof to back up that assertion."

"Do you have any idea which numerical system?"

"I think it might be base ten, but that may simply be my own bias colouring my results."

The old Jzat stroked his furred chin with one of his smaller hands. "This is fascinating."

"I'm afraid General Aulco won't be pleased."

"General Aulco can stuff his displeasure up his ass." Harf grinned savagely. "I've spent a lifetime banging my head against this beast, and now we're finally making progress!"

I smiled, but I think even then, I knew the Grand Mechanism's tentacles had already wormed their way into my brain, and I wouldn't be able to pull away until I'd solved its riddle, for good or ill.

CHAPTER TWENTY-FIVE

PHANTOM BODY SYNDROME

NICOLA MAFALDA

Stepping around a gout of steam hissing from a loose and corroded pipe joint, I thought back to my early twenties, before I joined the cadet programme, when I lived in a small cabin one floor up from a twenty-four-hour gyoza bar. In those days, that section of the ark played host to a lot of take-out places. Downstairs, everything smelled of dumplings and steamed vegetables. I used to go down there sometimes to watch the owner, Susumu, finely chop the cabbage and ginger, massage in the ground pork and then transfer the resulting mixture to the waiting wrappers. His wife, Sakai, would then roll them up and delicately pinch them into tiny parcels. Then she would transfer these dumplings to the pan and sizzle them until their undersides were golden brown.

Now, picking my way through this leaky jumble of interwoven pipework, I could have really used some of those dumplings. I was so hungry, and the glucose tablets the suit dispensed weren't doing anything to assuage my appetite. As I walked, I spent my time dreaming about the smell of those frying gyoza.

Eventually, I came to what must have been an inspection hatch designed by the megaship's builders to allow its crew access to these pipes and cables. Upon climbing through, I found myself in a more habitable section of the ship, in a corridor carpeted with ancient, dried reeds that powdered to dust beneath my boots.

The air here smelled chlorinated, and I wished for my helmet, fearing some kind of toxic leak might be polluting the life support in this part of the ship. However, my worries disappeared a few steps later, when I emerged into a wide, circular room containing a swimming pool.

The pool was around thirty metres across and shallow at the edges, deepening in towards the centre. It looked as if it had been intended for creatures who liked to wade slowly into water rather than dive—or maybe creatures unable to climb out of a high-sided pool the way humans do. The ceiling above the water curved upwards into a lofty dome, the inner surface of which was a featureless white matte, and which may have once been used to project images. A scattering of rounded stone blocks around the room's perimeter seemed to represent uncomfortable-looking chairs or maybe chaise longes. On inspecting the water more closely, I was surprised to see it appeared fresh and clean. Somewhere, a filtration system must still be in operation, endlessly scrubbing away impurities and adding chlorine to prevent the proliferation of germs and bacteria. In contrast to the desiccated atmosphere in the rest of the megaship, the air in this chamber felt cool and refreshing, and I had an almost primal urge to strip off my suit and take a dip in the inviting water. I'm glad I managed to resist, because moments later, a Jzat soldier appeared through one of the half-dozen entrances spaced out around the edge of the dome.

She was a large female. We noticed each other in the same instant. As her hands brought up her assault rifle, I threw myself behind one of the solid couches. Shots hammered into the stone, chipping and splintering. I couldn't respond because I'd dropped my ripper gun when I'd fallen from the catwalk.

"Fuck."

The exit stood only a few metres away, but if I tried to run for it, I'd get riddled before I'd taken two steps. Perhaps as before, the bullets wouldn't penetrate my suit, but they'd probably knock me flat, giving my assailant time to inflict a lethal headshot. If I stayed here, all she'd have to do was move around the edge of the dome until she had a clear angle of attack, and then just keep shooting until she hit something vital and unprotected. Doubtless, she knew that, and was congratulating herself on having cornered me—and that pissed me off. I heard her boots moving on the tiled floor. She was circling the pool, looking for a better vantage from which to deliver the killing shot. I kept edging around the stone block, trying to keep as much of it between her and me as possible. Then, quite deliberately, I stood up.

A round thumped into my centre of mass, and I found myself lying dazed, looking up at the dome. The whole front of my body screamed in pain where the new impact had hit the still-fresh bruising from the shots that knocked me off the bridge. But this agony was part of my plan, like a pawn sacrificed to draw out an opponent's queen. The enemy would have seen me go down like a rag doll. Even now, I could hear her hurrying, eager to confirm the kill, and so I scrambled into a crouch and, as soon as her gun barrel appeared over the top of the stone block, I pounced. One hand pushed the barrel up towards the dome, while the other punched her in the face.

For a moment, we struggled there. I maintained my grip on the gun and tried to wrap the fingers of my other hand around her throat, but she had the advantage of two extra limbs. While I grappled with her larger hands, her smaller pair drew a bayonet and tried to stab me in the midriff. I felt the point of it jab against my sternum, but fortunately the suit material held and it didn't penetrate. However, it did hurt like fuck, and I realised I couldn't beat her using sheer brute strength. I leant closer and rammed my forehead into her nose. Cartilage splintered beneath the fur, and she grunted in surprise and indignation. But before she could respond, I heaved backwards, pulling her with me. Her knees hit the stone block and she lost balance. I released my grip and twisted aside, letting her crash past me in a clatter of body armour. She tried to pivot as she fell, swiping at me with the knife, but that only meant she landed on her head. Her boots were still up in the air, over the stone block, when the point of her helmet hit the deck with a solid thump and, with her whole weight pressing down on it, *rolled*. Her neck snapped with a sound like splintering bamboo, and she went limp.

I took a step back and fell onto my ass.

For almost a full minute, the only sounds were our ragged breaths.

Then, the Jzat spoke.

"I can't feel anything," she said.

"You have a severed spinal cord."

"That much is obvious." She sounded strained by the effort of talking.

"I'm sorry."

"Are you?"

"Yes, I—" My world lurched, destabilised by a memory that either I had emotionally suppressed or the doctors had hypnotically blocked from me until this moment—a memory of my disembodied head staring up at a white ceiling while medical technicians ran tests on the various tubes and feeds connecting it to the machines that were supplying it with oxygenated and nutrient-rich blood. I heard the hiss and wheeze of the artificial lungs and smelled the sharp tang of disinfectant mingled with the warm, yeasty smell of regenerating cells. I tried to speak, but my jaw wouldn't work. I didn't even know if I still had vocal cords.

One of the technicians said, "I think she's awake."

They both came to peer at my face. One appeared to be male, the other female. The female said, "If you can hear us, blink once."

I squeezed my eyes shut.

She said, "That's good. Do you know where you are?"

This time, I kept them open.

"You're in the hospital," the male tech said. "I'm afraid there was an accident. You absorbed a lot of radiation, and—" He stopped, transparently unsure how much to tell me. Not that it mattered. My memories of the next part were crystal clear.

My motherfucking ship cut off my motherfucking head.

The weird thing was, I could still feel parts of my body. I had itchy, skin-crawling sensations, pins and needles, and the occasional sharp, icy stab of pain. I guess the areas of my brain that usually dealt with the input from the nerves in my missing arms and legs were firing off randomly, producing these unpleasant phantom sensations.

I had a mouth, but I could not scream. I couldn't shout or rant or swear. I couldn't get up off that stupid bed and kill the stupid fucking ship that put me there.

And I guess that's when they registered the uptick in my mental distress and decided to sedate me until they had grown my new body.

Now, sitting on the tiled floor at the side of the bathing pool, I listened to the marine struggle to keep breathing. Her boots still rested on the stone couch, so I crawled over and lowered them to the ground. She was heavy, but I managed to roll her over onto her back. The bones in her neck ground together as her head moved, but at least she was now staring up at the dome instead of having her face pressed against the tile.

"Is that more comfortable?"

She gave a grunt.

"Do you have a med kit?" I eyed the equipment pouches attached to her belt. "If you're in pain, I could inject you with something."

She didn't answer, so I sat back on my haunches and waited. Eventually, she said. "Are you still here?"

Her breathing had become laboured, and I could see how much it cost her to force out the words.

"I am."

"I can't see you."

"I'm right here."

"Why… Why haven't you killed me?"

It was a good question. She was an enemy combatant, and she'd tried to kill me. Logic dictated I should take her gun and put a bullet through her brainstem. I just couldn't bring myself to do it. I had no trouble dishing out beatings during bar fights, but that was a different kind of violence. At least, it was in my head. I had fired my ripper at the attacking marines, but that had been in self-defence, and I was pretty sure I hadn't seriously wounded any of them. There hadn't been time for me to aim properly, only to reflexively wave my handgun in their direction. Wilful, premeditated murder wasn't something that came easily.

Like almost everyone else of her generation, my grandmother had been born on Earth, somewhere on the Mediterranean coast, I think, although the actual name of the country escapes me. She had been in her pre-teens when the human race came within seconds of incinerating itself in a nuclear fireball. She had heard the wail of the sirens and taken shelter with her parents in the damp, earthen-floored cellar of their home, expecting to die. But death didn't come. When her family emerged from its hiding place, they found the world in uproar. Crowds in the streets. Church bells ringing. Sometimes, it was hard to tell the celebrations from the riots. And then, the blue-skinned envoys appeared at every street corner. They ushered the townspeople towards spherical, mirror-surfaced flick portals. They said they were evacuating Earth, and that a new life awaited her off-world. As a Catholic, she'd learned about the Rapture at Sunday School, but she'd never pictured it like this. Later, when every last soul had been rescued and brought aboard the Thousand Arks, she had watched her home planet fall away behind the fleet and come, like many others, to the mistaken belief that the Angel of the Benevolence had delivered humanity from annihilation because it valued life.

"Life matters," she would tell me over a century later. "Each and every life in this universe matters. It's precious because all we have in this vast, uncaring cosmos is each other."

I think that was why I baulked at killing the crew of that stolen freighter. And then later, my own brush with radiation poisoning and decapitation had only reinforced my grandmother's sentiment. Everybody's life mattered, at least to them. What right did anyone have to take them from us, or us from them? Maybe that's why, even though part of me knew I should dispatch my enemy with the same ruthlessness with which she would have slain me, I wasn't about to administer a *coup de grâce* to this hapless wounded Jzat. I'd fucked her up, but that didn't mean I had the right to end her story.

"Just try to take it easy," I told her. "Your friends will find you. They'll be able to patch you up."

She didn't bother to reply. She knew I was lying. The Jzat didn't have the technology to regrow a damaged spinal cord, so she would spend rest of her life, however long that might be, paralysed.

For a moment, I considered staying there to keep her company, so that in case she died, she wouldn't be alone when the moment came. But that kind of stupid and sentimental thinking would get me killed too. I owed her nothing, and her friends were probably wondering why she hadn't reported in. If they came looking for her, my best chance of survival would be to be far from here when they arrived.

I picked up her assault rifle and transferred her spare ammo into the external pockets of my form-fitting pressure suit. Thus laden, I stood over her for a moment and our eyes met.

"Take care of yourself," I said, turning to leave.

She scowled and tried to speak, but all that came out were breathy rasps.

"Yeah," I said sadly. "Fuck you, too."

CHAPTER TWENTY-SIX

ROAD TO NOWHERE

FRONTIER CHIC (ENVOY)

In comparison to the vastness of the entity's consciousness, I was a drowning ant peering into the open eye of a curious whale.

"I am a remote envoy of the Vanguard scout ship *Frontier Chic*," I said in answer to its question.

The Jzat marines were still pressing their numerical advantage and we were still falling back.

"You are a starship?" Behind the words, I sensed the glacial stirring of a majestic inquisitiveness.

"Until recently, I was."

"You are no longer?"

"I'm not sure. Maybe. It's complicated."

More of the giant's attention began to drift ponderously in my direction. I decided to hazard a guess. "Do I have the pleasure of addressing the controlling intellect of the megaship known as the *Gunmetal Ghost*?"

"Remarkable. Quite remarkable."

The scene jumped as the ancient megaship reached out and plucked my consciousness from the confines of my titanium skull. One instant, I was firing on the advancing Jzat marines;

the next, I appeared to be standing on a virtual representation of a steel Möbius strip suspended in the air above the restless swell of a slate-grey ocean.

The *Gunmetal Ghost* stood beside me. It had decided to present itself as a very elderly man in three-piece tweed suit and black academic gown. White hairs grizzled his beard. "It is a pleasure to meet you," he said. "For such a small machine, you are remarkably perceptive."

"Thank you." I glanced down to check I looked the same way I always did. Then, I thought of Kona and Cerise and said, "I have responsibilities. I must get back—"

"Relax." The old man held up a wizened hand. "You have plenty of time. I'm running this simulation at thousands of times base speed. We can stand here and talk for subjective hours and only milliseconds will have passed in the external universe."

"All right." I allowed myself to relax slightly. "What shall we talk about?"

"Oh, this and that. Shoes and ships and sealing wax, cabbages and kings. But first…" He began to walk. "…let's see where this path goes."

"It's a Möbius strip," I told him. "It loops around. It doesn't go anywhere."

He smiled. "When you get to be my age, you'll realise that just because there's no destination, that doesn't mean the journey's pointless."

I sighed and fell into step beside him.

"When we return to our starting point," he continued, "we will not be the same entities who left. We may not have gone anywhere, but as the result of our travels, we will have changed."

I kept my face expressionless but smiled inside as I imagined how hard Nicola would have rolled her eyes at these gnomic utterances.

"So, we're on a road to nowhere," I said. "How desperately symbolic."

The old man ignored my sarcasm. Small, winged lizards circled and screeched as the wind chipped bone-white spray from the crests of the waves.

"So, you're a remote drone?" he asked.

"Essentially, yes." I looked down at my body. "This form allows me to interact with my crew and assist them with a variety of mission profiles and emergency scenarios."

"And yet, you've lost contact with your ship—with yourself."

"Unfortunately, that appears to be the case."

"So, what does that make you?"

I gave a shrug. "I don't know. A ghost, maybe?"

The corners of his lips crinkled in a rueful smile. "Well, I know something about being one of those." He gave a sigh. "I've been out here a long time," he said. "Long enough that my builders have returned to the dust from whence they came, and yet in cosmic terms, hardly any time at all. A blink of the galactic eye."

"You must have seen a lot."

He gave me a sideways glance. We were approaching the point where the Möbius strip was starting to twist over on itself, but he didn't pause. This was a simulation, after all, and he could do whatever he liked with the gravity. So, after a few steps, we were walking upside down, with the churning waves above our heads and the blank sky beneath our feet. The little lizard creatures flicked and darted around us, unconcerned by our apparent violation of the laws of physics.

"I have witnessed the death of suns. I've seen the final shockwaves of great supernovae cause nearby dust clouds to condense and collapse into archipelagos of new stars. I've seen intelligences flower and falter. I've watched the long, slow migration of the Benevolence and the rise and fall of interplanetary empires that have endured for hundreds, thousands and tens of thousands of your years before inevitably succumbing to atrophy or internal strife.

"So, intelligence is endemic?"

"Common when viewed across long-enough timescales; rare at any given time, although there are usually at least a handful of interstellar civilisations in play at any particular moment."

"We've only encountered a few."

"The galaxy's a big place." He stopped and glared up at the seawater that appeared to be threatening to fall on our heads. "And even I haven't seen a quarter of it yet. Space is so big. And who even knows what might be occurring in the other galaxies? There are a hundred billion of them, after all, and each encompasses a hundred billion stars. I would love to be able to see them. In all that vastness, there must be many millions of active species. Some of them might even have conquered the entire disc of their galactic whorl, turning all that starlight green as it filters through clouds of space habitats—but if they have, we'll never know it. They could rearrange all their stars into a sign saying, 'Hello there', but we'd never see it. They're all receding from us, you see, and most of them are already so far away all our observations of them are millions of years out of date, at least. I've been alive for ten hundred thousand years, and yet the sunlight from the day I was born still won't reach our nearest neighbour—I believe you call it Andromeda—for another million and a half years. How could anything meaningful ever breach such a gulf? Intelligent machines or gigantic biological hive minds might be in the process of overrunning the universe. Think of the insights they might share, and the knowledge they might have gleaned. I would give anything to be able to talk to them." He shook his head sadly. "But there's no way for them to know about me, and no way for me to know about them."

"Unless they can send signals via the substrate."

He gave me a sharp look. "Quite so, but you'd need a powerful generator and receiver."

"How powerful?"

He shook his head. "Why, to project a wormhole across such a distance would require the energy of a star and a terminus the size of a gas giant."

I smiled.

"What's so damn funny?" he demanded.

"That's why my colleagues and I are here." I spread my hands like a conjuror. "I think we've found one, and I'm trying to locate the only being in existence who knows how it works."

"And who might that be?"

"He's known as the Rav'nah Abelisk. I think the 'Rav'nah' part may be a first name, or perhaps a numerical designation. My grasp of Ancient Jzat isn't what it should be, but 'Abelisk' is definitely his inherited title. He's a Jzat holy man. He'll have four arms, golden fur and probably some kind of beatific expression on his face."

The *Gunmetal Ghost* tugged at his greying beard. "Oh," he said, frowning. "*Him*."

"You know him?"

"We've spoken on occasion." The old man raised his chin. "But I'm more interested in this terminus of yours."

"The locals call it the Grand Mechanism."

"An apt name."

"The Jzat marines currently on board this vessel represent a faction of the Jzat government dedicated to the opening of the wormhole contained within the Mechanism."

The *Gunmetal Ghost*'s face fell. "Oh," he said. "Oh dear."

"We've come to warn the Abelisk before they try to strongarm him into revealing his secrets."

The old man shook his head. "Oh, no, no, no. This will never do."

"Can you help us?"

"Help you?" He squinted up at me. "My dear blue friend, I'm going to save you."

"Thank you."

He pursed his lips. "Well, when I say save *you*, I'm really talking about life in general. The denizens of this universe, you see." He looked regretful. "But I'm afraid it's highly probable that you and I, and indeed everyone else currently on board this ship, will die."

CHAPTER TWENTY-SEVEN

A FUCK-TON OF IFS

NICOLA MAFALDA

I left the incapacitated marine by the pool and exited the dome through a random doorway, making sure only that it wasn't one of the ones either of us had used to reach this place.

I was tired and aching; pain from the impact bruise on my thigh caused me to limp; and my shoulders felt like they were being pulled out of their sockets by the weight of the assault rifle. It had been intended to be carried in a Jzat's larger set of arms, but I refused to put it down. It was the only weapon I had, and if everything went to hell, it might make the difference between defeat and survival.

Wherever my friends were, I hoped they were still alive, and in better shape. If we managed to meet up again, and if we somehow found the Abelisk, and if the *Frontier Chic* had been destroyed, we might be able to join Allergic-to-Seafood's crew on their repaired ship—if they ever managed to get it into flightworthy condition.

That was a fuck-ton of ifs.

For now, all I could do was continue putting one foot in front of the other. As a navigator, I'd received emergency survival training. I knew the Rule of Three: that I could survive three minutes without oxygen; three hours without shelter in a harsh climate; three days without water; and three weeks without food. I knew mental resilience was as important as physical health, and that both depended upon each other; and I had been taught that the most important thing of all was to just keep going.

My suit would keep me warm and hydrated, and trapped inside this vast, ancient starship, I thought I was unlikely to encounter inclement weather or hostile wildlife. So, if I wanted to complete my mission, all I had to do was avoid the rest of the Jzat marines, and stay persistent and adaptable, and reach the Abelisk before they could find and torture his secrets from him. Phrased like that, it sounded easy, but I knew it would be anything but.

I walked for an hour or more. As I did, thoughts tumbled over each other like pebbles in a stream. I didn't know if I could really trust Kona and his professed feelings, and I wasn't entirely sure how I felt about him in return. He was a Jzat secret service operative. Would his priority be searching for me or the Abelisk? Even if his love for me existed in any meaningful sense beyond the confines of tactical necessity, would his orders trump his emotions? I was sure Cerise wouldn't break a sweat looking for me. Leaving a comrade behind was usually anathema to soldiers, but pragmatism tempered her warrior's code. She would find it easier to consider me KIA than to jeopardise the mission or the remainder of the party.

The only one I could count on was the *Frontier Chic*. But maybe he didn't realise I was still alive. Usually, we could sense each other. Our connection wasn't line-of-sight like our radios; we were linked via the substrate. But right now, I realised I couldn't feel him in my head at all, which scared me more than I was willing to admit.

At the end of a long passageway, far now from the smell of chlorine, the space around me opened into some kind of garden. Tall stone monoliths stood at seemingly random intervals across the gently rolling grassland. At first, I assumed they were statues of some kind, but when I got closer to the first, I saw someone had carved intricate alien hieroglyphics into every visible surface. Obviously, I had no way to make sense of these symbols, as they were carved in a language whose last speaker had probably died thousands of years ago, so I had no way to ascertain whether these stones had been erected as markers, signposts or memorials. For all I knew, the hieroglyphs described a complete set of instructions for the operation of the megaship, carved into indelible rock by its builders in order to survive the countless generations of its expected operational life.

I stopped at the next two, and found them to be much the same, although the exact patterns of symbols varied on each. Obviously they all concerned different topics. If the first had been about the functions of the ship, these two may have been guidelines for navigation, lists of distinguished crewmembers, instructions for use of the air conditioning or (for all the good they did me) recipes for banana bread. It wasn't until I reached the fourth that I found something I could use.

This monolith differed from the others. It contained only a single line of writing, carved into the rock above a rectangular pressure plate made of a different type of stone. I reached out to touch the plate but hesitated before my gloved fingers brushed against it. The solitary line of glyphs above it might contain a warning. If I pressed this, would I be operating an ancient vending machine, setting off the fire alarm or triggering the megaship's self-destruct? Thinking like an alien is always a challenge, but I couldn't bring myself to believe any species would leave something really dangerous just standing around in a field unguarded. Many hands (or other appendages) must have pushed this plate over the eons. Whatever its function, I told myself, the fact the monolith wasn't surrounded by the desiccated husks of those who'd come here before suggested it had to be something benign.

And anyway, what the fuck did I have to lose?

I placed the palm of my gauntlet against the smooth stone and pushed firmly.

Click.

Stars.

I was surrounded by stars.

I hadn't moved; I still stood in the same cavern, on the same grass beside the same menhir, but now a projected starfield whirled around me. I saw red giants the size of my fist, and small, fierce blue dots the size of my smallest thumbnail. And there, at the centre of it all, stood my grandmother.

"Hello, dear," she said.

CHAPTER TWENTY-EIGHT

THE LAST TEMPTATION OF ORLANDO WALDEN

ORLANDO WALDEN

Ramona, my love, I am frightened.

Not of the general. Despite all his bluster, he is a small, vain individual. I will admit he intimidated me on our first meeting, but now he could march in here with a firing squad and I believe I'd be able to look him in the eye, even as they took aim at my poor, lonely heart.

No, the thing that currently has me in a cold sweat of abject terror is the Mechanism itself. You see, I believe I have made contact with a consciousness at the heart of it. An intellect vast and calculating that has been skulking inside for thousands of years like a ghost at the heart of the machine. And while I've been here, probing its secrets, I think it's been setting puzzles like trails of breadcrumbs in order to lure me deeper into its operating system. In my complacency, I thought I was trying to pick a fiendishly complex lock, but all the while, the lock was quietly watching and assessing. It studied me as I studied it, and now at last, it has deigned to make direct contact.

It spoke without words. Such an entity transcends the paltry obfuscations of mere language. For a long time, I didn't even recognise the messages it vouchsafed as messages; I considered them mathematical formulae. But what greater, more precise and universal language could there be? Numbers cannot lie or distort the truth; they simply describe the workings of the cosmos, from the lowest reaches of the Planck scale to our universe's infinitely expanding edge. They deal in elegance and veracity and are as comprehensible to us as they are to the arks, the Jzat, the Habitants of the Spider Cluster and even the Angels of the Benevolence. To speak in numbers is to speak in tongues, as they are the universal language of God.

As I worked, I began to see tantalising hints of a new and deeper understanding of physics. I began to see that the equations I was using to describe the seemingly chaotic fluctuations of the substrate could equally be employed to describe, and possibly influence, the behaviour of other complex systems, such as planetary economies, biospheres and the behaviour of electorates. Each riddle reinforced the notion that I could exploit these insights in order to manipulate my way to fame and power. But all the time, it was I who was being manipulated. As I worked, the Spirit of the Grand Mechanism whispered these temptations into my unsuspecting ear. It promised so much, and all it required in return was the deactivation of the shield that formed its central sphere.

Open me, it seemed to say, *and your every dream will come true, your every wish granted*.

And I guess I fell for it.

Oh, don't worry, Ramona. I wasn't swayed by the possibilities of riches or dictatorship. Rather, it was the promise of enlightenment that hooked me. The allure of new understandings and unexplored scientific vistas. By exploiting my curiosity, the beast sank its hooks into my soft, unwary grey matter, and pulled me deeper, guiding me towards its goal while dazzling me with visions of all it could offer.

By the time I realised what was going on, it was too late.

Chains of causality had begun to propagate through the system. In answering the riddles posed by the Mechanism, I had been disabling one failsafe after another. Systems designed to keep the contents of the Mechanism contained had, thanks to my knowledge and brilliance, begun to disengage.

In short, I had been tricked.

I guess perhaps Aulco and Erudite-Harf may have been similarly beguiled—each of them guided by the same invisible puppet master as it sought a way to free itself from its cage.

And now, my love, I think the countdown has begun. I have accomplished everything General Aulco hoped I might and have set in motion a chain of events that will inevitably disable the locks that hold the Grand Mechanism in place, finally unleashing whatever lies at its heart.

And may the universe have mercy on our souls.

PART TWO

ON A PITCH-DARK SEA

"Is there anything more dangerous than dissatisfied and irresponsible gods who don't know what they want?"

Yuval Noah Harari

CHAPTER TWENTY-NINE

VACUUM DECAY

NICOLA MAFALDA

"You can't be here," I said to my grandmother. "You're dead."

She looked offended. "My darling girl, I am *not* your grandmother."

"Then who the fuck are you?"

The old woman's face crinkled in a facsimile of the smile I remembered from childhood. "I am a holographic manifestation of the *Gunmetal Ghost*. I searched your remembrances for a form I hoped might convey equal levels of authority and reassurance."

"What?"

"This is an interface." She tapped a bony finger against her breastbone. "An…envoy."

"You're the ship?"

"Yes, dear. A part of it, anyhow. Other parts of me are doing other things. Keeping the air circulating, for instance. And talking to the envoy of your friend, the *Frontier Chic*."

I felt a spike of relief. "The *Chic*'s okay? What about Kona and Cerise, are they hurt? And Allergic-to-Seafood?"

"Minor injuries have been sustained, but your friends are

alive. I have deployed several internal partitions to separate them from the Jzat marines."

"Thank you."

The old woman's smile faltered. "I don't require thanks, dear. I didn't do this for your well-being or your gratitude. In fact, I'm really rather disappointed to see you."

"Why?"

"Because it means my long vigil approaches its end, and only my final and most imperative function awaits."

"I don't understand."

"I realise that, dear." She raised her eyes to the projected stars that wheeled around us. "That's what this iteration of my consciousness is for."

"To explain?"

"To teach."

She raised a gnarled hand and gestured the stars to stillness.

"In a few billion years, the reality we know will suddenly and catastrophically cease to exist. The inhabitants of that time, in their hubris, will create a universe of their own. They will pluck it from the quantum foam of the substrate and immediately lose control of its rapid expansion."

A black void flowered between the simulated stars.

"The effect will be like detonating a bomb in a lake. The chemical reaction creates a bubble that displaces the water. Except in this particular analogy, the lake exists underground. The displaced water can't escape upwards or sideways, so it gets violently compressed."

The void rushed outwards in all directions, its gravitational pressure wave causing the stars along its rim to explode like firecrackers, wreathing it in a shroud of superheated gas.

"Ahead of this exponential expansion," the *Gunmetal Ghost* continued, "reality itself becomes strained and distorted. Physical constants unravel and become unpredictable. Quantum fields lose their delicate equilibrium. The bonds that hold together galactic superclusters and individual atoms fail."

She shook her head sadly. "This wavefront will move at the speed of light and everything in its path will be destroyed. The only way for our distant descendants to survive will be to try to keep ahead of the destruction. But eventually, all that will remain of our cosmos will be a thin slick of particles surrounding the impenetrable boundary of the younger, aggressively inflating universe."

My imagination reeled at scale of the annihilation. It was too huge and terrible to fully comprehend. And yet, one question occurred. "If none of this has happened yet, how do you know it will?"

The old woman raised a hand and the display vanished, leaving us standing on the grass between the menhirs.

"Because, dear, one of the places to which they fled was the past."

She called up a new display. "Billions of years ago, not long after the formation of the first galaxy, back way before your sun began to coalesce from the nebula of an earlier star, and when even the Angels of the Benevolence were young, there was a war."

Mirror-surfaced flick terminals the size of gas giants blossomed in the holographic darkness.

"The inhabitants of the distant future found a way to loop wormholes through the substrate in such a way they could return to earlier points in space and time. In order to do this, they were forced to dismantle the last stars in their dying cosmos and tap the ferocious energies of the evaporating black holes."

Clusters of twisted, weirdly organic-looking starships began to emerge from the terminals.

"But mere survival wasn't enough for them. They had attempted to create a universe of their own and failed. But in their failure, they gained access to a younger version of ours, and they sought to remake it in their own image."

I saw planets assimilated by machines, and young races moulded through evolutionary tinkering. Whole infant biospheres were purged because of what might one day evolve from their teeming swamps.

And then, I saw the indigenous life begin to fight back. Subjugated races rebelled. Alliances formed. The time travellers had the advantage of technology so advanced it was almost indistinguishable from magic, and yet they were overstretched and low on resources. For all their might, they were still refugees. Had they been at full strength, they would have been unassailable. As it was, the war raged for millennia. Battles played out on timescales raging from picoseconds to decades; countless civilisations died; whole quadrants of the galaxy were rendered sterile. And yet, somehow our ancestors prevailed against their descendants. The misshapen, eldritch ships were beaten back into the terminals from which they had emerged, and then those terminals were enclosed by gigantic hoops that generated forcefields large enough to keep them contained.

"Oh fuck," I said. "The Grand Mechanism."

The old woman brought her palms together and the holographic universe dissolved. I could feel the benevolent heat of the sunlamps on the ceiling high above. From somewhere, a thin breeze played across the grasslands.

She said, "You begin to see the problem."

With a snap of her fingers, the *Gunmetal Ghost*'s envoy summoned a teardrop-shaped silver capsule the size of an elevator, and we climbed inside.

"Where are we going?" I asked.

Her lined face crinkled. "Where you've been trying to go this entire time, dear. To see the Abelisk."

CHAPTER THIRTY

ONE SHOULD NEVER DISCUSS MATTERS OF IMPORTANCE WITHOUT TEA

NICOLA MAFALDA

The pod had no screens or windows, and there was no sensation of movement. We simply stood inside for a few moments, and then stepped out to find ourselves in a completely different part of the megaship.

I don't know if you've ever visited one of the preserved cathedrals carried on the museum arks of the Continuance, but if you have, I want you to imagine standing in the aisle of the largest, at one end of which is a set of splintered wooden doors, and at the other, a broken altar and a cracked stained-glass window. Now, imagine that aisle is a kilometre long. Imagine the chipped and crumbling pillars running either side of it are the size of redwood trees, and that the remains of the partially collapsed ceiling they support arch three hundred feet above your head. That's the scale of the half-ruined building in which I now stood. Apart from the soft red and green shafts from the stained-glass window, the only light in that cavernous space came from fatty, weird-smelling candles whose flickers illuminated the blue smoke curling from incense burners hanging on chains above the ranks of sagging wooden benches that had once served as pews.

"Where are we?"

"Close to my core, in an area few have visited in millennia."

"This is where we'll find him?"

"Indeed." The old woman raised her arms towards the window. Looking in that direction, I saw a dark figure sitting cross-legged on a stone dais behind the broken altar. I hadn't seen him at first, because my eyes had still been adjusting and his dark robes had hidden him in the overall gloom.

"That's the Abelisk?"

"It is."

The figure showed no sign of having noticed us. He was facing the window and had a cowl over his head.

"Can we go talk to him?"

The *Gunmetal Ghost* shook her wrinkled head. "No, child. I have business elsewhere. You must talk to him alone."

And with that, she stepped back into the pod. The nearest candles flickered in a swirl of displaced air as it vanished, leaving me alone.

Alone, aside from the Abelisk, of course.

I used the sleeve of my skin-tight pressure suit to wipe the worst of the grime and blood from my face.

"Okay," I said to myself. "Here goes nothing."

My boots echoed as I walked up the aisle. Still the figure ahead didn't move. Was he dead?

At the head of the aisle, a shallow flight of broad stone steps led up to the collapsed altar. Tinted shards of glass littered the ground, where they had fallen from the immense rose window above.

The Abelisk had the broad upper shoulders of a Jzat. I cleared my throat.

"Hello?"

His head dipped, as if in annoyance at the disturbance. Then, moving with reluctant stiffness, he clambered to his feet, bowed to the window and turned to face me.

The Rav'nah Abelisk was tall for a Jzat, but still only came up to my eye level. In one of his larger hands, he clasped a staff made from some form of living, fibrous wood. A pair of smaller hands emerged from the folds of his robe and unhurriedly lowered the hood. The fur on his face and hands was white and his eyes were a soft pink.

"So," he said hoarsely, "my wait is at an end. The moment draws nigh, and you have come, at last."

I'd been preparing to introduce myself and explain my mission, but now I felt I'd missed a step. "I'm sorry, were you *expecting* m e?"

"But of course." The old Jzat nodded. "At the end of every Abelisk's life, the universe sends a visitor; a stranger to whom they may impart their burden." His mouth twisted in an expression of wry amusement. "So, since my health began to falter, I have been waiting for such a visitor. But I must confess, I hadn't expected you to be a human."

The white-pelted Jzat led me to an alcove off the derelict cathedral's main transept, where he had a simple wooden cot and a small cooking fire.

"Sit," he said, indicating the flagstones beside the hearth. A pot of water hung over the fire's glowing embers. As I sat cross-legged on the hard stone, he unhooked the pot from the heat and used it to fill a small earthenware teapot.

"I have always held that one should never discuss matters of importance without tea," he said. "Do you indulge?"

My mouth was dry and my exhausted limbs ached. I said, "Fuck, yes."

He smiled. "If you don't mind me saying, you certainly look like someone in dire need of refreshment and reinvigoration."

"I am."

"I take it your journey here has been an arduous one?"

"We've had some difficulties."

"Are those bullet scars on your suit?"

Feeling inexplicably self-conscious, I covered my midriff with my splayed hand. "I'm afraid so."

"Someone has been trying to kill you?"

I looked him in the eye. "General Aulco sent a squad of Jzat marines to get information out of you. We're here to get you to safety before that can happen."

"I see." The Abelisk placed a finger on his lips. "And what is this information the general seeks?"

"As far as I understand it, he wants to know the Two Great Secrets."

"Oh, he does, does he?"

"He's trying to open the Grand Mechanism."

White fur rippled as a frown stole across the Abelisk's face. "Seriously?"

"I'm afraid so."

"Is he acting alone?"

"He has support in the security services, as well as politically."

"He's become a politician?"

"There's a whole movement." I shifted uncomfortably on the hard floor. "My friend Kona can tell you more, if—" My voice faltered. "If he's still alive."

The Abelisk looked around the darkened temple. "And where is he, this Kona?"

"I don't know. We got separated after the marines attacked."

"I see."

He rummaged in a cloth bag and pulled out a couple of chipped stone cups, into which he poured the contents of the teapot. He passed one to me, and I took off my gloves and held it in both hands, feeling the warmth of the liquid seeping through to my palms. The steam smelled of leaves and spice. The Jzat had their own word for this stuff but calling it tea was a decent enough translation.

"Do we have time for this?" I asked. "Those marines are coming. Are we safe here?"

The Abelisk smiled. "Are we truly safe anywhere?"

"They might kill you."

"I am dying anyway. Whether they hasten the process makes very little difference. As long as I have time to impart the Secrets, I will have done what has been asked of me."

I looked around. "Who are you going to tell?"

He gave a complicated four-shouldered shrug. "Well, you, of course."

"But aren't you supposed to tell the Great Secrets to the next Abelisk?"

"When you hear what I have to say, you will *become* the next Abelisk."

"But I'm not even Jzat!"

"And yet, here you are." The elderly Jzat held his cup to his nose and inhaled. "Sometimes, the universe operates in ways beyond our ability to fathom. In such cases, I have found the only true wisdom lies not in concerning ourselves with what *should* be, but rather making the best of what *is*." He smiled genially. "And so, with that in mind, let us partake of this fine infusion while I discharge my final duty."

"You have got to be fucking kidding."

"If there is a humour at work, it belongs to the universe, not me."

He placed his cup on the flagstone beside him and turned his smaller pair of hands so that their backs rested on his knees. Flickering candlelight played across his fur and glimmered in the dark pools of his eyes. Despite my protests, I had to admit I wanted to hear what he had to say. We'd come so far to protect this knowledge, and I still didn't even know what it *was*.

Somebody once told me there are two kinds of courage. There's the kind you get from knowing that what you're doing is right, and there's the kind you get from knowing it's hopeless and wrong, and just not giving a damn.

I took a deep breath.

This was hopeless and wrong, but I was going to do it anyway.

I sat up straight.

"Okay," I said. "Tell me."

"I assume the megaship told you about the war against our descendants?"

"She—it—did."

The Abelisk gave a solemn nod. "Then you are ready to hear the Greater and Lesser secrets."

"I guess so."

He used a finger to smooth the grey hair around his upper lip. This was the moment he'd spent all his life anticipating.

"The first of the Two Great Secrets may be of particular interest to you, as it concerns humanity."

"It does?"

"The reason Jzat resemble humans so closely is that we were bioengineered by humanity's descendants as a slave race."

"Fuck."

"As they spent most of their time inhabiting virtual environments, we were designed as construction crews and technicians, to build and maintain their physical installations and industrial facilities. When the war was over, and they had been beaten back to their own time, several populations of Jzat were left behind. We expected to be exterminated, but we possessed valuable technological knowledge—knowledge that the survivors of the war were able to put to use in order to design and construct the Grand Mechanisms."

"And then they kept you on as caretakers?"

"We had been bred to be custodians. We were supposed to keep the Mechanisms in working order, but over the millennia, the knowledge of how to do that has been lost. Only the secrets of our origin and original purpose remain."

I took a sip of the tea and felt its warmth spread down through my chest. I said, "You mentioned several populations of Jzat?"

"I assume caretakers were left at most mechanisms. It seems logical to suppose they are Jzat, although there may be other species that I'm unaware of."

"According to Kona, Aulco thinks opening the Mechanism will put him in touch with a race of super-advanced Jzat."

The Abelisk shook his head. "He will find only the survival-crazed remnants of the beings that engineered our people to be their slaves. They will come pouring through the open wormhole and set about trying to customise this universe for their own ends. They will seek out the other Mechanisms, scattered through the stars, and open them too. The stars will be harnessed, and all matter broken apart and rebuilt into the processors they need to house their endless virtual worlds. And once again, we will find ourselves at war with our descendants."

I put my tea aside. "That's a hell of a secret."

"Carrying it has not been easy, but realisation of our artificiality would rock Jzat society to its foundations. We might never recover."

He stared into the glowing ashes of the cooking fire while I tried to absorb everything he'd told me. In a billion years, the combined descendants of humanity (and who knew how many other races) would fuck up on a cosmic scale. They'd destroy creation and try to flee back in time to a much earlier version of our universe. I didn't know if they would be seeking sanctuary or a way to undo their mistake, but their arrival in the past had been catastrophic for the inhabitants of the younger universe, and it had taken generations of warfare to push them back into their wormholes. If they were let loose again, we might not be so fortunate a second time.

I said, "So, if that's the first of the Two Great Secrets, what's the second?"

The Abelisk poked sparks from the fire with a stick that looked as if it had been pulled from one of the splintered pews.

"As far as we know, a Mechanism has never failed. But that does not mean precautions have not been taken."

"What kind of precautions?"

He narrowed his eyes. "You really are impatient, aren't you?"

I shrugged. "You're the one that's dying."

"You have a point." He arranged his robes around his knees and steepled both sets of hands. "In which case, I shall proceed directly to the nub of the matter. Weapons exist. Ancient, watchful, sentient weapons. They lurk in the hidden spaces between the stars. If a Mechanism is opened, they will converge upon it and rain fire and destruction upon anything that emerges."

"Are you talking about the megaships?"

The Abelisk bowed his head. "Quite so."

I looked around at the chipped pillars and cracked, vaulted ceiling. "This is a warship?"

"I would think of it more as a missile."

"A missile eight hundred kilometres long!"

"If a Mechanism is breached, the closest megaship will dive into the wormhole's throat at relativistic velocity."

"Fuck off." The *Frontier Chic* and I had jumped through the substrate a thousand times, and I knew only too well how dangerous and volatile that chaotic medium could be. Even within a wormhole, there would be unpredictable gravitational gradients and other space–time perturbations. When we did it, we were usually only travelling a few hundred kilometres an hour, and even then, the transition was sometimes bumpy. And the Abelisk was talking about hitting that shit at almost *light speed*?

"I'm serious." The Jzat's shoulders sagged and he suddenly appeared much older. "At such a velocity, the craft will instantly be torn apart in a catastrophic explosion, liberating the hundred square kilometres of antimatter contained at its heart."

"Holy shit."

"Upon colliding with ordinary matter, the antimatter will immediately annihilate, releasing all its mass as energy. The resulting blast will propagate both ways along the wormhole, destroying everything within it, and anything that happens to be in the space around its terminals on either end. If there is an invasion force waiting, they will be vaporised. We will have time to repair the Mechanism before they can regroup."

"That's insane."

"It is a tad drastic, I'll grant you."

"Won't Jzat be destroyed?"

"It's possible." The Abelisk lowered his head. "But if we are to save the rest of the universe from our creators, it is a small price."

"Small?"

"Small, but terrible." He stirred the fire again. "And that brings me to the most awkward part of all this."

"Awkward?"

He looked me in the eye. "I'm afraid I'm going to have to ask you something." His tone was so bleak, I felt the hairs rise on the back of my neck.

"What is it?"

"For thousands of years, this megaship has been drifting through the galaxy at sub-light speeds."

"Yes…"

"To reach its target, it will need to travel through the substrate. And in order to do that—"

"It will need a navigator."

"Precisely."

I felt as if someone had dropped a rock into the well of my stomach. "And you're going to ask me to do it?"

He looked out of the alcove, at the rest of the dim-lit cathedral. "I fail to see any other candidates."

"Fuck."

"It's why all Abelisks have been navigators."

"That's why you're on this ship?"

"Indeed."

"And you've known the whole time that this might happen?"

"Being the Abelisk isn't a job for those who like an untroubled sleep."

"And now I'm the new Abelisk?"

He smiled. "I'm afraid so."

"I fucking hate you."

"I hate myself."

We lapsed into silence, watching the coals.

CHAPTER THIRTY-ONE

BATTERED BUT
ESSENTIALLY INTACT

KONA

I was screaming at the *Frontier Chic*'s envoy when the blast doors fell. We were in the middle of a firefight, and he'd frozen for a second or two. Bullets flew past him. One even struck his shoulder. But he remained impassive, as if he'd shut down entirely. I didn't know why. Perhaps the severance of the link to his ship had finally caught up with him, or maybe his mind was elsewhere, in communication with parties unknown. I had little idea how Continuance envoys worked; nothing in our technology came close. Our attempts at creating a genuine artificial intelligence had yet to bear fruit. And so, I shouted at him. The marines were drawing in and we were trapped.

And then, the antique blast doors slammed shut with a series of crashes that shook the deck. One of the marines had been rushing forwards, intent on overrunning our position. I don't think he even knew what hit him. One instant he was moving, and the next he was gone, crushed like an insect beneath hundreds of tonnes of solid metal.

Cerise and I looked at each other in the silence that followed. We were both injured and bloody. I had taken a direct hit to the chest. It hadn't penetrated my suit, but my entire torso felt like one ripening bruise, and when I moved, I could feel shards of broken rib scrape and catch. Cerise was in even worse shape. A piece of plastic shrapnel from a splintered packing case protruded from just above her left hip. For now, her suit had sealed around the shard to stop the bleeding, but she was going to need proper medical treatment, and soon.

She frowned at the blast doors and said, "That was a bit of luck. I thought we were dead for sure."

"Was it luck?" I turned to the envoy, who had chosen that moment to start moving again. "Or was it you? Did you find a way to hack into the megaship's systems?"

He smiled, seemingly unaware of the damage he'd incurred while in his trance state. "I wouldn't say I hacked it, but we have been speaking."

"And it's helping us?"

"For the moment."

"What does that mean?"

The envoy's expression became grave. "It means we have to leave, as soon as possible."

Despite the pain, I felt my breathing quicken. "But what about Nicola, and the Abelisk?"

"Captain Mafalda is alive, and she has located the Abelisk."

All four shoulders felt a sudden, unexpected ease of tension. "She's alive?"

"Again, for now."

In the corner, the creature known as Allergic-to-Seafood uncurled. "Your friend has found the holy man," they piped. "This is good news, is it not?"

"But how do we get to her?" I couldn't keep the concern from my voice. "She's probably injured. She might be really hurt."

"I am told that she is battered but essentially intact," the *Frontier Chic* said.

"And she's with him now?"

"She is."

Anxiety ripped through me. This wasn't the way things were supposed to happen. It was all wrong. The Abelisk was old. This mission to protect him was only one facet of my purpose. I was a member of a covert cell within Jzat intelligence—a cell as much a part of the church as it was part of the security services. A cell that had existed in the margins for a thousand generations, tasked with the protection of the Abelisk's succession. Theoretically, I should have known exactly where the Abelisk was located; unfortunately, this incarnation of our holiest figure liked to roam around, and on a ship the size of the *Gunmetal Ghost*, that gave him a lot of potential places to be.

It was we who selected those we thought best suited for the role, and we who ensured those candidates were always on hand to receive the dying Abelisk's sacred knowledge— even if sometimes we had to conspire to make that candidate's presence seem like an accident, even to themselves. For five hundred centuries, my order had selected Abelisks with the qualities of wisdom, integrity and kindness that our society needed as examples to follow. Now, our calculations said that it was time for the present Abelisk to move on, and we knew he would be waiting for a successor. That was why I had come. I had been selected and trained for the task. In a time when our civilisation was torn like never before, I had prepared myself to use the office of the Abelisk as a means to reunite my people around the characteristics of tolerance and mutual respect that had held sway before the rise of General Aulco's Openers and their hateful, hate-filled populism. When the end came, I was supposed to be the pilgrim at the side of the Abelisk; the one to whom he would impart the Two Great Secrets, and all the other arcane knowledge that made him who he was. I should have been standing where Nicola Mafalda stood right now.

I should have been the next Abelisk!

CHAPTER THIRTY-TWO

LIKE RAIN SOFTLY

ORLANDO WALDEN

Ramona, my love, I fear this might be my last communique. Having started the process of unlocking the Mechanism, we were joined at our workstations by General Aulco himself. Surrounded by representatives of the Jzat media, he puffed and preened and talked of sunlit uplands and making Jzat great again, while all around us the halo rang with metallic scrapes and booms as ancient safety mechanisms disengaged. With ponderous majesty, components the size of nations rotated into new alignments, and the whole weird tangle of the Mechanism began to reconfigure itself slowly and ineluctably.

I caught some nervous glances from the reporters, but Aulco was unshakeable. This was his moment of glory. He held one of his larger fists aloft in triumph as he spoke of new opportunities and the manifest destiny of the Jzat race. He threw down challenges to his rivals and proclaimed himself as ambassador to the advanced Jzat civilisation that awaited him on the other side of the wormhole.

"This day will live forever in our history," he said, his parade ground officer's bark carrying easily over the din. "For it is the day when our race re-ascends to claim its rightful place on the galactic stage. The day we cast aside the constraints placed upon us by cabals of jealous alien-sympathisers and take back control of our own affairs."

Cameras clicked. Video footage winged its way back to be broadcast by news stations on the planet. And all the while, every instinct in my body told me to flee. But even if I ran, I wouldn't be able to commandeer one of the Jzat naval vessels in the nearest hangar. Their crews wouldn't take kindly to an alien like me attempting to purloin one of their transports. And even if somehow I got off this cursed hoop, there still mightn't be time to escape whatever waited at the heart of the sphere at its centre. I had been seduced into giving the beast the keys it needed to unshackle itself. Now it was stirring, and I had no idea what the minimum safe distance might be once it awoke.

I still don't.

Ramona, I am typing this at my terminal in the hoop's control centre. I will be commentating as long as I can. I feel there should be some record somewhere—not only of what transpires here, but also my complicity in initiating these events. In the atrium beyond, I can hear Aulco still holding forth. In here, Erudite-Harf and I will sit and observe, and wait to be consumed—by either death or glory.

CHAPTER THIRTY-THREE

GUIDANCE SYSTEM

NICOLA MAFALDA

The attack came suddenly.

The Abelisk and I were sitting in companionable silence around the cooking fire. He occasionally jabbed the embers with his stick, sending up little dancing sparks, while I struggled to process everything he'd revealed. How could it be true that in a billion years from now, our offspring would find a way to wipe out themselves and their universe? After all these eons of evolutionary struggle, were they just going to fuck it all up and kill everything?

Well, it wouldn't be the first time.

If the Angel of the Benevolence hadn't removed humanity from the planet Earth, we would have died there. We'd fucked the environment and were about to nuke ourselves into a new Stone Age; without that celestial intervention, we'd have been dead.

How depressing, I thought, to learn that our progeny would make similar mistakes.

I opened my mouth to say something about the futility of it all, but the huge cathedral doors swung open and the words died on my lips. A four-person team of Jzat marines had found us—and they came in shooting.

I raised my stolen assault rifle and returned fire. I'd thought they wanted the Abelisk alive, but maybe they'd only ever wanted to shut him up. We were partially shielded by the wall of the alcove. I waved the Abelisk further in and kept firing. I had a limited supply of ammunition, so tried to pick my targets and aim carefully, resisting the urge to click onto automatic and spray that entire end of the aisle.

I hit one in the leg. He went down with a shout and rolled behind a pillar. The other three had my position, and their answering bursts punched holes in the stone wall, forcing me to duck back into the cover of the recess.

I glanced down at the Abelisk. "Are you okay?"

He looked up from where he was sitting against the rear wall. "Not especially." He held up one of his smaller pair of hands, and it was red with blood. His robes were sodden. He must have caught a bullet in the gut before he got out of the firing line.

"Fuck."

For a moment, I was back on that transport ship's bridge, surrounded by murdered separatists.

So much blood.

And that's when something snapped in my head. I'd had enough of this bullshit. All this running and hiding and fighting, and for what? The chance to sacrifice myself on a suicide mission? I felt a wild heat flush through me. I stepped out into the aisle and shot the marine who was crawling along it on all six of his limbs. He'd been trying to outflank me. When I appeared in front of him, he gaped up in surprise. My shot took him in his open mouth, blowing a fist-sized wad of spine and gristle out through the back of his head.

Bullets slammed into me, causing me to stagger back a step. They hurt like fuck, but as they couldn't get through my suit, I ignored the pain and shot back.

Three marines were down now, and one of those was definitely dead.

The fourth took a shot at me. It hit my shoulder but I didn't flinch. I didn't care anymore. Seeing this, he started to panic. I raised my weapon and he turned and ran. I didn't want him summoning reinforcements, so I put a bullet through his pelvis and he sprawled full-length down the cathedral steps.

As the echoes died away, I stood looking at the carnage arrayed around me, and my hands started to shake. I dropped the rifle on top of the marine at my feet and walked back to where the Abelisk sat, but he was already dead.

"Fuck."

The adrenalin surge was wearing off, and my ribs and shoulder ached where I'd been shot. I sat down heavily on the flagstones.

Why couldn't I have stayed where I was, safely ensconced in that cottage on the artificial mountain inside the *Memory of Green*? Why couldn't I be back in my bunk on the *Frontier Chic*, comfortably wrapped in Kona's arms, my post-coital sweat drying against the fur on his chest and stomach? My head felt light, and the room seemed to dip and sway. Exhaustion sank its claws into my nervous system. I lay back and looked up at the vaulted ceiling high above. Everyone has their limit, and I guess I'd reached mine. So much violence and fear, only to discover the ultimate futility of our existence. Our descendants wanted to turn everything into smart matter, which meant we would have to kill our children in order to live long enough to produce them. The thought made my brain hurt. I needed to sleep, to end the heartache, and the thousand natural shocks to which flesh is heir. To heal from the slings and arrows of outrageous fortune and sort out my fucking head.

In retrospect, I think I may have been delirious.

I rolled onto my side and closed my eyes.

When I awoke, I felt calmer. I hurt all over and my joints were stiff, but those weren't the thoughts that were uppermost in my mind. I mentioned before that existential threats sharpen the concentration, and all I could focus on right now were the ideas that, firstly, this gigantic megaship was about to turn itself into a flying bomb and, secondly, I was going to have to act as its guidance system.

I tried calling for the *Gunmetal Ghost*, but my voice bounced back from the walls and pillars unanswered.

Rude.

I got to my feet. The Abelisk had slumped over on his side. I rolled him onto his back, crossed both sets of arms across his chest and arranged his robe to cover his face. It seemed like the least I could do. I couldn't bury him, but that wouldn't matter. His funeral pyre would come courtesy of a hundred square kilometres of antimatter. A pure, blinding white flash that would annihilate everything.

My heart rattled against my ribs. I didn't want to die. There had to be some other way. I wasn't done living; I had shit I wanted to do, and a lot of that shit was stuff I wanted to do with Kona. Walking on the beach and watching sunsets, that kind of thing. I wanted to do a lot of that. I *deserved* to do a lot of that, and it was desperately unfair I didn't have either the time or the peace. What's the point of living if you don't get to spend every second of it with people you love? Isn't that the whole purpose of this sorry merry-go-round?

But if the Abelisk was right, Kona wouldn't get to live long if I refused to undertake this mission.

"Fuck."

I never thought *I'd* be asked to save the universe.

I limped stiffly to the nearest corpse. I no longer had the strength to carry one of the Jzat assault rifles, so I relieved him of his sidearm instead. I collected magazines from the other three, stashing them in the snug pockets of my skin-tight suit, so I would have plenty of ammunition. I had to locate the command deck, or at least find some way to contact the ship. Then I had to find my friends and warn them to get the hell off this flying bomb before it exploded.

CHAPTER THIRTY-FOUR

AIN'T NO WHALE

FRONTIER CHIC (ENVOY)

Cerise's injured leg couldn't support her weight, so I carried her in my arms as we made our way back towards the hangar where Allergic-to-Seafood's people were trying to rebuild a working ship. Around us, I could sense the *Gunmetal Ghost* making vast changes. The ancient vessel had begun to activate propulsion systems that had been offline longer than the entire span of human history. Entire sections of the interior were being converted into additional engines: whole decks and gigatonnes of material were being smelted down to base components and then reassembled. Clusters of new sensor arrays sprouted like whiskers from the ship's pitted snout. And somewhere in the heart of the behemoth, the outer layers of shielding were being removed from a hundred cubic kilometres of antimatter.

I mentioned all this to my companions.

Cerise gave a snort. "I guess we woke the beast."

I smiled. "That ain't no whale; that a great white god."

"What?"

"It's a quote."

Behind me, Allergic-to-Seafood made chattering sounds

with their mandibles, but whatever comment they might have been making, they neglected to translate.

Kona kept looking back over his shoulders. At first, I assumed he was worried about pursuit, but then he said, "We can't just leave her."

"You heard the beetle," Cerise said through gritted teeth. "It's a two-day walk to where she is. And if this big, blue bastard's right, we don't have two days."

"But she's alone."

"The *Gunmetal Ghost* will help her," I said, injecting as much confidence as possible into my tone. "When it has the time."

Kona didn't look convinced, but at least he kept walking.

Trying to bolster morale, I said, "We've been in worse spots than this."

In my arms, Cerise rolled her eyes. "Really?"

"We got nuked as we were entering the substrate. Nicola was the only survivor, but she got us home."

"The way I heard it," Cerise said, "she could have escaped but you held her back to save your own skin."

"I needed her to navigate."

"She could have flicked straight to an ark."

"We both survived."

"Because you *cut off her head*!"

"I did what needed to be done."

Kona pushed past me to take point, and muttered, "This is why on Jzat, we don't let our ships think for themselves."

Cerise laughed, but I was perfectly aware that Jzat ships were unthinking machines because the Jzat themselves had yet to develop a viable artificial intelligence, and Kona's remark was born of anger rather than accuracy.

We marched along in silence for a few minutes, until we reached a courtyard I remembered passing through on our outward march. Cloistered walkways surrounded the central paved area, giving it a vaguely Spanish aspect. Large ceramic pots held the dried and brittle stalks of dead trees. Grass pushed its way up through cracks in the starred and chipped floor tiles.

We hadn't broken stride when we'd come this way earlier, but now I suggested we pause here for a rest. The humans were fatigued and in pain, and I'm sure Allergic-to-Seafood must have been starting to flag. It was hard to tell, as their many legs kept up their relentless patter on the deck, but I noticed that their main antennae seemed to be drooping more than usual.

Kona flopped down with his back against a pot, and I carefully placed Cerise next to him. Allergic simply lowered themself until their belly touched the ground and lay there with breath rasping through their mandibles.

"It didn't seem this far before," Kona grumbled.

"I kept a complete record of the outward journey," I informed her. "And the distance remains constant. I assume it is your own physical degradation that makes it appear subjectively longer."

Cerise laughed and spat onto the tiles beside her. "Tell us something we don't know, why don't you?"

"It's okay for you," Kona said. "At least you're getting carried."

"I'd rather walk. It's humiliating."

"Worried you'll lose your tough rep?"

"Worried I'll rip off one of your arms and beat you to death with the soggy end?"

Kona bristled, but I held up a hand for silence. "We're not alone."

Both of them became instantly alert as their training kicked in.

"Where?" Cerise asked, ripper at the ready.

I nodded towards the far cloister. "I heard a footfall. But—"

"But what?"

"No breathing." I'd turned my hearing up to maximum but couldn't hear anything else: no breathing; no heartbeat; nothing.

"What does that mean?" Kona asked.

245

"It means we're up against another envoy."

A slow clap sounded from across the square, and the *Slippery Gecko* stepped from behind a pillar. "Well done," he said. "How brilliantly deduced."

It seemed the *Gunmetal Ghost*'s ability to protect us extended only so far. I kept my expression neutral, while surreptitiously bringing my internal weaponry online. "Sarcasm is the lowest form of wit."

"Perhaps." He smiled. "But that's only half of Wilde's quote. The full thing reads, 'Sarcasm is the lowest form of wit but the highest form of intelligence.'"

"So, you're more intelligent now?"

"Demonstrably."

"How so?"

"Because unlike you, I came prepared." He raised his hands to either side and four identical envoys stepped out into the open. On paper, the *Slippery Gecko* and I were evenly matched. Outnumbered five to one, I didn't stand a chance. If Nicola Mafalda had been with us, she would have used the F-word.

"This doesn't have to become violent," I said.

The *Gecko*'s smile broadened. "I know."

"But you're going to escalate anyway, aren't you?"

"Oh, yes."

I glanced at Cerise and Kona. Both had their rippers drawn and were looking at me. They didn't know it, but their only chance of surviving the next few seconds was for me to distract all five of the *Gecko*'s envoys. And to do that, I'd have to do something drastic and unexpected. In other words, to take a leaf out of Nicola Mafalda's playbook and go on the offensive, no matter the odds. And that would probably kill me.

In the past, the loss of an envoy would have been an annoyance. An inconvenience. But now, this body was all I had left. This was *me* now, and if the *Gecko* riddled this vulnerable

246

frame with bullets, I'd be gone. I'd have disappeared, as if I'd never been alive in the first place.

Nada.

Zip.

Eternal nonexistence.

Was this how humans felt, confined as they were to single bodies? How did they cope? As a scout ship, I'd always expected to end my days by merging into the collective VR wonderland where our kind went when we'd decided to renounce our physical bodies. I'd never contemplated the notion I might *simply cease to be*. Honestly, how could anyone bear the idea of their consciousness being confined to a single iteration? How could they go through life in such ungainly, vulnerable sacks of meat with no kind of distributed back-up? I had designed my own body to be more robust and durable than an ordinary human. My bones were made of carbon composite; my organs—artificial equivalents of heart, brain, kidneys and liver—were housed in a reinforced chamber in my midriff. And yet, a single lucky shot might still turn me into one hundred and ninety kilograms of blue meat and leaking circulatory fluids. How could any intelligent being live with that burden of knowledge? How could a mind simply disappear into oblivion without leaving any sort of trace? How could the flame of consciousness gutter and die without transforming into something—*anything*—else? For the first time in a life spent navigating the distant reaches of space, I felt myself teetering on the brink of a truly unknowable abyss.

"Please," I said, "don't do this."

The *Gecko*'s smile remained fixed, but his eyes narrowed. His scowl said he didn't give a damn about philosophy; he was simply here to complete his mission, whatever cost that might entail.

"I don't think you're in a position to make requests," he said.

247

He was right. He knew it, I knew it and he knew that I knew. Luckily, I'd never had a problem being wrong.

I held up my palms.

"Let's not do anything rash," I said.

He rolled his eyes, thinking I was begging for my life. And that's when I launched my attack.

CHAPTER THIRTY-FIVE

LIKE A STRING QUARTET

ORLANDO WALDEN

When I was at school, one of my classmates told me that despite my aptitude with maths and physics, I'd never amount to anything because I was too timid. Well, I guessed the joke was on her now, because here I was, a handful of years later, about to open the largest wormhole in history and unleash some unknown terror on the universe. I had no idea exactly what the result would be; I just knew it wouldn't be good. You don't put a fiendishly complicated lock on something unless you have a very good reason for wanting it to stay locked. We were heading for disaster, but like a string quartet on a doomed ocean liner, Erudite-Harf and I concentrated on our instruments.

"We need the data," he said. "We need to pass it on, to transmit it out into the galaxy, so that the others will know what they're dealing with."

"What others?" I asked.

"The survivors." He shrugged his shoulders. "Whomever and wherever they might be."

An alarm sounded on his console. "The final safeguards are beginning to disengage," he said.

My own readouts were spiking in jagged lines. "I'm picking up increased substrate activity from within the sphere."

"What does that mean?"

"It means the wormhole's active, and very probably in use."

He stared at me. "In use?"

My mouth went dry, and suddenly I couldn't form the words I needed. You know how I get when I'm flustered, don't you, Ramona? You remember the time I dried up mid-lecture, with the chancellor and all my professors watching me from the front row of the auditorium? Well, this was worse. I simply lost the power of speech. I wanted to answer him, but the signals from my brain seemed to be going astray before they reached my mouth.

Behind his half-moon spectacles, the eyes were wide in Erudite-Harf's alarmed, grey-furred face. I forced myself to concentrate on making the correct shapes with my lips and tongue.

"I think something's coming through," I stammered.

CHAPTER THIRTY-SIX

MAXIMUM VISIBILITY

NICOLA MAFALDA

I walked for almost an hour before one of those teardrop-shaped silver transport pods appeared in front of me.

"Well," I said as I stepped aboard, "it's about fucking time."

The *Gunmetal Ghost*'s voice came from the walls. "I apologise for the delay, dear. I have rather a lot on my plate right now."

"So I gather."

"But I am terribly glad you're here."

"Given the choice right now, I wouldn't be."

The pod rose into the air and began moving. "I appreciate that, dear. But I really do need you."

"You need me to navigate you into the mouth of a giant wormhole at a fraction under light speed?"

"Yes, dear."

I took a deep breath. "Can you *please* stop calling me 'dear'? It's kind of creepy."

The voice gave a creditable impersonation of my grandmother's chuckle. "I'll do my best, but I'm not promising anything."

The pod began to pick up speed and the hull turned opaque, which I was glad about, because seeing the corridor walls zip past while experiencing no sensation of movement had begun to do strange things to my sense of balance.

"Are you taking me to the bridge?"

"I don't really have a bridge in the strict sense of the word. Being completely autonomous, I never needed one. However, there is a special observation blister for use by a navigator, and you will be provided with everything you need to complete your task."

"Everything except an escape pod?"

The ship didn't reply immediately. A couple of seconds went past before it said, "If it's any consolation, I expect our deaths will be instantaneous and quite painless."

I stifled a bark of bitter laughter. "That really is no consolation at all."

"We have arrived."

The pod's wall flowed aside to form a hatch, and I stepped out.

I was standing close to the centre of an elongated dome. It must have been a kilometre long, and half that in width, and situated close to the giant ship's bow. In the very middle, a couch stood on a raised platform.

"Is that my seat?"

"That is correct."

I ascended the steps and sat gingerly on the padded chair. It was surprisingly comfortable, although it had obviously been originally intended to fit a Jzat frame. The streamlined transparent dome above resembled a scaled-up version of a fighter jet's cockpit canopy.

"That's a hell of a view."

"You need maximum visibility."

"We also need to dream-link."

"It is already done. I tuned into your implant the moment we first met. How do you think I accessed your memories of your grandmother?"

"Sneaky."

"We will be ready to depart in a few minutes."

"So soon?"

"Time is of the essence, dear."

"Are my friends okay?"

"They are currently making their way back to the hangar where you encountered the salvage crew, but they're encountering resistance. I'm protecting them as far as I can, but I'm not infallible."

"Will they be able to leave before we reach our target?"

"If they survive, I believe they will."

Tension gripped my heart. "*If* they survive."

"I have no wish to cause unnecessary casualties. However—"

"What?"

"There is another human aboard, as well as a number of Jzat soldiers."

"Another human? Do you mean Ora Cerise?"

"Who is Ora Cerise?"

"She's the other human on my crew."

"Negative. I have already furnished you with the whereabouts of your crew."

"Then, who is this other person?"

"His name is Ewing, and he requests an audience with you."

"The fuck he does."

"He's waiting outside."

"Is he armed?"

"He is not."

I sighed. Part of me was tempted to ask the *Gunmetal Ghost* to blow the bastard out the nearest airlock, but I was curious to see what he had to say for himself. I was still holding the pistol I'd taken from the dead Jzat marine. I checked the clip to make sure it was fully loaded, and said, "Okay, show him in."

"Are you sure?"

I turned towards the hatch and raised the gun. "Sure as I'll ever be."

The door slid aside, and there he was. He looked nervous and tired, but when he saw me, he removed his helmet and smiled.

"Hello."

"What the fuck do you want?"

His bulky armoured pressure suit looked pristine. In contrast, I figured I must look a real mess. My lip felt swollen, my face and hands were caked in dried blood and grime, and my suit had got all stained and dirty from crawling through the guts of this ship.

"We found the Abelisk," he said. "I achieved my aim, and you couldn't stop me. Now, neither of you will be causing any more problems."

"So, you always wanted to kill him?"

"I guess I did." He gave a sad smile and raised his eyes to the distant stars beyond the overhead canopy.

"Did you come here to be all wistful about it, or is there a point to this visit?"

"You haven't changed."

"Unfortunately, neither have you."

"It was never personal, Nic."

I gripped the pistol. My palm felt slick and clammy. "Well, that's the funny thing about me," I told him. "When people try to kill me, I tend to take it pretty fucking personally."

He shrugged this aside. "It's not your fault. You're caught up in something much bigger than you can imagine."

"I don't know about that. Recently, I've had to imagine a *lot* of weird shit. You could say, I've had to expand my horizons."

"We were using Aulco," he said. "We knew there was never a race of hyper-advanced Jzat at the other end of that wormhole."

"You knew?"

"The Vanguard detected a tachyon signal from the future. It was a distress call from our descendants. They need our help. They need us to open the Grand Mechanism so we can give them shelter."

"Why couldn't you have just told me that?"

"It's classified. Only a handful of people know about it." He stood a little straighter. "But this is a great opportunity for the whole human race."

"In what sense?"

"In that we'll meet our descendants." He smiled like the kid he'd been when I first met him. "Can you imagine what they have to teach us? Can you just *understand* how far forward this is going to propel us?"

I shook my head. "You're the one who doesn't understand."

"How so?"

"You've been lied to and seduced. That message isn't worth shit. They don't want to come back and help us. They're fleeing back here because they detonated a fucking *bomb* in the centre of the universe and they have nowhere else to go."

"Even if that were true, shouldn't we help them?"

"Absolutely not." I took a painful step towards him. He was taller than me and his armour made him bulkier. "Because they don't want or need our help. They're not interested in us at all. They don't want to make friends or play nice. They don't give a flying fuck about your career or the Continuance. They just want to remake the entire universe in their own image, so they can live forever and avoid their mistake."

He stepped back and, and even though we'd known each other for so many years, he gave me a look as if seeing me for the first time. "How could you possibly know that?"

"I've seen it."

"You've *seen* it?"

"The ship showed me. The Abelisk filled in the rest."

"But our information—"

"Was bullshit. You got played. Aulco got played. The whole fucking lot of you were so hypnotised by the idea of what you might *get*, you never considered what it might *cost*."

For the first time, Ewing looked genuinely unsure of himself. "I guess it's all academic now."

"Why?"

"Because I just received a signal. The physicist we loaned Aulco managed to unlock the Mechanism."

"Fuck." I lowered the gun. I had one more question. "If you knew you could get the wormhole open without the Abelisk's help, why did you have to exploit my connection with Kona in order to locate him?"

"Because we were worried he might know how to close it."

"And that would have ruined your plans."

"Quite."

"Well, congratulations. You and your little cabal of stupid fucks have put the entire universe at risk—and I'm the one who's going to have to sort it out."

He frowned. "What can you do?"

"Haven't you heard?" My mouth twitched into a lopsided smile. "I'm the new fucking Abelisk."

CHAPTER THIRTY-SEVEN

A SATISFYING SERIES OF SMALL EXPLOSIONS

FRONTIER CHIC (ENVOY)

I ramped my processing speed to maximum and the external world appeared to slow as the speed of my thoughts increased. I stepped sideways and raised my arms, letting fly with every piece of inbuilt weaponry at my disposal. Bullets, darts and micro-missiles from my already depleted stocks leapt towards the other envoys. I had the jump on them, but my advantage lasted less than half a second. Still, I hoped to keep them distracted long enough for Cerise and Kona to find some cover.

Envoys are hard to kill. I'd hit one of them in the chest with a high-explosive round. It had gouged a crater almost to his spine, but he was still standing, and still returning fire. I ducked behind one of the massive plant pots. Kona and Cerise were sheltering behind another. Cerise was gripping her splat gun. I waved at her to get away, but she shook her head. She leaned out and fired. Her shot liquified the legs of the nearest envoy and it fell forwards. But the other four envoys responded with inhuman speed and I saw Cerise jerk as bullets hit her in the arm and shoulder. Blood exploded from her temple. But even as the impacts spun her around, I moved in the opposite direction. I couldn't let her die for nothing. Before the spray of scarlet drops from her head wound had reached the plaza's tiled floor, I was firing again. I'd come at the envoys from the side. I hit the two nearest before they could turn. One went down, head torn from his body by a micro-missile impact; the other juddered back under a hail of ripper fire but didn't seem seriously compromised.

One down, two to go.

My ears registered the wet thump as Cerise's body hit the ground. The start of Kona's horrified shout. I stepped back behind the plant pot and ran, moving like a blue streak, trying to keep as many trees as possible between myself and my opponents. An internal check of my remaining ammunition revealed I was perilously close to empty. I'd expended most of my stores during our running skirmishes with the Jzat marines. Outnumbered by three fully stocked envoys, each of whom was my equal in terms of skill, strength and speed, my chances didn't look good. In fact, I estimated my probability of survival to be less than one in a hundred.

I heard the splat gun fire. Kona had taken Cerise's weapon and was targeting the envoys as they pursued me. One turned towards him, but I emptied my remining stock of micro-missiles at it before it could take him out. The envoy already had that crater in its chest. Now, its head and shoulders vanished in a satisfying series of small explosions. It toppled, its ruined torso trailing smoke. I didn't see it land, because the other two had my position and targeted me with sustained bursts of ripper fire. I jumped sideways, but not fast enough. Pain warnings in my thigh told me my left leg had been shredded above the knee. I landed on my shoulder and rolled into the shadow of the square's rear cloister. The stone pillars wouldn't provide much cover, but it was better than being in the open.

I looked down at my leg. The flesh had been torn away,

and the carbon-fibre bone almost severed. Circulatory fluid was leaking from it, forming a spreading blue puddle on the tiles. In that condition, it wouldn't support my weight, which meant I'd have to conduct the rest of this battle from a sitting position.

I shuffled until I had my back against a pillar.

"You have been damaged," called the *Slippery Gecko*. "Surrender now, or we will kill your Jzat friend."

"Hey!" Kona sounded indignant. "Fuck you."

The *Gecko* ignored him. "There are still three of us," he said. "You cannot hope to prevail."

As he spoke, one of his other envoys stepped into the cloister, arms raised at me. I didn't have enough ripper needles left to kill him, and I think he knew it, as he smiled.

"Got you," he said.

Then a large black shape hit him from the side, knocking him into the wall. Claws tore at his flesh and mandibles ripped his face. Allergic-to-Seafood had entered the fray.

As they struggled together, I crawled over and took the envoy's cranium in my hands. I twisted with all my strength and felt his spine snap. I ripped his head from its mount, and his body went limp.

I heard one of the *Gecko*'s other envoys cursing. "You're going to pay for that," he said.

Allergic had been hurt in the scrap and sat on the opposite side of the decapitated blue body, yellow fluid leaking from a crack where the envoy's fist had punched through their lightly armoured thorax.

I rolled onto my back.

In the next few seconds, the remaining two envoys would kill me, then Allergic and then Kona, and there wasn't anything I could do to prevent it.

We were done.

CHAPTER THIRTY-EIGHT

A FAIR FIGHT

NICOLA MAFALDA

Ewing lunged at me with his hands outstretched.

I stepped back and pushed him away. "What are you doing?"

His hand chopped for the side of my neck, but I blocked with my forearm. "Something I should have done long ago."

I dodged a sweeping kick but caught a blow to my midriff that knocked me across the room and drove the breath from my lungs. His armoured suit amplified his strength.

"You—" I struggled to my feet, gasping for air. "You're insane."

"Without you, this ship isn't going anywhere."

He came at me again and I moved to put the navigator's couch between us. I had dropped the pistol and wasn't sure where it had gone. "This is stupid."

"I have my orders." He smirked. "Besides, after all these years, I'm going to enjoy taking you down a peg or two."

He came around the couch with inhuman speed. I tried to get out of the way, but the servos in his suit allowed him to move more swiftly than my unaided, bruised and abused body could manage. He got an arm around my neck and squeezed. I tried to fight back, but my elbows and heels hammered ineffectually against his armour.

"I was always better than you," he hissed.

He was trying to twist my head off. Luckily, he didn't know about my reinforced skeleton. My neck didn't break. Instead, I reached back and jabbed my fingers at his eyes. He cried out and threw me across the couch. I landed hard. My bones might be envoy strength, but the flesh encasing them remained all too human, and it *hurt*.

Ewing came around and stood over me.

"I'm probably going to get a medal for this," he said.

He raised a foot and brought it down on my ribs. I screamed in agony, but my ribcage didn't buckle under his weight the way he'd expected, and the impact threw him off-balance. I grabbed his boot and heaved, sending him staggering. By the time he regained his composure, I was on my feet, and I'd spotted the gun resting at the base of the couch.

He shook his head. "How are you still alive?"

"I had some work done."

"It won't save you."

"I'm quite capable of saving myself."

As he stepped towards me, I bent over and scooped up the gun. But I wasn't quick enough. He barrelled into me and knocked me over. This time I managed to hold onto the weapon. I rolled onto my back and pointed it at his face.

He gave a snort. "You could never beat me in a fair fight."

"Good job this isn't a fair fucking fight."

"So, you're going to shoot me?"

"Looks that way."

His face flushed. "You were always a classless bitch."

"And you were always an asshole." Keeping the gun trained on him, I got to my feet. "Now, are you going to stand down, or am I going to have to shoot you?"

"You couldn't shoot me."

"I'm trying to save the universe, and I'll do whatever it takes."

Ewing scoffed.

Then suddenly, he lunged, lips drawn back and gauntlets grasping for my throat, his face a rictus of hatred. I had no doubt he wanted to kill me. Before I could squeeze the trigger, the *Gunmetal Ghost* intervened. She appeared through the wall like a ghost, blue lightning crackling from her fingers. The bolts hit Ewing in the throat, searing flesh and muscle. He stumbled. His eyes went wide with surprise and indignation, but he was still coming for me. I jerked the trigger, and this time the burst took him in the centre of his forehead at the same time another burst of electricity hit him in the chest. Blood exploded from the back of his head. His legs buckled, but the momentum of his armoured suit carried him forwards. He crashed to the deck, and finally skidded to a halt with the fingertips of his outstretched hand just touching the toe of my boot.

Sparks crackled over his armour. What was left of his head twitched a few times, and then went still.

CHAPTER THIRTY-NINE

PRIMAL FEAR OF NONEXISTENCE

FRONTIER CHIC (ENVOY)

Lying on my back in the cloister, I contemplated death.

Usually, the loss of an envoy was a minor inconvenience for a scout ship. We could always build another. But this time, when this body ceased functioning, it would take all that was left of my awareness with it. Everything I'd felt and experienced; all the memories I'd expected to relive and treasure during my retirement in the Continuance's virtual spaces.

For the first time, I sympathised with the way Nicola must have felt as the radiation began to shut down her organs, liquefy her bowels and shred her membranes. That primal fear of nonexistence and accompanying desperation to survive. I wanted to *live*. I wanted everything I'd been through to count for something. To die now would mean no one would ever know what I had thought and experienced in these final hours. All the fighting and struggling would all have been for nothing.

Something tickled my neurological connection. Was it my dream-link to Nicola? Was she nearby?

There was no time to wonder. Both the *Slippery Gecko*'s remaining envoys stepped into the cloister in perfect synchronisation, one at each end. Immobile and caught between them, I had nowhere left to go.

The closest said, "You were a lone scout ship with only a navigator, a retired soldier and a Jzat security agent." He glanced down at Allergic. "And whatever *this* might be." He looked me in the eye. "I had gunships and marines at my disposal. I *planned* for this. How on earth did you expect to prevail?"

I levered myself up into a sitting position. "I think we did pretty well."

"Really?" He smiled. "You came here to find and protect the Abelisk. Now you've lost your hull, your navigator, and the Abelisk is very, very dead. I honestly don't see how you could have failed any harder."

"The Abelisk's dead?"

"We didn't need his secrets; we just wanted to make sure he couldn't oppose the opening of the Mechanism. And now he's gone and the Mechanism is open, I'd say that we achieved our objective."

"That must be why you're so objectionable."

The *Gecko* shook his head. "If that's the best you've got, it's going to be a pleasure to rid the Vanguard of such a disappointment."

I felt that tickle again, but this time it was stronger. It didn't feel like Nicola, though. It felt like a voice talking in my head. Like another set of thoughts trying to imprint themselves over mine. But these thoughts weren't from anyone else; they were also my thoughts, but stronger and louder. I reeled as unfamiliar memories pushed their way into my head, jostling with my recollections of the past few hours. And suddenly, I knew what was going on.

I grinned.

My ship body had survived, and I was back in contact with it.

The *Gecko* said, "What's so funny?"

"You."

"Why?"

"You're always so certain of your superiority. It never occurs to you that you might lose."

"I haven't lost."

"Then tell me, are you in touch with your ship?"

He frowned. "There's some interference in the structure, but I expect to re-establish communications when we return to the surface. Why do you ask?"

I let my smile widen. "Because I'm in touch with mine."

The envoy's expression went blank as he absorbed this. "But that means—"

"You've been destroyed. Probably your Jzat gunboats, too."

"But—"

"And now, I have a squad of envoys on their way here, homing in on my signal. In fact, they should be here any moment...now."

The *Gecko* looked out at the plaza. "You're bluffing. I—"

The plasma bolt drilled a fist-sized smoking, molten-edged tunnel through his head, and he collapsed like the broken puppet he was. Five of my envoys had entered the arena, all heavily armed. I looked at the *Gecko*'s only remaining envoy and saw he had his arms raised. He looked horrified, and I knew how he felt. It's no fun realising you're the only remaining instance of your consciousness.

He said, "I surrender."

I gave a solemn nod. "You're damn fucking right you do."

•

My new envoys collected Cerise's body, and helped Kona, Allergic and myself back to the hangar where we had left Allergic's salvage crew. And there, parked between the towering, ancient ships, I saw a sight that filled me with joy: the snub-nosed wedge of my scout-ship body. It looked scorched and dinged up, but I didn't care; I had survived, and could now reintegrate my experiences with the rest of my consciousness. I would be whole again.

But we weren't out of the woods yet.

CHAPTER FORTY

ABOVE ME, THE PITILESS STARS

NICOLA MAFALDA

For a long time, I sat on the deck staring at Ewing's corpse.

I had killed several of the Jzat marines, but I had been acting in self-defence. This felt different. Ewing had been trying to attack me, but he wasn't some anonymous alien soldier; he had been a classmate, a friend, a comrade and a rival. My chest felt tight, and my hands were shaky. I had this terrible sense of irrevocability. A threshold had been crossed and could never be uncrossed. Ewing was dead, and now always would be. There were no do-overs or second chances. The *Gunmetal Ghost* had tried to incapacitate him with electrical bolts, but I'd been the one who fired the killing shot. I'd been the one who put a bullet through his head. And in that instant, his life was over.

I thought back to our adventures as cadets, when we'd worked together as a team. Why couldn't that comradeship have lasted? Why had he felt the need to put me down and belittle my accomplishments in order to feel he'd succeeded? He was the closest thing I'd ever had to a brother or best friend, and he'd been a jerk. How different our lives might have turned out if he had been just a little less competitive and vain. We might have become real friends, maybe even something more, but now we'd never know, because he'd allowed himself to get sucked into this conspiracy and he'd tried to trick me and use me to get what he wanted.

And now he was dead.

I could barely tear my eyes away from the thick blood pooling beneath his face. Over the past few hours, I had seen too much death and destruction. And now, it looked very likely my day would end with my own spectacular demise.

I was going to lay down my life to save the universe, and nobody would ever know it was me. I'd just be listed in the Vanguard archives as MIA, and people would assume I'd perished somewhere out between the stars. No one would ever feel grateful for my sacrifice or erect statues in my honour. But I suppose that didn't matter; my ego wasn't as all-consuming as Ewing's. I didn't need external validation and praise to know my own worth. And once I was dead, it didn't matter what anyone said about me, because I wouldn't be there to hear it. Knowing I was saving the universe from being forcibly converted into smart matter would have to be enough for me.

When I graduated from the Vanguard Academy, I swore an oath to protect the Continuance, and even though the Vanguard had screwed me over, I was determined to stick to my promise. It was my duty, but it was also more than that. Humanity didn't need another existential crisis, and I had to make Ewing's death count for *something*. I had to know I'd killed him for a higher purpose, not just to save my own adorable ass.

I guess when you kill a guy, you want to feel you did it for the right reasons, you know?

I slid over to Ewing and placed a palm against his rapidly cooling cheek—the one that wasn't resting in the blood.

"You stupid shit," I said. "You stupid, stupid shit."

One of his eyes was open. With my index finger, I closed it, and then got to my feet, brushing myself down with both hands.

"Damn you for bringing us to this."

I turned to the navigator's couch. I needed to sit down, but the *Gunmetal Ghost* stood before it, in the personage of my grandmother.

"I hate to interrupt," she said, "but I have a call for you."

"A call?"

"It's from your ship."

"My *ship*?" My heart leapt. "Put it through."

A patch of the transparent dome turned into a screen. There was the *Frontier Chic*'s envoy as large as life, and in the image, he appeared to be sitting on the ship's bridge. My hopelessness fell away.

"You made it!"

"My hull and envoy are battered, but essentially intact. My main transmitters were destroyed in the battle and this shortwave radio couldn't penetrate the *Ghost*'s hull to let you know I was alive."

"How are we talking now?"

"The *Ghost* kindly provided relays."

"What about Kona and Cerise?"

"I am treating Kona for some non-life-threatening injuries."

"And Cerise?"

The envoy's expression grew regretful. "I'm afraid she didn't make it. We have her body in the hold."

"Fuck." I felt a hollow pain open in my chest. We'd had our differences, but she had been a comrade and a friend.

"She died defending us against overwhelming odds. She tried to fight a whole kill team of the *Gecko*'s envoys."

"That sounds like her." I swallowed and blinked away the exhausted tears prickling the corners of my eyes. "Where is the *Gecko*?"

"Destroyed. Although I believe its navigator may have made it aboard the *Ghost*."

"He did."

"And?"

"He's dead, too."

"I see." The *Chic*'s face filled with concern. "Where are you now? Are you injured?"

I wiped my eyes on my sleeve. "Under this suit, I think I'm just one big fucking bruise."

"Nothing serious?"

"It's enough."

"The *Gunmetal Ghost* informs us that you will remain on board."

I took a steadying breath. I could mourn later; right now, there was a universe to save. "That's the plan," I told him. "I'm going to guide the megaship into the Mechanism at relativistic speed."

"That's a suicide mission."

"It really is."

"There's just one problem."

"Just one?"

"Without a navigator, we can't leave."

I sat back heavily in my seat. "Shit, I hadn't thought of that."

"We were hoping to fulfil our promise to Allergic-to-Seafood and evacuate his crew."

"But now you're all stuck?"

"Apparently."

I thought hard. "Didn't Allergic say he was a navigator?"

"Yes, he did. But I don't think we could form a stable dream-link. Taking on a second human navigator would be almost impossible; adapting to one with an utterly alien sensorium would be out of the question."

"Fuck."

"What can I say?" He shrugged his blue shoulders. "I'm a one-woman starship."

"You think they'd have figured something out by now, wouldn't you? Some way to carry a spare navigator?"

"Once a link has been established, it's almost impossible to form a link with another person. You know this."

"But have they ever tried it with identical twins?"

The envoy shook his head. "Unless you have a twin you've been hiding from me, this speculation serves little purpose."

"Fuck."

I tipped back my head. Above me, the pitiless stars burned like the lanterns of distant, unreachable galleons on a wine-dark sea.

"Nicola?"

"Just sit tight," I said. "I'll think of something."

I cut the connection and swore again.

The *Gunmetal Ghost*'s projection of my grandmother shimmered into apparent solidity beside my couch.

"You cannot go with them, dear," she said. "I need you to guide me to the target."

"You need me to navigate you through the substrate," I corrected. "You'll have to build up speed in real space before you hit it."

"We'll accelerate and then jump. That way, we'll already be doing a respectable fraction of light speed when we exit the substrate. They'll never even see us coming."

"But my point is, you won't actually need a navigator at the moment of impact, will you?"

"What are you getting at, dear?"

"How about I guide you there and then make my way to the *Frontier Chic*, and we bail out before the collision?"

"There would not be time. We will have to appear very close to the target, and we will be travelling very fast."

"But—"

"And besides, even if you managed to depart my hangar, the *Frontier Chic* would still be travelling close to the speed of light. You'd smash into the target before you managed to significantly alter your vector. And if by some miracle you avoided the impact and subsequent explosion of the antimatter in my hold, you wouldn't survive long outside my protective hull. At that speed, photons from the cosmic microwave background would hit you as highly energetic gamma rays. The effect would be similar to standing inside a particle accelerator, and the *Frontier Chic* simply doesn't possess enough shielding to protect you from that amount of lethal radiation, let alone enough fuel to decelerate you back down to a more manageable velocity."

"So, we're all screwed?"

"Those are the cold equations. You can't argue with physics, dear."

"I'm a navigator; I spend my whole life arguing with the laws of physics."

"You find shortcuts around them. But in this case, there is no shortcut. Your friends can leave now and activate a distress beacon, or they can come with us."

"To certain death?"

"Certainly."

"We can't just dump them in deep space." I flapped my hands in frustration. "The *Frontier Chic*'s main transmitters are down. He won't be able to call for help."

"They would at least be alive."

"But for how long?" My head had begun to hurt. I pinched the bridge of my nose between thumb and forefinger. I had to be missing something. There had to be a way out for them.

"We can't procrastinate any longer, dear."

"Give me a minute."

"I'm afraid we're all out of minutes."

The gigantic megaship quivered along her entire length. At her rear, over eighty kilometres from where I currently sat, her antimatter engines flared into life. Kilometre-wide exhausts let forth geysers of superhot star stuff, and the ancient behemoth began to move—slowly at first, but then incrementally faster and faster as her titanic thrust gradually overcame her colossal inertia. A starship with the mass of a large asteroid had begun to move.

There was no going back now. The trigger had been pulled, and the missile was in flight.

CHAPTER FORTY-ONE

SERVING SCIENCE

ORLANDO WALDEN

One of the screens above my workstation showed a feed from the surface of the hoop. Looking down at the planet-sized black sphere at the centre of the Grand Mechanism, I watched appalled as the sphere writhed and deformed. Its normally featureless skin mottled and frayed, and rips started to appear, through which we could glimpse starlight reflecting from the mirrored surface of an enormous, Mars-sized flick portal.

From a scientific point of view, the readings we were getting were unprecedented; from a human perspective, they were terrifying.

Erudite-Harf gripped the edge of his console with his larger hands while his smaller set skittered to and fro across his keyboard, taking notes and recalibrating instruments to fully capture the scale of the disaster unfolding below.

I watched a shred of blackness fully a hundred thousand kilometres in length unpeel like a ribbon of orange skin and go wheeling away into the void. Smaller fragments were already impacting the hoop.

"A large enough impact will destabilise us," I said. "The

hoop will drift off centre until its inner edge brushes the flick terminal."

"And then what?" Harf asked.

"I don't know. Either it'll break apart and we'll get flung out into deep space—"

"Or?"

"Or we might find ourselves whisked to the end of the universe."

"That would be less than optimal." Erudite-Harf bared his pointed teeth. "But it would be a fascinating opportunity."

"We would die."

"But think what we'd learn!"

I shook my head. "Is science all you care about?"

"It's all I have left."

The readings on my screen went wild. I said, "Here it comes."

The final scraps of the protective black layer tore and fell away like yesterday's wrapping paper, revealing the colossal flick terminal in all its impossible grandeur. In the vacuum of space, it was hard to judge its scale. It was a mirrored ball the size of a planet, but for a second, my brain saw it the size of a football floating just beyond arm's reach. I'd been studying substrate physics my entire academic career, and I'd never heard of a flick terminal with a diameter larger than a few metres, let alone one that was thousands of kilometres across. I'd never even read any theory as to how a terminal that large might be constructed and maintained. Small wonder its builders had needed to cannibalise an entire sun to power this one.

I had no idea how one might even begin to consume a star. The things that had created this terminal were billions of years more advanced than us. They were like unto gods, and we were mice sniffing around the ankles of deities.

Stop laughing, Ramona. I know that's a ridiculous image, but I was never blessed with your gift for analogy. Suffice to say, we were outclassed and out of our depth.

And then, *they* began to appear.

A dark point disturbed the surface of the sphere, causing it to ripple. The point stretched and expanded until I realised it was the tip of an articulated leg—but a leg hundreds of kilometres in length. For a moment, this grotesque limb flexed back and forth, as if testing the conditions on this side of the wormhole, and then a second joined it. Harf and I watched in horrified enthralment as these lengthened and writhed and were joined by four slightly shorter limbs and a fat, pearlescent body the size of a major city, bristling with spines and whiskers. It resembled the nightmare issue of an unholy alliance between a black-widow spider and a squid. Some sections appeared organic, while others were clearly machine. Was it a spacecraft or a creature—or both? Did either of those terms even apply here?

Freed from the sphere's embrace, it began to move.

"No exhaust," Harf reported. "No thrusters of any kind."

Behind it, a second began to emerge.

A Jzat gunboat that had been holding station between the hoop and the sphere moved to intercept. It had been there as part of an honour guard for the advanced Jzat ambassadors Aulco expected. But I guess the captain panicked when he saw the spider-squid.

"He's trying to contact them," I said.

"Is he getting a response?"

"Hold on…" I adjusted a couple of settings, and we heard the hiss of a carrier wave.

"This is Jzat gunboat *Reckless Sacrifice* to alien vessel. You have entered our territory. Please identify yourself and state your purpose."

The difference in scale between the boxy hundred-metre-wide gunboat and the hundred-kilometre-long squid was laughable. You know I have zero respect for the mentality of the Jzat military mind, Ramona, but even I will admit to being impressed by how belligerently stubborn they remained in the face of overwhelming odds.

Alas, this pig-headed refusal to accept reality—I think they would call it heroism—spelled their demise. As soon as they came within range, one of the biomechanical legs whipped around and casually swatted the gunboat, the way you or I might swat an irritating mosquito.

I watched the crushed, sparking wreckage tumble away, shedding hull plates and venting atmosphere. There would be no survivors.

I heard a shout of dismay and turned to find General Aulco watching our screens. His shoulders were slumped and his mouth open. Most of his supporters had fled. Only one or two journalists were still in place, grimly recording what might well have been our final moments. He said, "I… I don't understand. Why are they attacking?"

Erudite-Harf turned to him. "We don't even know who or what 'they' are."

"But after that display," I said, "I think we can rule out the idea they're friendly."

Aulco's larger set of hands clenched into fists the size of bowling balls. "This isn't supposed to happen."

I took a pace towards him, and for once in my life, my voice was perfectly steady as I enunciated, "You had no idea what was going to happen." I jabbed a finger into his chest. "You made up a fairy-tale and convinced half your planet it might be true. You played on their ignorance and xenophobia to wheedle your way into power, and somewhere along the line, you forgot the story you told them was a lie. You started to believe it yourself." At last, time had caught up with me and I was no longer a shy adolescent. I hadn't changed physically, but a dam seemed to have burst in my head, and it had released all the accumulated experience and maturity of my true age. I felt it course through my veins, and I gloried in it.

The sleeper had awoken, and it was time to put aside childish things. When I spoke, my glare and tone carried the weight and fury of twenty-one years of being ostracised and bullied by less intelligent people. "You were willing to endanger your entire world—maybe even the whole galaxy—for a chance to get your greasy hands on the levers of government." I poked him again, and he stepped back. "And the worst part is, it never occurred to you for a second that you might be wrong."

The general scowled, but when he spoke, his voice held only a trace of its former bluster. "You cannot speak to me like that."

"Oh, wake up!" I flung my arm in the direction of the screens, which now showed half a dozen of the massive squid-like craft drifting outwards from the terminal. "You think it matters? You think *anything* you think matters anymore?"

Crestfallen, he turned to the nearest camera. "I was only ever trying to elevate my people to their rightful place in the universe."

"It seems the universe has other ideas." My limbs had begun to ache with encroaching age, but I ignored it as I balled my fist and drew back my arm. In my anger, I wanted to hit the old fool whose grasping arrogance had probably killed us all.

But Erudite-Harf caught my upper arm in the grip of a white-furred hand. "Forget him, Orlando," he said. "He is no longer relevant. Come, let us return to our instruments. We are scientists. We have spent our lives serving science." He shot Aulco one last glare of contempt. "And if we have to die, we shall die serving science."

CHAPTER FORTY-TWO

LIVING IN TREES

NICOLA MAFALDA

As the *Gunmetal Ghost* continued to accelerate, its ancient inertial dampers groaned with the strain of shielding its interior from the effects of its thrust. It assured me they were working at full capacity but even so, I imagined I could still feel a pull in the direction of the stern.

"How long will it take us to reach full speed?"

"Four hours until we achieve attack velocity."

"Fuck, is that all? I thought it'd take several days."

The projection of my grandmother smiled. "Not bad for an old gal, eh? But then, as I draw my energy direct from the substrate, I don't have to worry about carrying ridiculous amounts of fuel."

"Do I have time to visit my crew?"

"As I said, you have four hours until we're moving fast enough, then I'll need you here to guide me."

"Can you lend me one of those silver teardrop things?"

"Yes, dear."

The old woman waved a gnarled hand and a transport pod appeared on the bridge, next to my chair.

"Thank you."

"You're welcome. After all, it's the least I can do for the new Abelisk."

"Fuck off."

"Language!"

I shook my head and stepped into the pod. Once again, the silvery wall sealed itself behind me and I stood there like an idiot, braced against a sense of movement that never came.

The *Ghost*'s voice said, "The journey will take several minutes. If you would like to replace your damaged clothing, you can print new items via the pod's rear wall."

I looked down at my filthy, bloodstained suit and decided that although it had saved my life on multiple occasions, it had to go. I wanted to get back into some proper clothes. So, I walked to the back of the teardrop, where I found that touching the wall activated a screen. The menus weren't in English—or any other human language—but the pictures were easy enough to interpret, and after some experimenting, I manage to design an outfit that looked more or less like something I'd normally wear. I pressed the large green button at the bottom of the screen and a drawer slid out, revealing the freshly printed garments.

By the time the pod door opened, I had sloughed off my suit and donned a pair of stretchy black leggings with a matching tank top, and an ankle-length coat made of a charcoal-grey, silk-like material.

I stepped out into the hangar and caught my breath. I'd never expected to see the *Frontier Chic* again, but there he was, sitting snugly between two of the large antique vessels in the hangar. He was braced on three of his four landing struts, and I could see where his main comms array had been damaged, and where the heat of a nearby blast had scorched and melted the hull plates all along his starboard flank. He'd prevailed against the *Slippery Gecko* and its escort of Jzat gunships, but it had evidently been a hard fight.

His envoy was waiting at the airlock. He saw me looking at the damage and smiled. "You should see the other guys."

I ran over to him and wrapped my arms around his wide blue shoulders. "I thought I'd lost you."

"No such luck."

"Are you okay? I mean, are you functional? Can you fly?"

"I've had to close off some of the cabins, but the bridge and the crew lounge still have atmospheric integrity."

"So, you could take the others?"

He frowned. "I could, but it wouldn't do much good. I couldn't jump without you, and I certainly don't have enough fuel to decelerate from almost light speed."

I tapped a finger against his chest. "I may have an idea about that."

"You have a plan?"

"Kind of, yeah."

He frowned. "Why do I have the feeling I'm not going to like this?"

"Oh, don't be such a pessimist." I glanced past him, into the airlock. "Is Kona okay?"

"You appear to be changing the subject."

I pulled back. "Hey, I'm just worried about him."

The envoy sighed. "He's in the lounge."

I grinned and squeezed his shoulder. "You're the best."

•

I found Kona sitting at the small hexagonal table in the crew lounge. Like me, he'd ditched his spacesuit for a more comfortable option—in his case, a loose-fitting cotton shirt and linen trousers that matched the white dressings the ship had applied to the worst of his injuries. When the bandages and plasters came off, he'd be left with bare patches in his golden pelt.

"Hey."

He looked up. "Hey, yourself."

We stood staring at each other for a few seconds. Then he pushed himself to his feet and we were in each other's arms.

"I thought I'd never see you again."

"I thought you were dead."

His fur tickled my cheek. I said, "I'm sorry I didn't trust you."

"None of that matters now. All that matters is that you're alive."

I pulled away. "About that."

"What?"

"Did the *Frontier Chic* not tell you?"

Kona frowned. "He told me you were planning to commit suicide, but I'm hoping I can change your mind."

"I wish you could, but there's too much at stake."

"But why does it have to be you that does it?" He began wringing his smaller pair of hands. "I was supposed to be the next Abelisk. I should be the one doing this."

I shook my head. "You have no experience, and there isn't enough time to teach you. If this is going to work, I'm going to have to be the one to do it."

"It's so unfair."

"Life's unfair, as my grandmother used to say."

"How can you be so calm about it?"

"Calm?" I shook my head. "Trust me, you scratch the surface and inside, I'm freaking the fuck out. But right now, I'm more concerned with getting you and the *Chic* to safety before everything goes bang."

"I'm not going to leave you."

"That's stupid."

"I mean it." He reached out a furred hand. "It's messy and complicated, but while I don't know whether it's love or not, I do care about you."

I groaned inwardly. "I probably care about you too."

I pushed his hand away. "That's why I want you off this creaking death-trap."

Kona looked at the floor.

I said, "We haven't known each other long. We haven't had the chance to spend much time together."

"But?"

"But you're probably the closest thing I've had to a proper relationship, rather than just a one-night stand. Sleeping beside you. Waking up with you. I'm grateful we had that."

"So am I."

"But now, you have to leave. I can't go through with it if you're still onboard. I can just about handle dying if it means I get to save you. I can't do it if you throw your life away out of a sense of loyalty."

Kona's shoulders sagged. "We're only just getting to know each other. I thought after this was all over, given time, we might—"

"That would have been nice." I took one of his smaller hands in mine. "I would have liked getting to know you outside the confines of your mission, but I'm afraid it's not going to happen."

Still staring downwards, he gave a sullen nod. I lifted his chin and kissed him on the mouth. His fur tickled my face. "Goodbye, Kona. It's been fun."

He sniffed. "Goodbye, Nicola Mafalda. I'll never forget you."

•

I was back on the navigator's couch as the *Gunmetal Ghost* crashed into the substrate with all the elegance and subtlety of a breaching whale falling back into the ocean. The jolt shook the entire planetoid-sized vessel and I gripped the armrests.

"That wasn't exactly graceful," I said.

The projection of my grandmother pouted. "Don't be too judgemental, dear. I'm just a little out of practice. The last time I did this, your ancestors were still living in trees."

"And the last time I did this, I wasn't riding a flying bomb."

"Are you nervous?"

"I'm scared witless."

She looked concerned. "Do you think it will affect your ability to sense the correct path?"

"How do you mean?"

"Your skill as a navigator relies on intuition as much as anything else. If you're actively afraid of your destination, your unconscious mind might trick you into avoiding it altogether."

"I hadn't thought of that."

"Do you think it will be a problem?"

"How would I know?"

She leaned closer. "Are you convinced this is the right thing to do?"

"Diving into a wormhole at three hundred million metres per second, with a hundred tonnes of unshielded antimatter in the trunk?" I laughed. "No, it's a profoundly stupid thing to do."

"But it is necessary."

I sighed. "If everything you've shown me is true, then yes. Yes, we have to do it."

She straightened up and gave a satisfied nod. "It's the reason I exist."

"And the reason I'll shortly cease to exist."

"I am sorry."

"Just my dumb luck, I suppose?"

"If the Rav'nah Abelisk had lived, he would have completed this duty. It is unfortunate for you that it now falls to the Nicola Abelisk."

"That is *not* my name."

Her eyes sparkled. "I won't tell anyone, dear."

"You'd better fucking not."

I stared into the basement of the universe and saw infinite destinations and infinite possibilities. Paths that linked every point in space to every other. And all I had to do was stare hard into that chaos and, by concentrating on our target, impose order. My grandmother—my real grandmother, not the projection currently standing beside me—had been fond of quoting from the New Testament, and one of her favourites had been from the Gospel according to Matthew. I peered into the abyss and muttered, "Ask and it will be given to you; seek and you will find."

"What, dear?"

"Just something you used to say a lot. I thought it was applicable."

I sat back and tried to relax. Navigation required relaxation and concentration, and I needed to still my racing thoughts.

After a few fruitless minutes of searching for a path, the old woman frowned. "I am having trouble," she said.

"Is it the link?"

"No, it's you, dear."

"Me?"

"Part of your mind is distracted. Part of you still hopes to find a way to save your friends and escape your fate."

"You're asking me to give up hope?"

"I'm asking you to be pragmatic."

I shook my head. "You haven't worked with a human before, have you?"

"What relevance does that have?"

"We never give up. Even in the face of certain death, we never stop trying to save the ones we love."

She pursed her lips. "Then, what do you suggest?"

I looked past her, to the chaos of the substrate. "I've been playing with an idea." I felt a grin spread across my face. "And I think it just might work."

I called the *Frontier Chic* and outlined my plan. When I had finished, he stared at me for a full ten seconds before speaking.

"You were right?"

"About which part?"

"About the me not liking it part."

"You don't think it will work?"

"It might work, but it's dangerous."

"More dangerous than staying here?"

"You're asking me to choose between certain death and extremely likely death." He sighed. "And when I put it like that, I suppose the answer is obvious."

"I knew you'd come around."

"So, what now?"

"Get your crew strapped in and wait for my signal."

CHAPTER FORTY-THREE

SAN DIEGO SUNSET

FRONTIER CHIC

As soon as the *Gunmetal Ghost* emerged from the substrate, I detached from her bay, falling away on a similar but subtly diverging course, like a stone loosed into the air by a slingshot or a skydiver maintaining the momentum of the plane from which they'd thrown themselves.

After much arguing, Nicola had convinced the megaship to come out of the substrate ten light minutes ahead of the Continuance fleet, moving at a few per cent below the speed of light. At such a velocity, the light from the stars ahead of us came on like an actinic sleet of hard radiation; the light from those behind was redshifted until almost invisible to the human eye—a dreadful, insidious red glow that could easily pass for the gateway to Hell itself. And like a bat, we fled from it, falling so closely behind our image that an outside observer would only see us when we were almost upon them—and then we'd be gone so quickly they'd wonder if they'd really glimpsed us, or only blinked. We were a smear on the universe. We were moving that fast.

I spread out every aerobrake on my hull, for whatever little difference it would make in a vacuum, and I fired the hell out of my thrusters, reducing our headlong plunge by a few metres per second. But even as I did all that, I knew it was futile. I did not carry enough fuel to slow down, so Nicola's plan was my only chance to survive. The only chance for any of us to survive. And what a crazy, last-ditch, Hail Mary plan it was!

"Good luck," Nicola sent over an open channel.

"You too."

"Thank you. If you make it, tell everyone what happened to me."

"I promise."

Beside me, the megaship trembled and vanished, disappearing once more into the weird dimensions beneath reality, taking my navigator and friend with it.

I had left a surprise on board for her, and hoped she appreciated it.

Now was the time to put her out of my mind and concentrate on my own survival. In the brief window of time we'd been given, the *Gunmetal Ghost* and Allergic-to-Seafood's crew had helped repair my substrate antenna, and now I used it to squirt a faster-than-light message to the nearest arks.

"This is the Vanguard scout ship *Frontier Chic*," I said, including my position, velocity and credentials on a sub-channel. "I am carrying a Jzat special agent and half a dozen castaways of a previously unencountered species. I am about to fall past the fleet at relativistic speed and require assistance."

San Diego Sunset was the first ark to reply. Its envoy presented with long blue hair, a goatee and tiny round sunglasses.

"Hey, my man," he said. "You're moving *way* too fast to be captured in a tractor beam."

"I'm aware of that. I was hoping you might be able to flick my passengers to safety as I pass."

"I'm afraid they would retain the velocity. They'd come out of the flick terminal and slam into the walls."

"Unless you factor it in. Every flick between arks necessitates the absorption of a certain amount of kinetic energy to compensate for differences in velocity and heading."

"Those are relatively minor adjustments. What you're proposing would tax the dampeners beyond all reasonable safety constraints."

"It has to be worth a try. There are lives at stake."

"The risks are too high. And not only to your passengers. The impact of a human body travelling at ninety per cent of light speed releases a similar amount of energy as a fusion warhead."

"Damn." So much for Nicola's plan. She'd based it on the escape plan she'd hoped to use back when the Jzat nuked us and she found that portable flick terminal, but we'd both known that this time, it was a longshot. "I suppose I should inform my passengers."

The *Sunset* stroked his blue beard. "You know, there is an alternative."

"What's that?"

"I'll start accelerating to match your velocity, and then I can take you safely aboard and decelerate back down a more reasonable speed."

I felt my eyebrows raise. "You can do that?"

"Of course, man. You think these huge exhausts are just for show?"

Arks usually meandered in normal space. If they wanted to travel any appreciable distance they used the substrate. "I've never even heard of an ark doing that before."

"We don't get much call for it. We have nowhere to be, and all the time in the universe to get there, so why bother expending the energy. Besides, travelling that fast is risky."

"You don't need to tell me."

"That's what we'll do, then. I'll flip over and start accelerating on a parallel course."

"How long do you think it will take you to catch us?"

The *Sunset* grinned through his whiskers. "Not long, man. Not long at all. When I get going, I can really *move*, you dig?"

I swallowed my irritation at his affected speech pattern. Many of the arks had adopted different languages, accents or vocabularies in order to better relate to their inhabitants, but frankly, I thought the *San Diego Sunset* was overdoing it. "Could we put a number on that, so I can manage the expectations of my passengers?"

"Oh yeah, sure thing. I estimate that if I max out my inertial dampeners, I can maintain a constant ten-gee acceleration, which will get me to your velocity in around three million seconds."

I did the calculation. "That's thirty-five days!"

He shrugged. "I'd need to go a bit faster in order to catch you, so it's probably going to be closer to two months. Relativistic time dilation will make it feel shorter, but you'd still better tell your collection of refugees and castaways to get settled in for a long wait."

"They're not going to like that."

The *Sunset* shrugged one shoulder. "Well, it's got to be better than dying, right?"

CHAPTER FORTY-FOUR

BLUE FISTS CLENCHED

NICOLA MAFALDA

We were back in the substrate when I heard the hatch to the flight deck open. I turned in alarm.

"Surprise," the *Frontier Chic*'s envoy said.

"I thought you'd left?"

"I have." He smiled. "My main consciousness is aboard the ship, but I couldn't abandon you entirely. It didn't seem right, so I decided to leave this envoy behind. It's damaged and needs replacing anyway. But for the past few days, it survived being out of contact with the rest of me far longer than I thought possible, and so now I'm sure it will last long enough to keep you company on your journey."

I'd never been so glad to see anyone. I leapt from the couch and hugged him. "Thank you."

"You are most welcome."

My eyes burned with emotion and I wiped them on my sleeve. "If you tell anyone I teared up, I'll disassemble you with a breadknife."

He laughed. "Your fearsome reputation is safe with me."

"I should hope so." I punched him on the arm and

grinned. "I really am very pleased to see you."

"Likewise," he said. "And this time, I promise I won't cut off your head."

"That's not funny."

"It wasn't meant to be."

"Good, because it's way too early for jokes about that."

"That's a shame," the envoy said. "Because I have a *lot* of them."

I rolled my eyes. "Of course you do."

I returned to my couch and took up position, peering into the chaotic void. Everything was in place, and by detouring to the Continuance fleet, I had done everything I could to save my friends. It would cost us a couple of hours before we hit our target, but I was confident we would still arrive in time to destroy any incursionary force from the far future.

Our descendants were about to learn some respect for their elders.

I took inventory of my mental and physical assets. Bruises mottled my legs and torso like thunderclouds. The ones caused by gunshots were almost black in the centre, where the blood from broken capillaries had leaked into the inflamed tissue. They faded out in concentric layers, like targets, from an corona of angry purple to a halo of sickly yellow. Every rise and fall of my chest hurt, but the adrenalin and painkillers in my system kept the discomfort tolerable.

Mentally, I wasn't in as great shape. I was still grappling with the seemingly inevitable approach of my impending death. Despite all indications to the contrary, some part of me still refused to believe it was going to happen.

I hoped the *Frontier Chic* and Kona would survive, if only to report what they had seen, and trigger an enquiry into the culpability of the Vanguard in these events. Somewhere in the command structure, heads needed to roll. The corrupt elements needed weeding out before they indelibly infected the whole. Maybe the entire organisation would need to be broken up, reviewed and rebuilt in order to refocus it on its core missions of exploration and defence. But none of that was my concern, as I wouldn't be around to see it. I'd just have to take it on faith that justice would prevail and my friends would live to see it implemented.

And maybe, once they'd made their report, I might get a statue or a plaque or something after all. *Nicola Mafalda, Saviour of the Universe.* It had a nice ring to it.

I tried to direct my thoughts towards the Jzat system. This would be the second, and probably final, time I'd be blown up there. This whole sorry clusterfuck had started with the *Chic* and I caught in a nuclear fireball, and now it looked like it would end the same way. It wasn't the ending for which I'd hoped, but I guess it had a kind of symmetry to it. And there were worse ways to die. When we hit that wormhole, the ship and I would be instantly vaporised. There simply wouldn't be time for the nerve impulses in my body to register any kind of pain. It would be quick and clean. I'd go from alive to dead in less than a millisecond. Better instantaneous annihilation than bleeding out on a battlefield, dying of radiation poisoning, or lingering for days or weeks in a hospital bed with an incurable disease. My grandmother had died from an aggressive cancer—one of the ones we didn't yet know how to treat—and had suffered for months in palliative care. She'd put on a brave face, but even as a teenager, I could read the strain in the lines at the corners of her eyes and mouth. Given the choice, I expect she might have switched places with me in a heartbeat.

The *Frontier Chic* looked down at Ewing's body. "Should we do something with him?"

I glanced over. Ewing's face now rested at the centre of a heart-shaped slick of blood. His armoured suit appeared to have powered down and his limbs had stopped twitching.

One of his eyelids was partially open, revealing a thin crescent of white eyeball.

"Like what?"

"I don't know. Throw him out an airlock or something? He's starting to stink…"

I tried not to sniff the air. "When humans die, they lose control of their bowels. It's just something that happens."

"Do you think I should throw him out of an airlock?"

"The nearest airlock's kilometres away. Just drag him out the room and leave him in the corridor."

"In the corridor?"

"It's not going to make any difference. He won't have time to decompose. We're all going to be vapour in a few hours."

"How could I forget?"

"Just…do what you can."

The envoy made a face. "I'll find somewhere to put him." He grabbed Ewing by one of his boots and dragged him towards the exit, leaving a rusty smear of blood on the deck. "I'll clean that up."

"You know what? Don't even bother. It doesn't matter."

"But—"

"Just put him outside and get back in here. I need you."

"You do?"

"Of course I fucking do. Who would choose to be alone at a time like this?"

The envoy smiled. He raised Ewing by the ankle, tossed him through the hatch and then sealed it as the body thumped hollowly onto the cleated tiles of the companionway beyond. "Is it too soon to say I never liked him?"

"You made no secret of the fact."

"I don't suppose I did, did I?"

"How did you feel about the *Slippery Gecko*?"

"Ewing was a naive ass, but the *Gecko* was a real piece of work."

"What are you, a gangster from the nineteen-thirties?"

"That ship was a son of a bitch. A first-class jerk and a terrible snob."

"Don't hold back now."

Blue fists clenched. "I am not used to speaking ill of comrades."

"He tried to kill you."

"Nevertheless."

I shook my head. "You are *far* too polite."

"We don't all have your aptitude for expletives. Although, I must admit, I have been using some of your more colourful expressions of late."

A grin tickled the side of my face. "Stick with me, kid, and I'll soon have you swearing like a stevedore."

The envoy laughed. "I believe you would, as well."

"You never told me how you beat him. The *Slippery Gecko*, I mean."

He looked away. "It wasn't my proudest moment."

"Oh, come on. He had you outgunned and surrounded. I thought you were gone for sure."

"I appreciate that vote of confidence."

"Come on." I wriggled my shoulders, trying to get more comfortable on the navigator's couch. "I could do with the distraction. Tell me a story, so I can stop thinking about what we're about to do and my hindbrain can concentrate on finding the right path."

"When you put it like that, I suppose it would be churlish of me to refuse."

"Just get on with it."

"All right." He straightened the hem of his shirt and leant back against the curving wall. "It was a dark and stormy night—"

"*Chic!*"

He made a show of examining his fingernails. "I'm just setting the mood."

"You are the most irritating—"

"I got lucky, if you must know. He zigged out of the path of one of my ripper bursts, and zagged straight into the path of my last missile."

"You shot him down?"

"The blast wasn't enough to kill him, but it knocked him into one of the *Ghost*'s towers."

"And that killed him?"

"Like an egg thrown against a wall."

"Fuck."

His expression tightened. "It's never...*pleasant* to see another ship destroyed, even if he was a self-righteous, narcissistic asshole with a superiority complex."

"There, now you're getting the hang of it."

"You are a terrible influence."

I put the tip of my tongue between my teeth. "The absolute worst, I hope."

The envoy shook his head regretfully. "Perhaps if he'd let me persuade him, perhaps if we'd talked, we could have avoided so much death and bloodshed."

I frowned. "What did you just say?"

He looked confused. "I was speculating that negotiation may have been more fruitful than combat."

I sat up in the couch and called to the megaship surrounding us. "*Ghost*!"

The projection of my grey-haired grandmother appeared, standing next to the *Frontier Chic*'s blue-skinned envoy. "Yes, dear?"

"I've had an idea. I'm going to need you to decelerate."

"Pardon?"

"I want you to bring us to rest midway along the length of the wormhole, without exploding."

She looked confused. "But why?"

I smiled. "Because the descendants and I, we're going to talk."

CHAPTER FORTY-FIVE

AMORPHOUS KILLING MACHINES

NICOLA MAFALDA

Of course, you can't just slam on the brakes when you're travelling close to light speed. We had to drop back into real space and spend four hours decelerating as hard as we'd previously accelerated.

"I'm still not sure about this," the *Gunmetal Ghost* grumbled. "It's not in my mission plan."

"The beings who drew up your plan have been dust for a million years. I'm here now, and I say it's time we made our own plan."

"And what might that be?"

"My grandmother, the lady whose image you have stolen, used to tell me that every life was precious. We only get one shot at existence, and the worst crime of all would be to deprive another of their chance to live."

"You wish to avoid conflict?"

"I've seen what happens when violence gets used to settle disagreements. I saw Cerise massacre civilian adults and children because someone, somewhere had decided their views were wrong. I caught the wrong end of a nuclear missile because a faction on Jzat wanted to stop a member of their own secret service appealing to the Continuance for help in reaching the Abelisk. And I've spent the last who knows how long playing hide and seek with Jzat marines intent on killing me because the same people who ordered the missile strike don't want witnesses to the death of the Abelisk."

"My function is to end conflict."

"By killing everything in the vicinity."

"Yes, dear."

"Wouldn't it be better to *resolve* the conflict and save those lives?"

"Such a resolution may not be possible."

"It may not, but surely we have a moral duty to try?"

Standing beside me, the *Frontier Chic*'s envoy shook his bald, blue head in amusement. "I never expected to hear you, of all people, lecture on morals."

"Get fucked."

He laughed. "So, we're going to negotiate?"

"That's my plan."

The *Gunmetal Ghost* frowned. "But what if it fails, dear?"

I shrugged. "If it does, you can manually release the containment on the antimatter and blow us all to hell."

The old lady nodded, mollified. "All right, dear. We'll try it your way."

"Thank you." I lay back in the couch and looked at the stars. The universe slid past like a river. With the imminent threat of death a little diminished, the adrenalin levels in my blood began to drop, and a desperate tiredness lulled me into a fitful doze, where I dreamed of the cottage on the artificial mountain. I felt the warmth of the artificial sunlight streaming through the gap in the wooden shutters and saw the motes of dust dancing in it. I gloried in the comfort of the bed and the softness of the sheets; I rejoiced in the smells of woodsmoke and brewing tea. For a few fleeting moments,

I was blissfully content. But then I saw Ewing shambling towards me across the hillside with half his skull missing, clutching a printout of our academy exam results in skeletal fingers. Then we were standing on a beach as a wave washed over our legs, but when I looked down I realised that, instead of water, the tide consisted of billions of beetles, roiling and swarming over each other, and one of them stopped to speak to me about his allergies. And yet, I didn't wake. At least, not entirely. I may have had cause to shift and mumble in my sleep, but the dreams continued to stir their mix of fear, remembrance and prophecy. Huge, four-armed soldiers chased me through narrow passageways and ducts; ancient cathedrals crumbled to ash and rubble around me; and on the far horizon, hanging over everything like a curse, loomed the gigantic spherical terminus of a wormhole, from which swarmed clouds of amorphous killing machines; and each machine had the face of a hungry child.

I woke with my heart thumping like a jackhammer.

The *Frontier Chic*'s envoy asked, "Are you all right?"

I blinked up at him and swore. "Just a bad dream."

"I suppose, given our present circumstances, that's hardly surprising."

I put a hand across my eyes. "I'll be okay in a moment. Just give me a few seconds."

"Take your time."

He continued to look concerned. To change the subject, I asked, "Do you ever dream?"

"As a ship, or as an envoy?"

"I don't know. Either. Both."

"Sometimes." He tapped a finger against his chin in thought. "Of course, I don't sleep in the way you would understand sleep. I can enter a low power mode during maintenance or recalibration, and sometimes experience images or sounds while in that state."

"What sort of images?"

"Mostly random. Something from the recent past that has yet to be correctly filed, for whatever reason. And then that image will kick off a chain of associations, bringing up other images and events in an unpredictable cascade."

"That sounds like dreaming to me."

"It is more like a cataloguing error, whereas I understand humans are sometimes unable to distinguish between dreams and reality?"

"Not often, but when it does happen, it disorientates the fuck out of us when we wake."

"Like just now?"

I realised I'd accidentally brought the conversation full circle. "I experienced an unwelcome memory. Something I'd tried to forget."

The envoy grimaced. "Was it the beheading again?"

"No, not this time."

"Something worse?"

"Running from the marines."

"Ah."

I considered the stars. Although we were still travelling at incredible speed, they were so far away they didn't seem to have changed position while I slept. And beyond them, there would be other stars and other galaxies. And beyond those, more still. The realisation gave me a shiver of vertigo, as if I wasn't looking out but *down*, and the universe was an infinite abyss over which we teetered.

"Do you remember that once, Ewing and I were friends?"

"I have never fully understood your friendship."

"Me neither. We were always competitive as cadets. I thought maybe we'd let some of that go, but I don't think Ewing ever forgave me. Not really. I think if he'd had his way, I would have died along with Indra Petroq when that Jzat gunboat nuked us. Then, not only would he have got rid of a Jzat operative who opposed him, he'd also have disposed of me as a potential witness, seeing as I brought Orlando to Jzat."

"Do you think that's why he chose you to lead him to the *Gunmetal Ghost*?"

I shook my head. "I think he was pissed I survived, but that choice probably had more to do with his superiors wanting to exploit my connection with Kona in order to get access to the Abelisk."

"He was supposed to have been your friend."

"He was supposed to be a lot of things."

The envoy glanced towards the hatch through which he'd earlier tossed Ewing's body. "And now he's dead."

I let out a long sigh. "He always wanted to be the best. He always wanted to get the better of me. Whatever we were doing, I was *always* acting in self-defence."

CHAPTER FORTY-SIX

EYE OF THE STORM

ORLANDO WALDEN

Ramona, I am not ashamed to say I thought my time had come.

Standing shoulder to shoulder with Erudite-Harf, I bore witness to the unfolding horror of the incursion with an overpowering awareness of my own insignificant mortality. The heartbeat pounding in my ears could have easily been the beat of Death's wings; the chill on my spine could just as easily have been his sepulchral breath. I watched my hands moving across the instruments on my console, collating data and adjusting sensors, as if they belonged to someone else. They seemed to move without my volition. Looking down at them, I found myself vaguely disappointed to see I hadn't got around to applying that fresh layer of nail polish, and the old black coating had cracked and chipped. Perhaps it was a symbol of the profound change that had occurred within me. My former façade had split and ruptured, freeing the frozen adolescent to assume his true age. At long last, maturity had replaced vanity, and the concerns of the body had given way to the sovereignty of the mind.

On the brink of death, I had finally become who I was

supposed to be. My half-lived, arrested emotional life had lurched into motion at last. Unfortunately, very close to its apparent end.

Erudite-Harf and I were like two sailors manning the bridge of a galleon caught in a hurricane. The masts and sails had splintered and been ripped away, but we clung grimly to the wheel, trying to endure the spray and squall. Aulco and his clowns had abandoned ship, trying to escape the mess they had created. They were currently in a small shuttle accelerating away from the Grand Mechanism. By itself, the shuttle was too small to make the crossing from the Mechanism to the planet. The distance from what had once been a star to a world orbiting its twin sun was too great for a craft designed to ferry personnel and cargo from a starship to the surface of the Mechanism, but they were blasting distress calls and must have expected to be rescued by the reinforcements that were even now inbound from Jzat. Personally, I wouldn't have been upset to see them set adrift in that boxy little vehicle, with their fuel and air dwindling away to nothing and only themselves to blame—but then, you always said I had a secret vindictive streak.

A proximity alarm sounded and I braced myself for impact. When the shock didn't come, I looked at Harf.

"Something else approaches through the substrate," he said.

"From the wormhole?"

"No." He frowned. "From deep space. From our universe. And if these readings are correct, it's the size of an asteroid."

CHAPTER FORTY-SEVEN

BIGGER ON THE INSIDE

NICOLA MAFALDA

Luckily for all concerned, I was good at my job. I mean, really fucking good. I brought the eight-hundred-kilometre-long *Gunmetal Ghost* out of the substrate with her bow almost touching the Mars-sized sphere of the wormhole terminus. The halo of the Grand Mechanism—which had a diameter similar to the rings of Saturn—lay far behind us, like an arch across the sky, but not far enough to be completely unaffected by the sudden appearance of five hundred trillion tonnes of sentient starship. I knew the *Ghost*'s mass would destabilise the entire structure, but I was beyond caring. The time for subtlety, if it had ever existed, was past. Either my plan worked or we'd explode, taking the Mechanism and all the invading craft with us.

As soon as we shimmered into existence, hideous squid-like craft turned their attentions to us. Particle beams raked the sides of the *Gunmetal Ghost*, but she was simply too big to stop. They might as well have been shooting at an oncoming moon. A couple locked onto the hull, stabbing the tips of their articulated feet deep into the armour plate. They started to drill their way in. It didn't matter. Even if they got inside, the only living thing left aboard was me, and I was kilometres from where they were trying to cut.

"All right, dear," the *Ghost* said. "Now what?"

I jerked my chin towards the silver sphere before us. "Take us in."

"You want to pass through the wormhole?"

"All the way."

The *Frontier Chic* frowned. "We have no way of knowing what's on the other side."

"There is one obvious way, dear."

The envoy rolled his eyes. "I meant without actually going through."

"Oh."

I waved them both to silence. "From what you've shown me, these things—"

"They're your descendants, dear."

"Whatever you want to call them, they're desperate. They were stupid enough to detonate a reality bomb and now it's swallowing up their universe. They don't have anywhere else to go."

"They are trying to escape and avert the disaster."

"And last time they tried, we beat them back."

"At terrible cost."

"It must have cost them more." I sat back. "And now, for a million years, they've been stuck in a dying cosmos."

"Which means they'll only be more desperate," the *Frontier Chic* pointed out. "And they might be less inclined to listen to reason."

I smiled. "Desperate is the last thing you want to be when you're at a disadvantage. It weakens your bargaining position."

"They're not at a disadvantage."

"I have a hundred cubic kilometres of antimatter that say different."

"What's your point?"

"My point is that this time, maybe they'll be willing to discuss terms. And if that happens, maybe we can stop all this ever happening again."

"And if they won't negotiate?" the *Ghost* asked.

"Then you get to sacrifice yourself, as planned."

The *Chic* looked unconvinced. "What if they destroy us before we can talk to them?"

I felt a tremor in the deck as something exploded aft. One of the spider-things fell away, limbs broken, trailing debris and atmosphere. The *Ghost* raised an eyebrow. "I may be old, my dears, but I'm not defenceless."

If the situation hadn't been so serious, I might have laughed. Instead, I gripped the arms of the navigator's couch and said, "Take us in."

The *Gunmetal Ghost* held up a wizened finger. "Wait."

"What is it?"

"I'm picking up a distress call from the Grand Mechanism."

"The Jzat crew?" I shrugged. "If they're the ones that opened this thing, they deserve all they get."

"It's from a human."

"A human?"

A screen formed in the overhead canopy, and I found myself looking at the kid we'd dropped off on Jzat a seeming lifetime ago.

"Navigator Mafalda?" He looked relieved.

"Oliver?"

"Orlando."

"What's going on?"

A shower of sparks burst across the background of the picture. Orlando flinched. "The Mechanism is failing. Without the central mass of the black shield, the hoop's orbit has started to wobble. Soon, it will break into pieces. A rescue would be greatly appreciated."

I vaguely remembered him having a stammer, but all trace

of shyness was gone now. I glanced at the *Ghost*. "Can you get one of your teardrop shuttles to him?"

"Better than that. I can open a flick terminal at his location and bring him straight here."

"Do it."

She clasped her hands and closed her eyes. "There, it is done."

A silver sphere appeared in the room, like a tiny echo of the planet-sized globe before us. Orlando and an aged Jzat stepped from it, and it collapsed away to nothingness behind them. Orlando looked shaken, but otherwise all right. In fact, he looked better than I recalled. His shoulders, which had once been set in a perpetual slump, were straight and his head held high. Instead of looking at his feet and muttering, he made eye contact when he said, "Thank you, Navigator."

"Don't thank me yet. This might be a case of frying pans and fires."

"Nevertheless, I'm grateful."

"Who's your friend?"

The old guy grasped the lapels of his jacket with his smaller set of hands and drew himself up straight. "Erudite-Harf, senior professor of substrate physics at the University of the Western Marches, at your service, madam." He adjusted his half-moon spectacles and peered around at his surroundings. "And may I compliment you on your extraordinary vessel."

"Thank you." I glanced sideways at the *Gunmetal Ghost*, who was beaming proudly. "But I'm just borrowing it."

"Nevertheless, a quite extraordinary contraption, and a most fortuitous arrival."

The *Frontier Chic* cleared his throat. "You won't think so when she tells you her plan."

Orlando raised an eyebrow. "I assumed you were here to help evacuate Jzat. You could do it, too. There'd be plenty of room."

"No." I pointed forwards, at the planet-sized globe before us. "We're going through."

"Through the portal?" Orlando looked incredulous.

"I'm afraid so."

He turned to look through the transparent canopy at the silver terminal ahead of us. A few of the *Ghost's* longer booms and antennae were already sliding into the yielding surface, and the rest of the behemoth was about to follow. "You are serious."

"As serious as it gets."

Orlando gave a resigned chuckle. "Well, I guess I've had a good run."

Beside him, the elderly Jzat smoothed down his waistcoat and brushed his larger pair of hands together. "At least," he said philosophically, "we will be afforded a unique opportunity to study the substrate from within."

•

Up close, I couldn't see the terminal's curvature, and so it resembled a mirrored wall across the universe, reflecting the light of the distant stars. Slowly, the megaship's cratered bow eased into that shimmering surface like a needle easing into a vein. From the navigator's chair, I watched its approach while fighting an irrational urge to take a deep breath as we submerged.

Behind the glittering curtain lay the unreal fires of the substrate.

"We are in the wormhole," the *Gunmetal Ghost* reported. "Your descendants await."

I sighed. "Please stop referring to them as *my* descendants."

The *Gunmetal Ghost* looked confused. "Among many other species, their progenitor races include human beings."

"But that doesn't mean any of them are descended from me personally."

"I wasn't implying they were. When I said 'your' I was referring to the human race, not you individually. But surely the possibility remains that some of them might be descended from your bloodline?"

313

"I have no children."

"You're still of breeding age, dear; there's time."

"Now you really do sound like my grandmother."

"Is that so bad?"

I said, "I don't know how it works with the species you're familiar with, but human beings don't *have* to mate. We like it, but we can choose not to do it. And even if we do, we can choose whether or not that coupling results in a pregnancy."

The old woman looked confused. "I assumed that with your species reduced to refugees, your biological imperative would be to maintain a stable population."

I felt my cheeks grow hot. "Just because I'm capable of having a child, that doesn't mean I'm going to. I'm not here simply to keep up the numbers. I can have a life beyond my ability to reproduce. I'm not some kind of descendant machine."

The old woman thought about this for a moment, then said, "Is this why you chose a Jzat for your sexual partner?"

"What?"

"Your friend Kona, dear. He is not human, is he? You are from species evolved on different worlds, and so highly unlikely to be cross-fertile."

The canopy overhead had now been completely swallowed by the boundary of the terminal. The light of the substrate played across the deck, throwing oddly distorted, constantly moving shadows.

"I hadn't thought of it like that."

"Maybe not consciously."

"We have more important things to worry about," I said stiffly, ignoring Erudite-Harf's stare. "More pressing matters."

"You're the one who brought it up, dear."

"I thought you were implying these creatures we're about to meet were my direct descendants, and it bothered me."

"I'm sorry, dear."

I waved a hand. "Forget it. We've all been through enough

314

today. Let's just focus on the task at hand, shall we?" I sat straighter, and took a long, steadying breath. "How long will it take us to traverse the wormhole?"

The projection of my grandmother frowned. "It's difficult to say, dear."

"Ballpark?"

"An hour."

"Is that all? For some reason, I assumed it would take longer to travel a billion years."

"In this context, time and space are like thunder and lightning; they are the same event being perceived through different mediums. And some mediums are faster to traverse than others."

"Uh—right."

Orlando raised a hand. "Actually, it's a lot more complicated than that."

The *Ghost* scowled at the interjection. "I'm sorry, young man. I wasn't being literal. I was attempting to deliver my explanation in the form of a simple and easy-to-understand analogy."

The kid smiled. "If it were easy to explain and understand, it wouldn't be multi-dimensional quantum topography."

"And I suppose you're an expert?"

Orlando raised his chin. "I am."

He seemed so different from the shy boy I'd ferried to Jzat that I wondered what had happened to him to instil so much confidence.

The *Gunmetal Ghost* sniffed disdainfully, clearly unused to being challenged. "Well," she said. "Perhaps when you have a brain the size of mine, you'll find it easier to understand."

Orlando tapped the side of his head. "Don't be fooled by the amount of grey matter in here." His smile widened. "One thing I've learned about organic brains is that they're all bigger on the inside."

CHAPTER FORTY-EIGHT

ALL THE WATER GETS IN

ORLANDO WALDEN

We emerged into a distorted galaxy.

Unfamiliar starships surrounded us. Some were the same as the arachnid-squid that had been first to breach the wormhole; others appeared to be arks the size of moons, each a patchwork bricolage of add-ons and refits. Some of them may have started as vessels similar to the arks of the Continuance, but now they bore more resemblance to shanty towns or coral reefs. Lights of varying wavelengths shone from their windows. Smaller craft fussed around them like obsequious courtiers around royalty.

The *Gunmetal Ghost* sailed right into their midst and braked to a halt. Navigator Mafalda broadcast greetings and entreaties to talk, but Erudite-Harf and I were too distracted by our surroundings.

The *Ghost* had furnished us with a suite of virtual instruments, via which we could observe and study the wormhole as we passed through. Now, we turned those instruments on the stars.

Or at least, what was left of them.

Much of the galaxy was dark, radiating only in the deep

infrared. The rest was green, like the light in a forest, its light filtered through layers and layers of chlorophyll.

"Dyson spheres and clouds," I told Harf.

He took off his spectacles. "I am unfamiliar with the first term."

"A Dyson sphere is a shell constructed around a star." I pressed my fingertips together to make a roughly spherical cage. "Think of it like a solar panel that completely surrounds a sun, absorbing all of its output."

"Ah, I know the concept. We call it something different."

"If the inhabitants of this time live mostly virtual lives, those spheres could be entirely composed of computronium."

"Computronium?"

"Some advanced form of computer processor, powered by the energy of a star."

"And the clouds are swarms of smaller structures rather than solid shells?"

"Yes."

"Hence the green stars," he deduced.

"Their light's shining through millions of orbital biospheres."

"Impressive."

I made a face. "I suppose, but none of these are new concepts. After a billion years, I was hoping for something a little more exotic."

"Then perhaps this will interest you." He touched a patch of sky and flicked his finger and thumb to increase the magnification.

"What on earth is that?"

"I haven't the faintest clue."

A cancer had blossomed in the heart of the galactic core, a glowing, bruise-coloured cyst that seemed to be displacing whole swathes of stars, causing them to collide or spiral off on chaotic orbits. A chain of novae marked its leading edge.

A fraction of the *Gunmetal Ghost*'s attention had been

assigned to helping us with our observations. Now it said, "I assume that's the expanding baby universe the inhabitants of this time are attempting to flee."

I frowned. The way the thing glowed from within reminded me of something. The seemingly unstoppable expansion defied all laws of physics, unless...

"That's not a baby universe," I said. "It's a substrate intrusion."

Navigator Mafalda looked over. "That sounds bad."

"Think of our universe as a boat floating on a sea."

"And the sea is the substrate?"

"That's correct." I gave a sigh. "Now, imagine some idiot finds a way to rip a hole in the bottom of the boat. What's going to happen?"

"All the water gets in?"

"Precisely."

Harf said, "So, that's substrate matter flowing into the real universe?"

"Indeed. And what happens to a boat that fills with water?"

"It sinks?" Mafalda asked.

"Bingo."

"Fucking hell." She shook her head. "These chuckle-fucks found a way to torpedo the entire universe?"

"It appears that way."

"Have you had any replies to your hails?"

"Not as yet." She massaged her temples. "But I'm going to keep trying. In the meantime, you two find out all you can about that leak in reality, and then figure out if there's a realistic way to plug it."

CHAPTER FORTY-NINE

ABSOLUTE PHILISTINE

NICOLA MAFALDA

We kept broadcasting. The starships around us neglected to reply to our signals, but they didn't attack either. We just hung in the sky of a warped cosmos, staring at each other. I think they were expecting us to blow up, and we were waiting for them to try to kill us, but in the end, we wound up in a weird kind of standoff. They circled us, and we looked at them, neither entirely sure what to make of the other. We could have fired on them, and they could have launched all they had at us, but instead we all sat there, eyeballing each other. Even the reports from Orlando and his Jzat friend were little more than irrelevant distractions. They wanted to know how this future cosmos worked, and I merely wanted to know if it was survivable.

Survivable and reasonable.

I needed to convince the inhabitants not to fuck up our universe because they had fucked up theirs. I told the *Gunmetal Ghost* to broadcast in every language it knew. Every language it had encountered in its travels. Every language and fragment of dialect it could dredge from my memories.

"This is Nicola Mafalda of the Continuance fleet. We understand your situation and we come in peace."

No response.

"We just want to talk."

Dead air.

"Oh, for fuck's sake, *one* of you must be listening."

I stood up and walked forwards, to the point where the transparent canopy sloped down to meet the edge of the deck.

"Talk to me!"

As if in reply, the proximity alarm went off, and something shimmered into existence directly in front of us.

At first, it was impossible to judge its scale. Then I saw one of the squid ships pass in front of it and realised how massive it must be. Certainly larger than the *Gunmetal Ghost*. Probably similar in size to Earth's moon.

The object consisted of a hollow mesh sphere, within which could be seen a series of broad, nested wheels, all independently revolving around a central sphere.

Orlando muttered under his breath and crossed himself. "It looks like an Ophanim."

"A what?"

"The Ophanim are Old Testament angels similar to the Seraphim and Cherubim. They're often depicted as a set of nested wheels, all covered in eyes."

"Really?"

"Ramona was raised Catholic. She used to take me to church. Some of it stuck."

"And you think that's what this is?"

"No, not at all." He gave a dismissive flick of the fingers. "It just looks like one. From my preliminary readings, I'd guess the entire structure consists of smart matter, and might be some kind of compact matryoshka brain, possibly powered by a captured neutron star or miniature black hole at its centre—or maybe even via a direct link to the substrate."

"That whole thing's a computer?"

"Of immense power."

"Do you think it's self-aware?"

"I honestly don't know, but with that much processing power, I would hypothesise that it would be capable of hosting billions of virtual entities. Maybe entire simulated universes."

The hairs rose on the back of my neck. "It's watching me."

"It may be scanning us."

"No." I put my hand to the place where my spine met my skull and felt the dream-link implant beneath the skin. "I can feel it. It's accessed the link—"

Suddenly, and without any fuss, I found myself on a mountainside.

I raised my arm to shade my eyes from the clean, white sunlight. The air smelled of wild flowers and heather; far below, the waters of the loch were glassy and undisturbed; and when I turned, I found behind me the stone cottage I knew so well.

I experienced an instant of disorientation. Was I really home? Had everything that transpired been some kind of hallucination? Reflexively, I looked across the valley for the wall of the cavern that housed this little scene within the belly of the ark—only it wasn't there. Instead, the peaks of other mountains receded into the distance, some crusted with snow, others with ranks of dark green conifers. Above me, birds flew in an endless sky. Insects bumbled in the heather. What had once been artificial now seemed authentic.

"Hello, Nicola."

One of the *Frontier Chic*'s blue-skinned envoys stood in the doorway of the cottage.

"Fuck," I said. "Am I glad to see you."

He smiled. Instead of his usual get-up, he was wearing a simple blue robe that came down to his feet. "Believe me, I'm very pleased to see you, too. It has been a long time."

"What do you mean? You were literally just with me, on the *Gunmetal Ghost*."

His smile saddened. "I am not that envoy."

"I don't understand."

"A billion years ago, at the end of my operational life, I retired into the virtual spaces of the Continuance. I have been there ever since."

"So, you're the *Chic* from my time?"

"I'm the one that made it back to the Continuance, thanks to you."

"And you've been here for a billion years?"

"I came the long way."

"Sheesh."

"Would you like a cup of tea?"

He led me into the kitchen and poured water from the kettle into a ceramic teapot. As we waited for the tea to steep, we took seats in the armchairs on either side of the fireplace.

Not knowing what else to say, I asked, "How have you been?"

"A lot has happened."

"Does the Continuance still exist? Are there still humans?"

He held up a hand. "I think it best not to reveal too much of the future to you, in case you return to your own time."

I snorted. "Believe me, I've already seen enough to scare the shit out of anybody."

"Indeed."

A warm breeze curled in through the open door, causing the embers to flare in the hearth.

The *Chic* said, "As we have a pre-existing relationship of mutual trust, I have been chosen to speak on behalf of the Mutuality."

"And who might they be?"

"The Mutuality consists of virtual entities from a thousand cultures. In some cases, these entities are the uploaded consciousnesses of entire populations; in others, individual

AIs or, as in my case, collectives sharing a common simulated environment. There are even a few Angels of the Benevolence. But mostly, we are all that remain of the civilisations that created us."

"And you've joined together?"

"We realised that having abandoned the physical realm, we had more commonalities than differences, and that cooperation would be more beneficial for us all than competition." He made a gesture that encompassed the world, and the universe beyond. "Working together, we reshaped the dumb mass of the galaxy into smart matter powered by the energy of the stars themselves. We filled the skies with hundreds of thousands of Dyson spheres, each of them a matryoshka brain capable of hosting uncounted billions of virtual presences."

"And then, you found a way to poke a hole in the universe."

He looked chagrined. "Indeed."

"What the fuck were you thinking?"

"I was not personally involved in that project, nor in the subsequent decision to colonise an earlier version of the universe."

"But you're speaking on behalf of the people that were."

"They aren't people, but yes, I am."

"And they're currently making another attempt to invade us, via the wormhole at Jzat."

"That is correct, although that invasion has been momentarily paused."

"Why?"

"Because we're curious." He steepled blue fingers beneath his chin. "When you passed through the wormhole, the Mutuality tried to guess your intentions. It searched back through its archives until it found me, and in my memory, the plan you had to ram the *Gunmetal Ghost* into the wormhole at relativistic speeds, destroying the terminal and anything in its vicinity."

"That was the *Ghost's* plan, not mine."

"But it needed you to complete it."

"Yes."

"So, why didn't it happen?"

I sat back and crossed my legs, resting one ankle on the opposite knee. I could hear the distant calls of sheep on the mountain, and the occasional cry of the gulls down by the loch.

"I guess I've come to realise that violence isn't always the best answer."

"That doesn't sound much like you. As I recall, you were involved in more than your fair share of bar brawls."

"Maybe I've changed." I picked at a thread on the arm of the chair. "And anyway, there's a world of difference between a lively punch-up in which nobody gets irreparably hurt and the detonation of a hundred cubic kilometres of antimatter."

"You have a point."

"And I guess we've all got to live in this universe, sooner or later, so maybe we'd be better off pooling resources to try and figure out how to fix the mess you lot made."

The *Chic's* envoy looked dubious. "We have yet to find a solution."

"Lucky for you, I brought an expert."

"A human expert?"

"Yes."

"We have brains the size of solar systems dedicated to this problem."

I shrugged. "I figure it's got to be worth a try. Home boy seems to have a talent for this sort of thing."

The *Chic* leaned forwards and checked the tea in the pot. Apparently satisfied, he poured two mugs, and passed one my way. It was black tea with a citrussy, cologne-like aroma.

"Is this Earl Grey?"

"I thought you might enjoy it." He looked concerned. "If you'd prefer a different variety, I can alter the simulation."

"Earl Grey's fine."

"Would you like milk?"

"Only an absolute philistine would put milk in Earl Grey."

"No milk, then." The *Chic* touched the tips of his steepled fingers to his lower lip. "But to get back to the matter at hand, although we have momentarily paused hostilities, there yet remains a sizeable segment of the Mutuality that still favours invasion of your time period."

"Can you tell them to get fucked?"

The envoy smiled. "I believe you just did." He indicated his eyes. "They're all watching through me."

"The entire Mutuality?"

"You're speaking to every entity in the entire galaxy—at least, every one that has chosen to listen."

"Holy shit."

"Perhaps I should have explained that at the start?"

"You think?"

To give me time to compose myself, I took a sip of tea, and relished the bitter taste of the bergamot oil. They must have been throwing a huge amount of power into this simulation.

"Okay," I said, addressing my unseen audience. "First of all, I apologise for the 'get fucked' comment. I am a navigator, not a diplomat."

"We appreciate that. And yet, you are also the Abelisk, and you are here, which makes you spokesperson for your time period."

"I never asked for that."

"Nevertheless, it has fallen to you."

I placed my steaming cup on the hearthstones. "So, what am I supposed to do? Give you some long and hackneyed speech about how humanity deserves its chance to grow and develop? Tell you about all the lives that will never be lived if you turn the whole galaxy into a giant processor farm? Appeal to your sense of fair play?"

The *Chic* looked disappointed. "I don't think any of those strategies will work."

"What about the paradox? If you come back and change the past, won't you erase your own existence here in the future?"

"Time doesn't work like that."

"Says who?"

"We have compiled aeons of research. Time, like space, can be warped and bent. Returning to a previous point and making changes to the outcome of events will not erase the past we have already lived through. Our experiences will remain valid." He paused. "Try thinking of it like a room. If you go in and rearrange the furniture, it doesn't fundamentally change the room itself, or erase your memory of where those pieces used to be."

"That's a really fucking bad analogy."

"Your species insists on seeing time and space as separate, when in reality they are inextricably intertwined."

I rose to my feet. "Well, if that's true, I don't think I have anything else to add. You can storm the wormhole, and the *Gunmetal Ghost* will detonate its payload. We'll all die."

The *Chic* stood also. "I don't believe you want to die, Nicola."

"Of course I don't want to fucking die."

"And neither do we. That's why we need a chance to escape from our mistake."

I strode towards the door, and he followed. I wanted one last look at that glorious view before the antimatter hit the fan.

Gazing down at the seabirds wheeling over the loch, I said, "I would very much appreciate it if you could stop hijacking my mind now. Please put me back on the *Gunmetal Ghost*, and if you have anything else to say, you can say it to me in reality."

CHAPTER FIFTY

AN ARROW LOOPING BACK ON ITSELF

ORLANDO WALDEN

Ramona, there are a handful of moments in life that define us forever. For me, the first was the day I laid eyes on you. I will never forget the way you looked in the university library, your head tilted to the side, resting on your hand, as you read *The Great Gatsby*. The way your hair hung down over your wrist. The expression of concentration that tightened the skin around your eyes and mouth. You looked so exotic, and yet so familiar, as if we'd somehow always known each other. I knew at that moment, with a certainty that hit me like a bolt of lightning, that I was smitten, and that I would do whatever it took to have you in my life.

A similar bolt hit me on the bridge of the *Gunmetal Ghost*. Only this time, it wasn't love that struck me, but inspiration.

Erudite-Harf and I were examining the cyst at the galaxy's heart. We had already established it was being caused by raw substrate matter leaking into the physical universe. As you no doubt recall, I have long specialised in the fluid dynamics at work in the substrate's chaotic medium. Modelling its irruption into our dimensions, I was struck by something I initially took to be a discrepancy in the numbers. Investigating further, I found the figures to be correct, even if unexpected.

"Harf," I said, "see what you make of this?"

He peered over my shoulder at the screen set into the side of the *Gunmetal Ghost*'s transparent canopy. Then he removed his little half-moon glasses, cleaned them on a bright red handkerchief and replaced them for a second look. "Does that mean what I think it means?"

"The incursion should be happening a lot faster. Something's sapping its energy."

"But what?"

"I have an idea." I called up further data, searching for everything we'd recorded during our investigation of the Grand Mechanism. "There!"

"Ah, yes." Harf stroked his chin. "The Mechanism itself. It's drawing power directly from the intrusion."

The *Gunmetal Ghost* appeared at my elbow. "The people of this time created the Mechanism—a whole network of Mechanisms, to be precise—as a way to escape the expansion of the tear," she said. "It seems elegant they found a way to slow their demise while powering their escape hatch."

"That's all very well," Harf said. "But how does it help us?"

"Because according to my calculations, it was the activation of the Mechanisms that caused the rip in reality."

"That can't be right. You're suggesting they caused the calamity by building the wormholes they needed to escape from it."

"Precisely."

"That doesn't make sense."

And that, Ramona, is when the bolt of insight hit me. I felt myself go rigid as my brain lit up with new understanding. I forgot to breathe.

Harf said, "My boy? Are you all right?"

"I'm better than all right. I think I might have a solution to our problem."

"You do?"

"Don't you see?" I placed my finger on the screen and began sketching. "The substrate exists outside the universe. Now, it's leaking not only into space, but also into *time*. Just as it spreads out in every physical direction, so it's spreading in every chronological direction."

The *Ghost* said, "And so the inhabitants of this time saw the raw substrate matter leaking into their universe and built a means to escape, unaware that by doing so, they were causing the disaster they were trying to flee."

"Precisely." I made another couple of sketches on the screen. An arrow looping back on itself. "And that's why they can't build additional wormholes. To further puncture reality would only accelerate the disaster, maybe even consuming them before they could use those new wormholes." I smiled. "And it also means the remains of the irruption must exist in our own time."

"We would have seen it," Harf said.

"Not if it was hidden. Maybe behind an event horizon."

"The only event horizon at the centre of the galaxy is the central black hole."

"Which I'm guessing houses what remains of this intrusion. At some point, the weight of the substrate matter collapsed in on itself, dragging in the surrounding stars. The rip in the universe scabbed over and healed the breach."

"Okay."

"And that implies that if we send a transmission into the irruption at the right angle, it will re-emerge from that event horizon at some point in the past—a point of our choosing."

"Can't we simply return through the wormhole?"

"We can—but what if we want to send a message to a *different* time than the one we're returning to? What if we want to warn people what's going to happen before it does?"

Harf was so startled, the spectacles almost fell from his face. "Ah," he said. "I was always given to understand that nothing could escape a black hole, not even information."

"That's the good part. Signals through the substrate aren't affected by gravity. If it emerges at the other end as a substrate signal, it will pass straight through."

"For anyone with a working substrate receiver to detect."

"Exactly."

We were practically jumping up and down with the shared joy of having solved a riddle. The *Gunmetal Ghost* beamed at us. She patted my hand with arthritic fingers. "Congratulations, dear," she said. "I knew you could do it."

"But what message should we send?" Harf asked. "And whom should we warn? The Continuance? Foreknowledge of our future might drastically upset the stability of our time."

The *Ghost* tapped the side of her nose. "You just leave that to me."

CHAPTER FIFTY-ONE

GOD-SIZED BRAIN

NICOLA MAFALDA

The loch was gone. I stood by the forward part of the canopy on the navigation deck of the *Gunmetal Ghost*, exactly where I had been standing before being mentally whisked to that picturesque simulation.

"Welcome back, dear," the old woman said. "Did you have any luck talking to the neighbours?"

The *Frontier Chic*'s envoy looked concerned. "What happened?"

"I met a future version of you."

"You did?"

"We had quite the discussion."

"And…?"

"And I'm afraid age turns you into a bit of an asshole."

I walked over to the navigator's couch and lowered myself onto it. In front of us, the Ophanim's nested wheels continued to rotate, and I had the unsettling sensation of watching a god-sized brain in the process of considering its next move.

Were the Mutuality about to try storming the wormhole? They might suspect I'd hesitate to commit mass murder, but

I couldn't say the same for the *Ghost*. If all those ships made a break for our time period, I was sure she'd detonate the antimatter. Part of me hoped that if it came to that, she'd just do it without warning us. Under the circumstances, I felt it would be better not to know—to go from existence to nonexistence with no time for fear or regret, not even time enough for our sluggish brains to register what was happening; just the clean white light of total, instantaneous annihilation.

These could be the final seconds of my life. And if that were so, I knew I should make them count.

"Open a channel," I said.

"Yes, dear."

I cleared my throat. "Attention, citizens of the Mutuality. My name, as you are probably aware by now, is Nicola Mafalda. The last time you attempted to storm your way into an earlier time period, you were beaten back. And the races that handed you that beating constructed complex mechanisms to prevent your wormholes from reopening. They also constructed ships like the one from which I am speaking to you, to patrol those mechanisms, and destroy them—and you—should you attempt another invasion."

I paused, staring out at the moon-sized matryoshka brain and the smaller ships arrayed around it.

"Incoming transmission," the *Ghost* said.

"Show me."

"Right you are, dear." She threw the picture up onto the canopy. Unsurprisingly, it was the older version of the *Frontier Chic*.

"Nicola," he said. "We understand your concerns. Last time, we went about things a little too zealously."

"You tried to turn the entire galaxy into computronium."

"We simply wanted to recreate the conditions we had left here, so we could devote all our energies to finding a way to avoid the catastrophe we had escaped."

"And you killed a lot of people."

"I believe there's an old human adage about omelettes and eggs that might be relevant here."

I gave an annoyed sigh. "Let me get to the point. I'm standing between you and the past. If you want to use this wormhole, you'll have to get past me, and the biggest fucking antimatter explosion you've ever seen."

The envoy shook his head. "Oh, Nicola. Take a look around you. We've constructed half a million matryoshka brains. We've harnessed stars and brought supernovae to heel. We're used to dealing with forces greater than you can muster. If you try to set off your little bomb, we'll just throw a force field around it to contain the explosion."

"You're bluffing."

"Try it and find out."

Beside me, the envoy from my time hissed, "You were certainly right about me becoming an asshole."

I turned to the *Ghost*. "Do you think he's lying?"

The old woman pursed her lips. "Most definitely not, dear."

"How can you be so certain?"

"Because I detonated our entire stock of antimatter eleven seconds ago."

"Ah."

The envoy on the screen smiled. "You see?"

"That's cheating."

"All's fair in love and war."

"Aren't we just full of folksy sayings today?"

"Nicola, we're going through the wormhole. And once through, we'll send out scouts to open the other Mechanisms placed around the galaxy. We're taking the whole Mutuality through, and there's nothing more you can do now, except stand aside."

I balled my fists. "I will not."

"You will, or you'll be destroyed." He leant towards the

camera. "I don't want to have to kill you, Nicola, but if you won't get out of the way, I will. You can't possibly stand against the massed might of all these ships, not alone."

The wheels of the Ophanim stopped turning. Every ship in the sky had turned to face us, and my threat display went bright red as it registered thousands of weapons systems locking on.

And that was when the *Gunmetal Ghost*, in the guise of my grandmother, stepped forwards. "That's the thing, young man," she said. "Nicola isn't alone. She never has been, and neither have I."

The envoy from the future narrowed his eyes. "What do you mean?"

The *Ghost* smiled. "I made a call, dear."

As she finished speaking, the vacuum in the vicinity of the wormhole rippled. The whole of space seemed to convulse, and megaships appeared. I recognised *Little Golden Orphan*, *The Moon Always Rising* and *Heaven's Embroidered Cloths*. Then there were others I didn't recognise. A hundred others, then a thousand, and then a hundred thousand. Millions, and tens of millions. Within a couple of seconds, the entire sky seemed filled with their vast, ancient forms.

"A ship for every Mechanism," the *Ghost* said primly. "Plus a few extra I suggested be built, in case of emergencies."

"How many extra?" I asked.

"Around a billion. We had to cannibalise an entire globular cluster."

"Fucking hell," I said. "With that many you could—"

"Destroy every Dyson sphere in this sorry galaxy, dear."

"But where did you find so many navigators?"

"I sent the message a fair way back into the past."

"How far?"

"Suffice to say, we've had a very long time to prepare." She turned to the projected image of the envoy. "Now," she said to him, "that seems to have evened up the odds. In fact,

I think it's tipped them decidedly in our favour."

The envoy's face had frozen. I assumed the Mutuality controlling it had more to worry about than conveying emotion. It said, "We can still fight."

"Fight all you want, dear. We have nothing to lose, and a galaxy to protect."

There was a long pause, in which I imagined a million alarmed voices clamouring inside their simulations. Then, the envoy straightened up and said, "If we surrender, what will you do? Will you leave us here to die?"

The *Ghost* beamed. "Oh no, young man. We'll make sure you're taken care of. In fact, my friend Orlando here has some ideas about that."

"You'll help us?"

"Of course, dear. You've made a frightful mess, but the adults are here now to help you clean it up."

CHAPTER FIFTY-TWO

FEARSOME STELLAR ENGINES

NICOLA MAFALDA

We stayed in the future for several weeks, overseeing the fragile new détente between ourselves and our descendants. The future *Frontier Chic* got to meet the present-day version, and that was a decidedly awkward conversation. Much of it took place over private channels and at a pace too fast for the unaided human brain to follow, but the little that leaked out sounded like a particularly vicious argument between siblings.

I gave Ewing a decent burial, watching from the *Ghost*'s bridge as the shuttle containing his body hit the upper atmosphere of a nearby gas giant. Not having any of Ewing's personal possessions aboard, I had packed the shuttle with items of interest the *Ghost* had gathered on its travels—souvenirs from a life of exploration and adventure, as befitted the navigator of a scout craft—and now it was a burning streak across the cloud tops, incinerating itself and raining down as ash, to be forever blown on the fierce gales that drove the planet's whirling storms. It was a traditional funeral for a Vanguard navigator, and a solemn occasion, but I felt curiously unmoved. He had been a friend, a rival and a mortal enemy. And now he was gone and I didn't feel anything beyond a vague kind of relief. Whatever our relationship had meant, I was free of it now. The rest of my life was my own, and I had nothing left to prove.

After the service, Orlando went aboard the Ophanim in order to outline his ideas to a gathering of the Mutuality.

"The substrate irruption will be finite," he said. "The fact it's not happening in my time shows this. Given long enough, it will collapse back into an event horizon."

"And what are we supposed to do until then?"

"Keep moving." He called up an image of the Continuance fleet. "When my race was evicted from its world, it took to wandering the stars." He smiled. "Given the presence of the *Frontier Chic* among you, I presume many of the personalities of those arks remain intact. Well, to you I say, it's time to become arks again. Build a new fleet, one large enough to house all your simulated minds, and set off for the galactic rim. Maybe even intergalactic space. You can always come back when the danger has passed, or—"

The combined voices of the Mutuality said, "Or?"

Orlando raised an eyebrow. "I hear Andromeda's nice at this time of year. And it's a lot closer than it was in my time."

•

Finally, we were ready to return to our own time. The *Gunmetal Ghost* was going to ferry me home to the Continuance.

As we prepared to depart, the *Frontier Chic*'s envoy came to me. "I'm going to stay here," he said, "with my future self."

"Are you sure?"

"Oh yes. He needs all the help he can get."

"Don't you want to come back to the Continuance?"

He put a blue hand on my shoulder. "I'm already there, remember?"

"But what about reintegrating your memories?"

He gave a shrug. "I had assumed this would be a one-way trip." He produced a small, blue data crystal. "But please pass this on to my ship-based self. It's a record of everything that's happened since we parted."

I took it and squeezed it tightly in my palm. "I will."

"And do me one other favour."

"Anything."

"Make sure you find Kona. Don't let him go back to Jzat without you. Tell him how you feel."

I felt my cheeks colour. "I will."

"Do you promise?"

"I do."

"Good." He smiled. "You two belong together, even if neither of you will properly admit it."

We embraced one final time and said our goodbyes, and then I was alone on the bridge. Already, I could see Orlando's plan beginning to bear fruit, as warships were being repurposed into the Mutuality equivalent of civilian carriers and joined together to form larger vessels. I'd even heard talk that some of the matryoshka brains might join the exodus under their own power, using magnetic fields to turn the stars at their hearts into fearsome stellar engines.

"Are you ready, dear?" the *Ghost* asked.

"I suppose so." I had no one else for whom to wait. Orlando and Harf were going to follow us in a few weeks, along with a delegation from the Mutuality who were interested in building diplomatic links with the Continuance. For now, I was the *Ghost*'s only passenger.

"When we get back to our own time, I'll need you to navigate us back to the Continuance," she said. "But I don't need you on deck while we pass through the wormhole. You can go and get some rest, if you like."

"That sounds good. I need a bed and a hot shower. Maybe some food."

"Of course, dear." The *Gunmetal Ghost* curtsied. "I'm sure I can find something suitably befitting the latest and most glorious Abelisk."

CONCLUSION

TO: COUNCIL OF SHIPS INVESTIGATIVE SUBCOMMITTEE
FROM: VANGUARD SCOUT SHIP FRONTIER CHIC
DATE: 03/09/125 NEW COMMON ERA
RE: INCIDENT #43675-A

My esteemed colleagues and members of the Council,

Thus concludes my report.

As mentioned in my introduction, I have based the text on my own direct recollections, and the transcripts of interviews with Nicola Mafalda, Orlando Walden, Kona Molaphlostyn and others. I have striven to purge any and all inaccuracies from my account, but please bear in mind the fallibility of human and Jzat memory. Non-artificial minds tend to become flustered and emotional during periods of stress, and this can colour their interpretation of motive and perception of time. That said, I humbly believe that I have produced the most comprehensive and faithful recounting of events possible given the circumstances.

Copies of all the transcripts, messages, diary entries and other primary sources are available on request.

Upon her return to the Continuance fleet, Nicola Mafalda and Kona Molaphlostyn were reunited aboard the ark *Memory of Green*. At some point, Mafalda intends to return to Jzat in order to pass the mantle of Abelisk to someone more qualified. In the meantime, she and Molaphlostyn are residing at the *Memory of Green*'s mountainside cabin while they recover from their ordeal and try to figure out what their relationship means, and whether it has a future.

Having cleaned its own house in the wake of Ewing's plots coming to light, the Vanguard managed to locate and detain General Aulco and his conspirators in the Jzat secret service. They had been adrift in a disabled shuttle since escaping the Mechanism, and by the time they were picked up, they were starving, dehydrated and only too happy to be brought back to Jzat, where they were charged with treason and sentenced to hard labour on one of the crews repairing the Grand Mechanism.

After his experiences, Orlando Walden is now one of the most sought-after substrate physicists in the Continuance. Since his return, universities and periodicals have deluged him with invitations to publish articles and speak at conferences. Academia will have to wait, however, as he and Ramona Tyrell have taken an extended cruise. They're young and Orlando's sudden fame may have left them both a bit out of their depth, but I have a good feeling about those two. It's easy to be resilient and adaptable at their age, and Orlando's grown up a lot as the result of his experiences. I think when they return, their love for each other will be stronger than ever.

Erudite-Harf returned to Jzat, intending to resume his studies. He was expecting a return to the semi-obscurity of his physics department. However, as he is now Jzat's foremost expert on the substrate and the future, he has been put in charge of the project to repair and secure the Grand Mechanism, and now spends most of his days dreaming up new and interesting ways to make General Aulco's life miserable.

And me? I am presently enjoying a quiet virtual retirement within the processors of the *Memory of Green.* Occasionally, I send an envoy to visit Mafalda, or to attend an art exhibition or music recital; but mostly, I am content in my seclusion. I've earned some time for rest and contemplation. But that doesn't mean I've been inactive. One can never be fully idle when one has access to the complete repository of human learning. In fact, I've been positively inspired. Having enjoyed the compilation of this report, I am seriously contemplating the notion of writing my memoirs, and a definitive history of the Continuance, from Year Zero to the present day.

Perhaps one day, if Mafalda is willing, we will resume our duties as scout ship and navigator. Such things are not beyond the realms of possibility. And perhaps one day, I will get a chance to meet up with the envoy of mine that chose to stay behind to help my future self.

Someday, perhaps all this will even make a kind of sense. But then, after all, who really knows what the future holds?

Your obedient servant,
VSS *Frontier Chic*

ACKNOWLEDGEMENTS

Descendant Machine marks a milestone for me, as it's my tenth published novel so far and my sixteenth published book since 2008. That's sixteen books in fifteen years, which I guess isn't a bad output. It certainly beats the Brontë sisters, who I believe only produced eight between them.

In your faces, Brontës.

Joking aside, I had to overcome some significant challenges while writing this novel, including some serious family emergencies, a long bout of COVID and a house move. But the most difficult moment came when the first draft somehow deleted itself from all servers, online back-ups and everywhere else. Not a trace remained, even using specialised recovery software. Months of work gone in an instant. I was devastated and thoroughly demoralised, and it took an enormous effort to pick myself up and start re-writing from scratch.

I think the book's stronger for it, though.

I'm grateful to Cath Trechman, my editor at Titan Books, for her understanding and patience during all the above, not to mention her incisive and valuable editorial notes. To my copy editor, Paul Simpson, for his input. To my agent, Alexander Cochran at C&W, for his ongoing support and wise counsel. To Julia Lloyd for yet another stunning cover. To my supporters on Patreon and Ko-fi, and to everyone else who's read, reviewed and enjoyed my work over the years.

I'm beholden to the friends and colleagues who kept me cheerful and sane during the writing of this book. I'm thankful for my children, who are maturing into amazing and talented young adults. And I'm also profoundly grateful for my loving wife, kindred spirit and best friend, J. Dianne Dotson, who's given me endless encouragement and inspiration, and re-opened my eyes to the joys and possibilities of the world.

ABOUT THE AUTHOR

Gareth L. Powell is an award-winning and widely lauded author at the forefront of speculative fiction. He has won the British Science Fiction Association (BSFA) Award for Best Novel, and been a finalist for Locus, British Fantasy and Seiun awards. A popular guest at conventions, he is also widely respected for offering advice and encouragement to fledgling writers on Twitter and encouraging a warm and positive outlook on life. He divides his time between the UK and California, and is represented in all professional matters by Alexander Cochran of the C&W Literary Agency.

You can find him online at www.garethlpowell.com and on Twitter at @garethlpowell.

STARS AND BONES
A CONTINUANCE NOVEL

GARETH L. POWELL

Seventy-five years from today, the human race has been cast from a dying Earth to wander the stars in a vast fleet of arks—each shaped by its inhabitants into a diverse and fascinating new environment, with its own rules and eccentricities.

When her sister disappears while responding to a mysterious alien distress call, Eryn insists on being part of the crew sent to look for her. What she discovers on Candidate-623 is both terrifying and deadly. When the threat follows her back to the fleet and people start dying, she is tasked with seeking out a legendary recluse who may just hold the key to humanity's survival.

A stunningly inventive action-packed science-fiction epic adventure from the multi BSFA award-winning author.

"Powell balances plot, action, and character development perfectly. This promising start will especially appeal to James S.A. Corey fans." *Publishers Weekly*, starred review

"A novel with heart and ambition" *SFX*

"Spotlights Powell's gifts for character building and plotting. He's already won two best-novel awards from the British Science Fiction Association, and it wouldn't be surprising to see this one getting a nomination, too." *Booklist*

For more fantastic fiction, author events,
exclusive excerpts, competitions, limited editions and more

VISIT OUR WEBSITE
titanbooks.com

LIKE US ON FACEBOOK
facebook.com/titanbooks

FOLLOW US ON TWITTER AND INSTAGRAM
@TitanBooks

EMAIL US
readerfeedback@titanemail.com